In Dreams We Trust

Created August 2019

by

Bruce Benoit

Chapter 1

In the center isle of the church, I stand as still as possible while the eeriness of the darkness surrounds me. The isle of this church is filled with nothing behind me and a haziness of light in front. Slowly, I walk towards the alter listening to little voices along the way not knowing if they are talking to me or to each other. The whispers continue as I walk forward glancing from side to side. The darkness behind me is making the hairs on the back of my neck stand up with chills running down my spine like little spiders racing across my bones. Both sides of the isle are pews filled with unexplainable shadows swirling around as if the wind was brewing up a storm. The thought of running was evident, but the physical ability was simply gone. Suddenly, black shadows rise from the pews as if a title wave was rising along side of me. But this was no title wave. Rising from the shadows were stretched out skeletal arms the length of several pews. They were barely covered by a black tattered cape that draped over each brittle bone of this creature's arms. The hands were huge with grey and white fingers sticking out from under the torn fabric as it moves closer and closer to where I'm standing. In only seconds, this mangled skeletal body stood more than twelve feet tall right in front of me. The head of this creature held a hooded covering with the skull that resembled anything but a face. With grayish, white eyes and no facial structure at all except for a skeletal resemblance, it glared down on me with identifiable evil. Running is literally impossible now and the feel of restraint holds me still. Looking away is my only option, but a greater force is making me stare. The voices have disappeared and formed into an extremely low, yet loud toned growl. Crashing down on me covering me in total darkness, the feeling of being completely suffocated by a large wet blanket overwhelms me. My voice disappears in a void as I try with all my might to scream.

Swiftly sitting up in bed with sweat rolling down his back, Tom reflects on some of the dreams that kept him up night after night for much of his life. The dreams during his childhood were all too familiar to the dream he just had. "It's the same damn thing," he tiredly mumbles. Getting more comfortable, he reflects briefly on his childhood.

Tom Chapman grew up playing baseball and other sports as a kid. He loved joining the games with all his buddies at the local community field where his friends would meet regularly even outside of the baseball team schedule. In general, sports occupied most of his time along with hanging out with friends, hiking in the hills and causing trouble. School, well school was just something that took up way too much time away from having fun and screwing around. Although school could be fun, it seemed to be a continued effort to get the paddle from Sister Mary Virginia King. As Tom recalls, she really hated him. Hate's a strong word of course especially for a Nun. Tom didn't see it any other way. But that statement was confusing because she was a Nun and they are supposed to love all children no matter what. Maybe there was an exception this time and God gave her permission to hate only him. In any event, Tom's childhood was really nothing too different from anyone else's, except for his dreams.

To Tom, his dreams were all too real. Most of his dreams were colorfully vivid which is odd due to research that shows most people don't dream in color. But Tom's dreams were wildly colorful and having such realistic dreams was only a small part of his concerns back then. Unfortunately, many of his dreams came to life which was devastating to him, especially as such a young boy. It was a secret Tom kept to himself for all this time simply because he had no idea what would happen if he even bothered to explain them to an adult. But because these dreams haven't occurred in such a long time now, he's concerned that this nightmare about the church might be the rebirth of these horrific experiences he had as a kid. He shakes the cobwebs from his head, gets up and heads for the shower to get ready for work.

In a small community not too far from the city, Father Stern is a Pastor at one of the local churches surrounded by a good, faithful congregation. Entering the church this morning as he's done for many years unlocking doors and turning on selected lights, he feels something a little different. Stern is a large man who has had religion and the belief of God as part of his life early on. During his young days as a teenage student, he was always sought after for the football team where he would've been the biggest lineman in the district. But Stern didn't believe in physical competition. It wasn't that he was scared of getting hit or even going up against someone in a competitive nature. In fact, Stern wasn't scared of anything which was a unique and calm quality about him. It was simply not his thing and of course, there was nobody that would give him a hard time about it due to his appearance and formidable size. With his full beard and mustache during his teenage years, he appeared quite adult like which scared most others. Truly, Stern was a gentle giant and was always the beholder of peace. At a young age, God somehow called to him and now his is a respected Pastor of his own church.

Getting the lighting just right in the back of church and all the appropriate doors opened, Father Stern headed for the alter for additional lights knowing people could be coming for their regular visits and prayers they perform each morning. Regulars would come to pray for many various reasons such as the passing of a loved one, safety and security for friends and family, wishing all happiness and health for all or just praying because they had nothing else to do. Some even prayed because they felt guilty that if they didn't, God would not love them. Either way, people had their reasons which is why the church opened its doors each morning to allow them this comfort. But for Father Stern, this morning was like no other. On his way to the alter, he felt a coldness in the air that made it nearly impossible for him to breathe. Almost sliding on the cold tile floor, Father Stern freezes in his tracks. Just a few pews from the alter, he glances down only to see a sight his eyes will never let him forget. Grabbing his mouth with both hands, he runs to the back of church to his office is and grabs his phone.

With police on scene evaluating every detail, Detective Butler re-enters the church after getting some fresh air from his first view of this terrible incident. The police just couldn't figure this one out. No broken furniture, no destructive evidence and no clues that would lead to a possible suspect capable of such a vicious crime could be found. Torn flesh, broken bones and shredded body parts scattered down the center aisle. Not only were the remains located only throughout the center aisle, but something even more disturbing was found, the blood. No blood splatter of any kind. Just small droplets of blood located by each body part was confusing and appeared to be too neat and tidy for such a violent and horrific crime scene. Carefully examined for clues, none of these parts showed any signs of bruising or a struggle or anything else that would help in this investigation. With such a mess on their hands and no possible clues of why or who, the police department were at a stand-still only hoping they would never see this again.

Chapter 2

After a long day at work, Tom drags ass into his apartment throwing his keys on the table by the door. He slides his coat off his shoulders and drops it to the floor. While unbuttoning his shirt and releasing the buttons around his wrists, he rolls up his sleeves and heads for the kitchen. Glancing around to decide what he's going to eat for dinner, he opens the fridge and grabs a beer. On the side of the fridge is a pretty cool magnetic bottle opener he received as a gift from a buddy as he uses that to pop it open. After taking a few long swigs, he decides to cook up a frozen pizza and dials the oven to 400 degrees. With the oven warming up, he walks to the living room and stares out at the view from his apartment window. Bothered by a somewhat stressful day along with the vivid dreams he had the night before, he wanders to the couch and flips the large, seventy-inch flat screen and scrolls to one of the local news channels. A "beep" comes from the kitchen as the oven is now at temperature. Tom places his beer on the glass table by the couch and walks to the kitchen placing the pizza in the oven. As he returns to the living room, he's stopped in his tracks from the voice of a brown haired man talking on the television with the latest news story…

"An incident at a local church involving a woman who was brutally attacked is under investigation. Sources tell us remains of this woman were scattered all over the center aisle of this church where Father Stern, the Pastor of the church, found her earlier this morning. So far, there is no evidence of a break in or a possible theft taking place. Details are limited at this time and the investigation is still under way. Due to the violent nature of this crime, the scene has been quarantined and the church is closed until further notice. There are no suspects at this time and we'll keep you updated as new information comes in."

In shock, Tom stands there as his blue eyes grow wide as his mouth drops open. "You've got to be fucking kidding me," he exclaims. Memories from his childhood come flooding in as he slowly leans towards the couch to sit down and breathe. Holding his hands to his chest, he gazes at the television not watching anything in particular as the news stories continue on to other topics. Many of the dreams Tom had as a child are now coming to mind all too clearly. Grabbing his lukewarm beer from the glass table, he pulls a few times trying to gather himself and come to his senses. Several minutes pass as Tom struggles to convince himself this has nothing to do with him. He tells himself it's just a coincidence and that those days of bad dreams and horrific events are far behind him. He looks at the ceiling with his hands on top of his head thinking this was just a really unfortunate situation for some woman in the wrong place at the wrong time. Running his hands through his thick, brown head of hair, he gets himself to relax, leans even further back on the couch and takes the last remaining sip of his warm beer. "Beep," the oven lets him know dinner is ready.

Wiping his hands from the saucy mess the pizza has made of his fingers, he swigs another couple times on an ice-cold beer that was replaced while grabbing the piping hot pizza out of the oven. Rubbing his full stomach while leaning back on the couch, his tired feet rest nicely on the dark brown, cloth ottoman. A full belly and relaxed atmosphere make Tom feel even better about the evening and the bad news he heard a short time ago. Reminiscing about his life these days, Tom realizes he's doing pretty well. With a lucrative sales position as a manufacturer's representative, he's able to enjoy many nice things including his downtown apartment. Naturally a talkative guy, sales fits Tom's personality very well. Working in the metro Detroit area has been rewarding to say the least. Growth in Michigan is on the upside and Tom is taking full advantage of the economy with startup companies, rebirth of the manufacturing business and many other small businesses eager to be part of this rapidly growing market. Looking around his apartment, he realizes the satisfaction of his job and the win is what motivates him. The income isn't so bad either.

Slowly sitting up on his couch after watching one stupid TV series after another, Tom raises his arms as high as he can to stretch. Yawning and moaning from sitting in one place the entire evening, he gets up from the couch, grabs whatever left over pizza there is sitting on the table, grabs his empty bottle of beer and walks to the kitchen. He places the dried up pizza in a zip lock baggy and stuffs it in the fridge next to the day old tuna sandwich he forgot to throw away. Dropping the bottle in the recycle bin with a loud "Clang," he closes the cupboard door and turns off the kitchen lights. Still feeling full from eating almost the entire ten-piece pizza and guzzling down a few beers, Tom adjourns to the bedroom and gets himself ready for bed. Still wearing the work clothes from the day, he undresses tossing his clothes on the chair in the corner of the room. Putting on some bright blue basketball shorts and a t-shirt, he heads for the bathroom to brush his pizza stained teeth and hit the john. Once done, he slowly slides into his nice king-sized bed covering himself under the plush, white comforter he got last year. As his head sinks into the large, soft pillows for the night, he clears his head hoping for a restful sleep. An early morning sales call requires getting some well-deserved sleep, but Tom still wonders how this night will go. Resting the comforter just over his shoulder while lying on his side, he gazes out the window to his left as he slowly falls asleep.

Standing at the bottom of the back stairway tiled in the old fashioned yellow linoleum flooring, I'm heading up from the basement. All I can hear is whining and high-pitched barking from puppies in the distant. With every sharp creak from the old stairway, the whining gets louder as I enter the window-filled kitchen area to find the puppies are not there. Continuing through the kitchen of this large, dark lit house, I'm guided towards the front door where the whining turns into barking and louder excitement from what sounds to be a pile of fun loving puppies. I cross into the main hallway where the dark brown stucco walls and poorly lit sconces are the only colors I see. Quietly, something stands behind me with shadows of blackness showing up in my peripheral view. I don't dare turn around as the hair on the back of my neck stands up and my skin crawls knowing it's something I see in many of my dreams. The eeriness of this monster behind me is all too familiar and frightening. Pushing me slightly from behind, I feel my body forcibly being moved towards the front door. Hot, steamy wet breath makes the back of my neck feel warm and moist. Moving faster towards the front glass door with my fingertips gliding along the uneven stucco walls, I'm unable to see through the glass door. That doesn't make sense. I should be able to see through glass. The barking and chattering from the puppies is much louder now and obvious they are just behind the door. Louder and louder these puppies get as I move closer to the door that leads to the front of the house. I'm only a few feet or so away from the door when suddenly, "Blast," the door flies open! Vicious dogs of all sizes come crashing directly towards me. I'm screwed. With blood stained teeth snarling and white drool dripping from each of their mouths and fangs, they lunge to drive their teeth into my flesh. Powerless, I have no retreat and no physical ability to get away. The sensation of being torn apart makes everything go completely blank.

Lurching out of his dream with his arms whaling around as if to protect himself from being attacked, Tom sits up in bed as he pushes all the pillows behind him for support. As he rests his head on the pile of pillows just below the top of the headboard, he fights to keep his eyes open to avoid going back into that horrible dream. Dim lighting enters his room from the moonlight just outside his large bedroom window. He scans from one side of the room to the other for any shadow like figures to make sure he's not sleeping. Not a thing, just a dark empty bedroom with only the sound of his pounding heartbeat coming from his chest. On the back of his neck, Tom finds moisture not from sweat, but from the disgusting saliva dripping off from the breath of that terrifying demon in his dream. Not wanting to fall back to sleep and with only a short time before he needs to get up, he lies there motionless cuddled between pillows and a comforter staring at the ceiling.

Walking as fast as he can without looking like one of those silly speed walkers, Tom finds himself cutting it close for his meeting after dozing back off and missing his alarm clock loudly trying to wake him. Fortunately, Tom only overslept thirty minutes or so, got ready in a flash and makes it with only moments to spare. Sprinting up the stairs to the third floor of this office building, he dashes through the cubicles arriving just in time for his meeting. Winning this order is a high priority and all seems to be going well during the meeting. But as the meeting progresses, Tom finds himself staring out the window of this large conference room losing total focus of his agenda and goals. Fears of this dream he had preoccupied his thoughts and make him stray from closing the deal. As the older, more sophisticated gentleman on the other side of the table is in agreement with the product fit and pricing model, he sits back in his chair and gives Tom the look that he is still a little hesitant to place the order. Tom sits quietly with his hands clasped together as if he's praying before eating dinner when he was a boy. Staring at the customer across the table, he doesn't implement his normally behavior and refrains from going in for the kill. Instead he says, "I'll tell you what. Think about what I've presented and let me know tomorrow. I'll give you a call later in the morning." An odd look is given from the customer as he responds, "that will be fine Tom. Thank you for coming by this morning." Leaving the conference room, Tom glances back at the gentleman who's wearing a comfortable knit sweater and says, "You're very welcome. Talk with you tomorrow." Pressing the large grayed out button to the elevator with his thumb, Tom enters the brightly lit elevator and leans against the cold marble wall as if he'd just finished running a marathon. "Ding," the elevator doors open to a beautifully decorated lobby entrance with warm features welcoming any visitor. Above the security desk at one end of the lobby, a large television rests against the wall where an old man sits wearing a dark blue vest and badge. On the way out, Tom glances up at the television as he passes the desk when a blonde talking head is describing the news of an incident that happened late yesterday evening…

"Action news is reporting a terrible incident involving a middle aged couple in a horrific dog attack on the East side. Details prove this to be a pack of wild dogs aggressively attacking and mangling the couple as they walked home from having dinner at a local pub last evening. The two bodies were found by neighbors after hearing the sounds of screams and what neighbors can only describe as the most vicious dog growls and barks they've ever heard. The couple was rushed to the hospital with injuries that would prove fatal. The couple also leaves behind an adult child not living in the area. Police are encouraging all surrounding communities to stay in-doors until these dogs are found, captured and destroyed. If you see any unusual animal activity, please report it to your local police department immediately and do not approach these animals. What a terrible incident. We'll bring you updates as information comes in."

Leaning heavily on the counter of the security desk trying to hold himself up, Tom sighs looking down at the floor. The security guard asks, "Hey, are you okay?" Not responding to the guard, Tom's blue eyes stare back at the guard with no response or reaction. Just a blank stare. Gathering himself, he straightens up composing his posture and heads for the revolving door. Once outside, Tom walks to the side of the grey stone building and leans against the wall facing the busy, car filled street. The sidewalk is filled with people of all types and sizes, but Tom barely notices. Looking down at the cement, Tom can only think of his worst fears. Across the street is a small common area filled with people, decorative landscape, benches and tables for people to lounge. While avoiding traffic, Tom rushes to the first available bench seat and clumsily sits banging his elbow on the black metal arm rest. Unable to breathe, he closes his eyes to regain his composure. "It can't be happening again, can it?" he mumbles to himself. His flush, red face overwhelms him as he thinks back to when he was young. A secret he's held for so many years he thought couldn't possibly be true. And until now, even Tom didn't believe it.

Chapter 3

As a child, Tom had reoccurring dreams almost nightly. The dreams kept him up and were so bad that he ran into his parent's room for safety. After having these same dreams over and over again, Tom started waking to them realizing they were just that, dreams and only dreams that couldn't hurt him. What he didn't realize was the fact that his dreams were hurting others in ways he couldn't imagine. One of the recurring dreams he had over and over again was when he got crushed by a car while riding across the street without looking. In the dream, he recalls hanging around with a couple friends from the block wondering what shit they're going to get into next. Since it was close to dinner time, most of them had to leave or get in trouble for being late for dinner. Tom and one of his buddies decided to ride to the corner store and get some candy before they had to head home. Because they were boys, competition was in every action. They raced as fast as they can to get there ignoring every stop sign or looking both ways before crossing the street. The eerie feeling he has during the entire dream bothers Tom. It was like something dark and troubling was right beside him the whole time. Almost as if something was following him and right on his tail. But Tom never looked back to see what it was. It was like running up the basement stairs knowing if you looked back, you'd see the boogie man chasing you. Tom only hoped it would've been his brother simply because it was his brother's bike he was riding. The bike was choice, as they used to say back then. It had all the cool decals and colors he wished he had on his bike. He also knew his brother would kill him if he knew he took it and was riding it without his permission. Tom figured he would ask for forgiveness rather than ask for permission. But as they came to the last corner of this high speed race, Toms friend was almost a house or two ahead and had already crossed the street. Racing across the street trying to gain on his buddy, Tom made a huge mistake. All Tom recalls in that dream is seeing a car only inches away from him. In his dream he wakes to the one and only, G.I. Joe! Yes, G.I. Joe hit Tom while riding his brothers bike. He recalls this huge man in fatigues sitting by his bedside while holding his head in his hands. There were many things in that dream Tom didn't remember, but G.I. Joe wasn't one of them. And if you don't know who G.I. Joe is, just search him and you'll find action figures created by a company called Hasbro from the early 60's. Unfortunately, Tom didn't actually speak to G.I. Joe in the dream.

It wasn't until later that day when Tom learned of a little girl in school who was hit by a car. She was crossing the street in the neighborhood when she was struck by a military vehicle heading back to base. This wasn't a military town, just close enough to a base where you'd see the occasional jet fly by, helicopter hover above or some sort of jeep or heavy duty military vehicle drive by. That was the odd thing about this. Of all vehicles to hit that little girl, why did it have to be G.I. Joes? The thought continued to cross Toms mind that maybe he had something to do with this little girl's death because of the dream. But that is really nonsense even for an 11-year-old. Dreams don't have that type of influence in real life. Sure, they are sometimes remnants of what we've done or from memories or from experiences we've had. But to have a dream that actually comes true after the dream? That's just ridiculous. Tom never did tell anyone about this and kept it his own little secret.

At the age of seventeen, Tom was now driving. He had a real piece of shit car for his first car like most kids did then. The Dodge Omni Shelby was one of Chryslers inexpensive and very economic cars at that time. However, it was also not a cool car at all. But this is what he was able to get and as a teenage boy, a car was a car. Now that Tom was mobile in his dark green so called sports car, there were so many more things he was able to do and places he could go. One of Toms hobbies was to hike in the hills with friends and including camping out for the night. Growing up in a small town, the country was where home was for Tom. He would test fate by enjoying nature at its best and its worst. Many times he'd venture out on his own which was riskier back then not having cell phones or ways to let people know if he was in trouble. That just didn't matter to him. On many of his hikes with friends, they'd encounter cliffs, caves and other obstacles that made their hikes both exciting and treacherous. Some were hikes in the evening which made things even more interesting when heading out of the woods in the dark. That was part of the thrill. Some of the experiences were so exciting and fun, Tom would dream about them all the time. Normally, people love dreaming about their fun times and places they've been. But not Tom. He didn't want to dream about anything. Way too many times he'd have a dream where someone would get hurt and the following day, that event would come true. It boggled Toms mind and scared the hell out of him each time. One of Toms dreams he remembers quite well was when he ventured out into the forest on a hike by himself. Now what he recalls about this dream doesn't make much sense, but they never really did.

He was only wearing hiking shoes, a pair of shorts and a T-shirt as he headed out into the wilderness. Obviously, very unlike Tom to go unprepared for a hike, but this was a dream. The thick woods made it nearly impossible to see more than twenty feet or so and it was dark from the beginning of his journey. With every step, the loud crackle from the branches below his feet breaking would echo through the forest louder than he has ever heard. It was a slow hike that seemed to take forever to go any distance and where he was going was terribly unclear. That was very unusual for Tom because as an experienced hiker, he knew where he was at all times. When he reached an area of the hills he's never seen before, he peered down a cliff that went on and on with no ending. "There's no bottom! Where the hell am I?" A loud, terrifying growl vibrated off the back of his neck as he stood looking over this cliff. Losing his balance trying to look behind him to see what this monster was, he begins to fall over the cliff grasping at every branch and limb he can find. The feeling of helplessness while falling with his arms and legs flailing through the air uncontrollably produces chills all over his body. The free fall never ends and Tom wakes up.

This is one of those dreams he remembers from childhood that he can never forget. The day after he had this dream, news of a young man falling to his death while hiking strikes him through the heart. He always wondered if it was completely coincidental or if there was something more. Because he was just a kid, it was more confusing than ever.

Chapter 4

Back at Toms office, Claudia, a striking young woman works diligently keeping busy with her administrative duties. She has a thing for Tom, but hasn't made her feelings known just yet. Flirting now and again is her way of letting him know she's interested, but she feels it's time to step it up a notch. It seems to her that Tom is just a little oblivious to her advances and that he's just not getting the message. Maybe he thinks it's just the typical office banter between friends and coworkers. Claudia is a petite little thing with long brown hair and big brown eyes. She has a smile that lights up a room and a body to go along with it makes every guy in the room turn into bobble heads when she enters. She isn't the type of woman to be out at the clubs and keeps to herself pretty well. However, if she gets the itch and wants to let loose a little, she easily does that while winning over any man that gleamed into those big beautiful eyes and that warm bright smile. There's no doubt she's uses those tools to her advantage. As managing office administrator, Claudia is super-efficient for all the managers and sales team combined.

She grew up in a small town just outside of Des Moines, IA with a population of around 8000. As a young girl, she didn't have the type of personality that most have at that age. Some were quite wild and out to have fun while enjoying their high school career more for the friends and social clubs than an actual high school education. Claudia was just the opposite with a side to her that was very warm and proper. She did the usual homecomings and proms, but it was mostly with a small group of friends she's known since she was very young. Unfortunately for her and her brother, their father was an abusive man. Verbally and even physically at times, he'd take his aggressions out on the kids and mother. To Claudia, yelling, screaming and fighting were a normal occurrence in the privacy of their home. Not many people in the community knew about it and it was something she kept secret for so long. During her senior year, Claudia knew she wanted to attend a college outside of the area and even outside of the state. Partly because she just wanted to get away. As an A student, she studied all the classes everyone else did with an exceptional ability to excel regardless of the curriculum. Needless to say, she took her studies a little more seriously than some of the others simply because she knew she would be leaving this small community for something better. A Michigan school is what she's always been thinking of. One of her close friends ended up playing football for a small division 3 school in Michigan. She visited from time to time taking in the area and the beauty of Michigan. Choosing Central Michigan for college, Claudia went as an excited little freshman ready to take the world by the horns. CMU is truly located right in the middle of the state. It's surrounded by corn fields, flat land, forest area and more corn fields. It does however, have some night life at the local casino along with a few local colleges and universities within short drives. During her college career, she was able to explore Michigan and all its beauty during each of the changing seasons. In the Fall, beautiful colors of the leaves changing make each landscape more colorful than can be imagined. During the Winter, layers of bright white snow cover the fields and hills for miles to see. Spring is even more beautiful with the sounds of birds chirping throughout the woods trickling springs flowing throughout the entire upper state. Spring in Northern Michigan was like watching the world reborn into gorgeous new colors, sounds and dreamscapes coming to life once again.

While adventuring out and learning more about Michigan, she was able to visit many of the major cities including Midland, Lansing, Traverse City, Grand Rapids and her favorite, Detroit. What touched her about Detroit was the continuous growth she watched as young people, couples and families crept back into the area. Detroit wasn't always the most desired location simply because of the common, stereotypical issues. Each major city has them. But

Detroit was on a positive path and Claudia saw that each time she visited. At graduation, she had already lined herself up with a small apartment right downtown where all the action was. This was quite different from where she grew up and exactly what she needed. Landing a job was one of her biggest accomplishments especially with one of the largest manufacturers in the Detroit area. Once she was able to establish herself within the company as one of the sharpest admins, she was able to advance little by little to now running all administration for managers including sales.

Socially, Claudia was doing pretty well with new friends and coworkers that enjoyed the night life of Detroit. Being able to walk, ride a bike or share a ride to local restaurants, watering holes and other interesting establishments, Claudia was having the time of her life. The one thing she felt she was missing was love. She has dated during her time here, but just hasn't found the one she feels connected with. Tom on the other hand, is someone she's had her eye on since she landed with this company. But the fact that he's a coworker has always kept them at an arms-length. Lately, she's been throwing vibes out to him to see if he'll respond.

Chapter 5

Swaying back and forth as the winds gust, branches on the trees move in harmony with each direction of the wind. I stand at the edge of an open field with trees behind me and a deep rich forest surrounding this huge opening. The field is filled with tall, light brown grass completely covering the ground clear across to the other side. Slowly walking towards the middle of the field, my finger-tips glide along the tops of the grass with a gentle tickle to each nerve throughout my hands. My legs are tingling as the stalks of grass rub gently against them. The sky is something I've never seen before with a haziness of blue and grey swirling around like tornados beginning to form. But with much less sound and not even a threat of a storm, it's all too eerie. In the middle of the field I see a swing hanging by ropes that lead to the sky. Not sure what's on the other end, but it reminds me of a swing set in a playground only there is no playground and there certainly is no swing set. The seat attached to the ropes is dirty red with old markings of an old piece of wood that has been used for years by all kinds of kids. With the wind making everything else move in the direction of each gust, the swing stood totally still and wasn't bothered at all. Looking full circle and seeing all the trees in every direction made me wonder how I got here. I'm an experienced hiker and this isn't anything I've noticed before. As I grabbed both of the ropes, I pulled myself up and popped my ass up onto the seat just as I did when I was a kid. The weather turned colder and the clouds began moving quicker in circles. Gripping tightly to the ropes, I gaze up to see where the swing goes. The ropes appear to be tied to a dark cloud in the sky that is circling around the ropes growing closer and closer to me. The wind suddenly stops and the clouds become motionless and black. A chill runs through my body I've never felt before when two large hands touch my back. With a force I can barely hold on, this thing pushes me into the air as I watch the field grow smaller and further away. I'm holding on with all my strength, but the feeling of being pulled away from the swing is too strong. In my body, I can feel the stress and impact from the speed in which I'm hurled. I lose my grip and can only hang on with one hand still moving at a tremendous speed. My other hand let's go from the pain in my fingers now soaring ever higher towards the blackness above. At this speed, it's difficult to maneuver my body as I'm spinning completely out of control. My eyes blurred with the wind, I'm able to see myself thrown into this cold, black cloud.

Another Friday morning in the office winding down the week with office politics and water cooler talk. Water cooler talk, an old expression used in the 80's and 90's where coworkers would stand around the water cooler and shoot the shit. Usually this would happen on a Monday so people could talk about their weekends. This Friday wasn't any different than any other, paperwork and follow up sales calls in preparation for the upcoming weeks. Being in the office wasn't one of Toms favorite things, however he did enjoy some of the banter with friends. Getting his calls done and any other miscellaneous work with the intent to get out of there by 2pm was always Toms goal. But this Friday may be a little different. Claudia was looking exceptionally nice today with the casual look in her tight jeans forming to her ass just right, comfortable shoes and a pretty pink blouse showing off just enough to catch an eye. Well, it caught Toms eye and he accidentally got busted looking. Boy did that bring a smile to her face, that big beautiful smile that Tom couldn't resist. He knew that though and for so long he admired her and was attracted to her, but would never let on. He knows he's slightly busted, blushes a little and turns away with a shit eaten grin. She returns to her desk, but keeps glancing over to make sure she saw what she saw. He's doing the same of course and now the cat is out of the bag. It's so fucking obvious, he thinks. There is no way in hell she didn't notice me checking her out! His mind wanders and he's getting nothing done at all. Sitting at his desk fumbling through paperwork, he decides to head to the kitchen for something to drink and to clear his mind.

Opening the refrigerator Tom finds the usual suspects, coworkers lunches, pop cans, plenty of water bottles, red bull drinks, a lunch that has been there for a week or so and a Snickers bar on the butter shelf. He grabs a bottle of water, glances at the Snickers bar just wondering who's it is and if they'd miss it and then closes the door. As he turns around to leave the room, there she is right in front of him. Claudia has come to do the same. Gee, what a coincidence, not! "Hi Tom," she says. "Hey Claudia, what's happening? Ready for the weekend?" "Oh hell yes," she says. "Ready for a weekend full of time to just catch up on some rest and some of the honey do list of things, but without the honey." Was that some sort of clue or prod to make me wonder even more about her? "How about you Tom? What do you have planned for the weekend? Anything exciting?" Tom stumbled a little on this one because it meant he'd have to open up on his personal life and he's not sure he wanted to do that just yet. "Well, not much on my end Claudia, just hanging around the apartment. Maybe getting out for a drink at some point." Oh crap, Tom thinks. That may have opened up an invitation that he may not be ready for. She peeks into the fridge, grabs a can of pop and the Snickers bar and turns to Tom. "Well, hope you're getting all your work done and can get out of here a little early today Tom." "Ya, me too and thanks." She turns and walks back to her desk. Now, Tom is even more intrigued by this woman. I mean really, she's got a great body, beautiful smile and from what he can tell, someone that likes candy bars. As he begins to leave the kitchen, Tom notices a breaking story on the local news channel.

Chapter 6

Action news reports the tragic death of a woman after somehow getting strangled on her children's swing set in the backyard. There are limited details, but what is known is that she was found by a neighbor while tangled in the ropes of the swing. At this time, there is no evidence of foul play and looks like a terrible accident or possible suicide. Due to the circumstances of how her body was tangled, investigators will be questioning the husband along with many of the neighbors for clues on this tragic event. More details to come as police continue this investigation.

Tom watches the news and quickly recalls his dream from the night before. His heart pounds and sinks to his stomach. Sick with fear, he bolts to his desk, grabs his keys and heads for the door. From the other side of the room, Claudia watches as he rushes towards the door without saying goodbye to anyone, not even her. Maybe he's got an emergency with a customer or a possible new client, she wonders. Either way, she now has his attention and can't wait for Monday to rekindle this flirtatious game.

Tom is struggling with the idea that his dreams are coming back to haunt him as they did when he was a kid. "Is this coincidence," he asks himself. "Or is this the start to another string of unexplainable accidents, murders and more of that fucking nightmare shit?" Tom is furious and starts thinking of how he can stop this before it gets bad like it did when he was young. Walking through the city to his apartment, he remembers the dreams along with the events that followed, like it just happened yesterday. He's horrified at the gruesome deaths that followed some of those crazy dreams. The dreams never made any sense and were endless counts of random bullshit. How could they possibly lead to someone getting killed afterwards, he thinks. It just didn't make sense. But this was the secret Tom's been keeping for so long. He enters his apartment, sits on a bar stool at the counter by his kitchen and stares out the window to the city. His apartment is actually pretty nice. On the 44th floor, Tom has a pretty good view of the city of Detroit. The city is growing at such a rapid pace that people are moving in more than moving out like they were in years past. Apartments and housing is getting harder and less affordable which is very good for residents in the city along with business owners and investors. With two bedrooms, a living room, dining room and a large kitchen, Tom feels right at home here and enjoys the view along with the luxuries provided on every block below. A gym on the top floor makes it even nicer for him to stay in the shape he's always been. Being six foot, Tom is built very well and enjoys working out to keep his muscles toned. With a full head of hair and blue eyes to go along with it, his confidence is much higher than most. Even his parking structure is attached which is extremely convenient. Being very organized, Toms apartment is quite clean and impressive when it comes to being a bachelor pad. All new appliances that are state of the art comfort him knowing he's got the best of everything including a 70" big screen tv mounted on the wall in the living room. His movie nights are amazing.

As Tom thinks about all the nightmares he's had in the past and even recently, he's bothered by one detail of those dreams. Something or someone is always there. Not just part of the dream, but something that is affecting the dream. Whatever this is, determines where the dream is going and what the outcome of the dream will be. Each time Tom gets chills that run clear down his spine, he knows whatever it is, is there. Cracking open a beer, he grabs a bag of chips munching them down like they were the last on earth. He's debating whether to turn on the tv because he certainly doesn't want to see any more of the destruction he's causing, or so he thinks. But his curiosity gets the best of him and he turns on the local news just to see.

Action news is reporting an update to an incident that happened at a local church where a local woman was found brutally attacked inside of the church. It has been determined that the Pastor, Father Stern was not involved and they still have no other suspects. Further details provided were that her body was torn apart or dismembered in a way the detectives have never seen before. Spread across the center isle of the church, they found a small amount of blood and no other clues implementing any suspects. "The scene was terrifying," says detective Butler of the Detroit police department. "It was nothing I've ever seen before. Body parts were scattered down the center isle, but there was little to no blood around them. It almost looked like someone had dismembered this woman, placed her body parts up and down the isle, then cleaned up before they left. It is one of the weirdest and most disturbing scenes I've come across. We will continue to investigate this until we find the individual or individuals that did such a horrific thing."

Watching this breaking story, Tom is bothered even more about the dreams and the real life stories that follow. He begins to wonder how his dreams are related, if at all to these terrible stories. It's like his dreams are the beginning of the story and then the real life events are the ending of the story. "Just doesn't make sense," he thinks. "Or maybe I have some supernatural abilities to see into the future through these dreams and somehow have to figure out how to save these poor saps from what is yet to come. Na, that's a bunch of shit. There is no way in hell I have any supernatural abilities!" So what the hell is really going on?

Chapter 7

The weekend is just another usual weekend hanging around the apartment, getting errands done and stocking up on food for meals during the next week. A couple of his buddies let him know they'll be heading out to watch the game Saturday at one of the local breweries and asked if he'd want to go. Of course, Tom is always up for watching a Michigan college football teams play while choking down some wings and enjoying an ice cold draft. They meet up at the brewery and pick a high-top table by the bar and away from the restaurant area to avoid the kids and boring people. The three of them each order one of the local brews along with some chips and salsa to chew on before they eat. As the game begins, the local crowd pours in to fill this place up in no time at all. TV's all around, decorations for all the local teams with flags and signs, waitresses that are pleasing to the eye and the all too familiar bar menus that really only give you a handful of items to choose from. The food is good and the beer is even better. Being a local brewery, they create new drafts often enough to keep people coming back to sample the latest and greatest. The flavor Tom enjoys is a golden ale with a hint of bourbon. It reminds him of a beer he had once down in Kentucky called the Kentucky bourbon barrel ale that was a little richer than his taste called for, but had full bodied flavor he enjoyed. The beers went down smoothly as they always did and it was about time to order some food. It's a good idea to get the order in before halftime simply because it seems to be the time there's a rush on food. Tom orders four buffalo, four teriyaki and four mango habanero wings along with some celery and ranch to go along with them. "Oh, I'll have some fries too." He finishes his beer, orders another and says, "I'll be back guys, got to hit the head." After shaking twice, he washes his hands and places them under the air dryer. This bathroom hand dryer looks like something from the stone ages. The air barely comes out of it making you rub your hands over and over again just to get them somewhat dry. "Oh for crying out loud," he yells. "Just dry my fucking hands already! Screw it." He rubs his hands on his jeans to finish drying them off and walks out the door.

"Holy shit, Claudia! What are you doing here?" Wow she looked good, I mean really good. Tight black jeans, hair pulled back in a ponytail, a Michigan jersey to match and that big beautiful smile that knocks me off my feet every time. "Oh Hi Tom, I'm here with some friends watching the game. I'm on the other side of the bar and saw you with a couple of your buddies, but didn't want to interrupt." "INTERRUPT," Tom exclaims. Oh shit, Tom thinks.

That may have been just a little too overzealous. He tones his voice down, "of course you wouldn't have interrupted me and my buddies, we're just hanging and watching the game too. You headed to the john?" Oh my god you idiot, what kind of question is that? "I mean when you're free, why don't you stop by the table, if you want?" "That sounds good Tom and yes, I'm going in to drop a deuce." They both start cracking up and walked their respective ways. Tom gets back to the table and begins telling the guys about Claudia. Their eyes are glued to Tom as he describes her as the hot little spinner she is. He continues to tell them how she is in the office, how they flirt from time to time and how she always looks so good that he has to be careful from getting caught checking her out. The football game continues and the wings show up at the table. "So good," he says while gleaming at the wings and fries not paying any attention to the celery that for some reason he feels he has to order when ordering wings. Are the celery sticks supposed to calm the hotness from the sauces or something? Whoever came up with the idea of celery with wings? In any event, he digs in.

The guys are pretty much finishing up their dinners, wiping their fingers and faces from the sauces with those little wet wipes restaurants generally provide. "I need to go to the john and get all this shit off my face in case Claudia comes over here," Tom says. "Oh really? Shit all over your face?" Tom's shoulders shrug just a little with a look of terror on his sauced up face as he hears that lovely voice from behind. "You heard that?" "Yes, I sure did Tom. Now why don't you go clean yourself up while I introduce myself to your two buddies." Tom is even more intrigued by the candor and social expertise Claudia is showing. What a chick, he thinks as he walks to the john to make sure he comes back looking his best. Claudia takes Tom's bar stool and begins shooting the shit with the guys. They are amazed how she's into the game as much as she is and how she's acting like one of the guys. Maybe she's trying to impress them and have them put in a good word for her when she ends up leaving. Tom comes back and stands by the high-top while Claudia and the guys are in the middle of a conversation having something to do with beer. She's describing the types of beer she enjoys and what she had to eat. Tom says, "you had wings? Okay, what are your favorite sauces? Do you like them hot or do you like the other sauces that give a lot of flavor?" "Oh I like'm hot, but they also have to have some flavor to them. So I usually order Asian Zing or Honey BBQ or something like that where I can get a good taste to them. Otherwise, they're just wings that burn your mouth off." "Ya, I agree," Tom says. Not really, he thinks. Love the hot wings that burn my face off! "Sometimes it's just too hot and you can't taste anything." Claudia laughs and continues to talk directly to Tom as if the other guys weren't there. The conversation flows smoothly as they discuss work, football and other non-interesting topics just to keep looking at each other not wanting the discussion to end. She then gets up from the table, turns and thanks the guys for the company and says to Tom, "I really enjoyed talking with you. Maybe we can do this again sometime." Tom was excited and terrified all at the same time. The terrified part was only because this was a coworker and those types of relationships never seemed to end well. "I'd really like that Claudia. Do I have your phone number?" Of course you don't you fucking moron, he thinks. "Well, if you did," she says, "you most likely stole it from the work listing and are getting ready to stalk me." That made his day. She's beautiful, sexy AND has a great sense of humor. "Oh," he laughs. "I didn't do that, but not a bad idea," Tom says. They exchange phone numbers, say a temporary goodbye and all three guys watch as Claudia walks away.

Chapter 8

Detective Butler has thoroughly exhausted all efforts in the case regarding the woman who was strangled to death in her own backyard by the ropes on the swing set. The husband was questioned along with neighbors and close friends that knew her well. During the investigation, he learned that this was a normal, happy family from what everyone described. It doesn't seem to look like anything other than a suicide or a terrible accident. But because the kids weren't present during this awful event, there has to be a reason the woman was even at the swing set. What was she doing there by herself? And how on earth did she get so tangled up? Those questions haunted the detective and not many of his previous cases did.

Detective Ray Butler grew up in Detroit being raised by his mother who also had three other boys. Charles was the oldest and James and Darius were twins and younger than Ray. His mother kept order in the household as much as she could with four boys and worked as a nurse at the medical center. Her job allowed her to work around the boy's schedules for the most part, but relied on Charles and Ray for help. When mom wasn't around, the boys had to raise themselves and stay out of harm's way. In Detroit and in the neighborhood they grew up in, it was easy to find trouble. Ray's older brother Charles was really the boss of the family given there was no father in the picture. All within just a few years of each other, the boys were very close growing up. All looked out for each other and no matter what, they had each other's back. Being the second oldest of the boys, Ray held some of that responsibility on his shoulders to make sure his two younger brothers kept out of trouble, got all of their homework done and pretty much stayed in line or else. The or else part was because if Ray's older brother found they were misbehaving, Ray would get it and Ray would just pass that discipline down to them. They all respected each other early on in their childhood simply because of the circumstances they were faced with. A mother that worked hard balancing a full-time job and raising four boys on her own was quite a task in itself. She was tough on the boys and they knew not to mess with mom. But they also grew up learning that mom was the shit and they loved her more than sons could ever love their mom.

In high school, Ray found himself spending most of his time playing football, studying and taking care of his two younger brothers. He was the one walking them to school in the morning and getting them home after school before he had to bolt back for practice. His mother, now taking on two jobs to make sure her boys were given every opportunity in this world to succeed, was busier than ever. Charles was now done with high school, working a part-time job at a convenience store and helping out around the house as much as he had time for. But the time he spent at the house helping out wasn't as much as what Ray would've wanted. He found that his older brother was spending more and more time with some of the guys in the hood and less time with him and his two younger brothers. His mother, relying on Charles to take care of the house and kids while she worked most of the day, was worried. Many conversations about responsibilities and what needs to be done while Ray was at school, football practice, the younger one's middle school, chores around the house, making sure everyone eats and finishes up homework, keeping each other safe and many other topics that were important to the family were somewhat ignored by Charles. He did take care of things at the house now and again. But it just wasn't enough. Charles struggled with working, living in this environment and the fairness in life. His thoughts got him to the point of considering other alternatives to make money which is why he was hanging with some of the other guys in the area. Charles thought he could make more money dealing drugs than working a shitty job at a convenience store. None of the other kids including Ray, knew what Charles was up to. He'd leave about the same time he was going to work and come back the usual time in the evening. Still, Ray had to do more for the younger boys than he wanted to. This was his time to enjoy high school, dating, playing sports and growing up as a teenager. Taking care of two middle school kids is not something he wanted to do, but he did it anyway because it's what needed to be done.

In his senior year, Ray was so accustomed to taking care of his brothers and people in general that he decided looking into this as a career after he graduated. His football career in high school was a lot of fun, but he knew it wasn't going to take him to the pro level simply because he never had the time to dedicate extra efforts to make that a dream. Some of the other guys in school were definitely more talented and dedicated all their time to the sport, one of the many things Ray admired. Reality was different for Ray, not bad, just different. He graduated with good grades and was proud to say he did it where many young men and women don't have the opportunity or just don't put the effort in to either stay in school or do well at it. He did both. James and Darius were entering high school now and would hopefully follow in Ray's footsteps. Charles on the other hand, didn't seem to be heading down the right path. For a while, there was more food on the table, more toys to play with, better shoes and name branded clothes along with just a little more cash around the house for the boys to spend. Nobody really questioned it and thought it was extra hours Charles was working, at least that was his story to his mother. He'd come home late at night now just in time to climb in bed without having to talk with anyone. When his mom asked him about work, Charles said he was picking up hours and working any extra odd jobs he could just to help out. She was proud of course, but also a bit concerned.

Chapter 9

Later that evening, Tom receives a text that simply says, "Hi." His eyes lit up a bit when he saw the name Claudia as the sender. "Just checking to see if you get this or if you gave me the wrong number on purpose." He laughs and responds, "who is this?" Waiting for the reply not knowing if she'll fall for that or not, she replies, "Oh I'm terribly sorry, I must have the wrong number, please forgive me." Tom immediately responds as if he's just made a big mistake by throwing her off and making her feel like he really did give her the wrong number. "No Claudia, it's me Tom. I was just messing around and thought that would be funny." She responds, "I know, I figured you'd do something like that so I wanted to play along to see what you'd do and well, you did exactly what I wanted you to do." "CRAP," he yells with laughter. "I can't believe I fell for that, I'm such a freakin idiot." The texting conversation goes on through most of the evening bantering back and forth while getting to know each other during the jokes. They find they are much alike and decide they should go out on a date, a real date and see where this goes.

Not so much in those words, but they bantered their way to this upcoming date.

The elevator's taking forever. Why is this so fucking slow? I've been on this stupid thing so many times and it's never taken this long to get to my floor. Finally, the digital message above the door reads 213 and the doors open. What the hell? Since when does this building have over two hundred floors and why on earth is there a floor 213? Most of the buildings in the U.S. skip the number 13 entirely. I get out of the elevator and begin looking for my apartment. Where am I? Did I get off on the wrong floor or something? It's a dimly lit hallway going in only one direction. The sconces on the walls flicker as if trying to stay lit under a power outage. Did we lose power? I walk down the hallway gazing at each of the doors just waiting for someone to come out so I can talk with them and figure out what's going on. There are hallways going only to my right which is weird because there are usually no hallways other than mine leading directly to my apartment. I turn down one of the hallways and notice the first door to my right close ever so slowly. Someone behind that door was watching me and didn't want to talk. But the image I saw just before the door closed made my skin crawl. A very skinny, older man gleamed at me as if I was someone dangerous. His skin was pasty white with moles on the top of his head along with big bushy, gross eye brows. As I walk past, the door re-opens showing three very large and gruesome fingers gently holding the top part of the door frame. I quickly turn and keep walking even faster so I can get the hell out of here. I certainly don't recall any weird or crazy neighbors and certainly don't remember that! I'm instantly back to the main hallway in which I started and I'm having a real hard time finding my apartment. Am I in the wrong building? The end of the hallway was extremely dark as if all the lights down there weren't on. Maybe the power is limited through here, but this still doesn't look like my floor. A slow, yet consistent rush of wind catches me as if someone opened a window in a high-rise hotel. I'm scared now because this isn't where I should be. The hair on my neck rises and the chill runs down my spine once again. Holy shit, I'm dreaming! I run for the door as if that's going to help and when I open the door to the stairwell, it sucks me in shutting the door loudly behind me. I have to get out of here, someone or something is right by me and I can't see it, I can only feel it. I run up the first group of stairs and continue to run as fast as I can. Each time I get to the top of the stair case, it seems as if I'm right at the bottom of the same stair case I just climbed. Faster and faster I run getting nowhere as each stair case grows harder to climb. Now I know something is behind me because I can hear whatever it is on the stairs below. Not being able to see what it is, I just run. I'm at a large black door with locks and hinges all over making it look completely impenetrable, but I can still hear something coming up from behind me. I gather up my strength and rush the door thinking I'll just bust it open. I'm standing on the other side of the door on the rooftop of this building. The short brick wall to my left is the edge of the building where you can see other buildings all around. The door slams behind me and what is standing in front of it I'll never forget. It's twenty feet or more away from me as I back up slowly wondering what this things next move is. Not knowing how close I am, my heels hit something hard behind me so I turn and look down at the back of my feet to make sure it's the wall. I immediately look back to see if it has moved and come face to face with this demon. It's leaning down looking right at me only inches from my face. The darkness of this demon was intense along with its size. His arms extended in each direction so far I couldn't tell where they ended. The hooded cape covered most of its face only showing dark, watery eyes and a mouth full of large discolored teeth. Scared out of my mind, I stumble backwards not being able to hold myself and tumble over the edge.

Literally jumping out of his dream, Tom wakes up grabbing his chest and looking at the ceiling recalling the exact details of that dream. "Holy shit," he exclaims. His heart is pounding and he's glad to be lying in bed instead of falling down the side of a high-rise building 213 floors up. But this was just another one of those bad dreams he didn't like to have. Worried about what was to come and the images of what he saw in his dream, he gets out of bed and jumps in the shower hoping to clear his head. It's Sunday and there's not much to do today other than watch an NFL game or get some stuff done around the apartment. "Ding," a text comes in. "Ding," and another. Tom gets out of the shower, dries himself up, slaps some deodorant on along with a little cologne for no apparent reason and heads for the kitchen. "Ding," the texting continues. It's Claudia! He picks up the phone and reads his texts from this little hottie. "Hi there, good morning." "Are you up yet?" "What the hell, did you go to church or are you just ignoring me?" Okay, he thinks. Do I respond with something fun or do I just say I was in the shower? "Hey there girl, just got done with church and on my way to volunteer at the homeless shelter down the street. After that, I'm heading up a retreat for opioid addiction and inviting them all back to my place for some really good stuff." No response, at least not for a few minutes. "Oh really, I didn't think you were the church going type or a volunteer. The rest, ya I believe that!" The "LOLs" start flying. Tom gets dressed and sits at the counter of his kitchen bar wondering what he's going to do today. He's thinking how nice it is to hear from Claudia this morning and wonders if this is now going to be a regular thing. I could get used to that, he thinks.

Chapter 10

Sunday is usually the shortest day of the week because nobody wants it to end. It just means going to bed at a decent time and wondering what the work week has in store for ya. Shortly before noon, Tom is wondering what he'll do today. Is it going to be a day to watch football or is this going to be one of those boring Sundays that move along accomplishing nothing and having the dread feeling of going to work the next morning. "Ding," a text comes in from Claudia. "Watching any football today big guy? I was thinking if you were free, we could go somewhere and watch the game for a bit." Well I'm watching football NOW, he says out loud all by himself. "Hey, that sounds great," he texts. "I was just sitting here wondering what to do today and wasn't sure if it would be chores, football or just nothing, LOL." He jumps to his feet now wondering what this day is going to be like. The excitement and nervousness he feels inside himself makes him smile and he can't wait to get this day moving. "Well that sounds great Tom. How about we meet at the sports bar and grill around 12:30pm in order to get a table or seat at the bar?" "Perfect, see you then," Tom replies. Getting ready to go watch a football game should take like five seconds. But this was different. Finding the right shirt, the right jeans and the right shoes was key. He sees this woman almost every day at work so why on earth would he be worried about what he's wearing. Regardless, he puts on his best pair of jeans, combs his hair just right, slaps on a little cologne and heads for the door.

Thinking he arrived early enough to grab a table by the bar for the two of them, he sits at the first open one he finds and positions himself to watch the game. That's funny, he thinks to himself, probably not going to be watching much of the game. The waitress comes up with a smile and a menu and asks if she can get him something to drink. He takes the menu and tells her he'll wait for his friend to show up before he orders. He's being so polite. The sports bar is filling up and table are hard to come by in the bar area. The bar area is the best because you don't want to be on the restaurant side where the obnoxious families are and all the kids that are running around yelling at their parents for quarters to play the only two arcade games they have in this place. You can see the restaurant section pretty well from the good side, but there's enough interference where you feel as if you are only in a bar. With televisions all around the bar and on the walls adjacent to the bar, you can see any game you're here to watch. The food is pretty good here considering it's just bar food, it's not like they have a specialty or anything. The atmosphere is what people come for, well, beer and the atmosphere. Suddenly, everything seems to go quiet. It's like the opening of a movie where the coming attractions stop playing and the beginning of the movie starts. The televisions go quiet, music from the jukebox stops and even the kids across the way stop yelling. She walks in the door and everyone including the wait staff stop, look and stare as she closes the door behind her. Okay, it wasn't quite like that. In fact, it wasn't like that at all, it just seemed like it. There she was! As beautiful as I recall and maybe even more so today. She smiled my way and headed for the table.

"Well hello handsome, this seat taken?" Who on earth would say no to that? "No as a matter of fact, I was just waiting for some lucky lady to come over and sit down. Looks like you're the winner!" She's really quite striking with her long brown hair, deep brown eyes and lips that kill. Her jeans fit nicely too, but I tried very hard not to look for more than one or two seconds. She also had a football jersey on which made the complete package just perfect. "So what are you drinking? Did you order yet?" "No," Tom said. "I wanted to wait for you." That must have hit home and may have been something small and stupid, but it meant a lot to her. "So you're old fashioned AND sweet, hmmm, another attractive quality I see." The waitress comes back and takes our orders of a couple beers and some chips and salsa. While waiting for drinks, they dive deep into getting to know each other. The game started some time ago and they're learning so much about each other they wouldn't have known with office conversations, bantering back and forth and the little flirting they've done. "It's so easy talking with you Claudia. Like we've known each other on a personal level for longer than we've actually known each other on a professional level." "I know," she replies. "It is really hard to get to know someone at work because you always have to be on good behavior for the most part and can't really, truly be yourself. I find it hard to show you who I really am at work because I think the others would see that I like you and have always been attracted to you." "Wow Claudia, that was really nice to say. I have to admit I've always thought you were attractive in the office, but didn't want to be offensive and make you feel uncomfortable knowing I thought so." "Oh my god Tom, you're so cute!"

The football game ends and people start to leave or transition to ordering new food and beverages for the 4pm game. Tom and Claudia are both wondering what even happened in the game they came to watch because they didn't even watch it. The glance up at the television and at the very same time say, "what was the score?" They laugh while looking at each other and realize they've taken up three hours simply enjoying each other's company. "Well Tom, we should probably get going. I still have some laundry, cleaning and some other shit to get done before I end up going to bed." "Ya, same for me, lots of stuff to do." Oh that was a load of crap, I didn't have anything to do and that was just to save face, Tom thinks. "It was really nice watching the game with you Claudia. Well, I mean it was nice being here with the game in the background and getting to know you," he laughs. "Maybe we can do this again soon or maybe even go out for dinner or to a show or whatever during one of our free evenings." "I'd like that Tom; I'd like that a lot. If you're in the office in the morning, I'll see you then. Until then, feel free to reach out anytime, I like talking with you."

Chapter 11

Now back to his apartment thinking of the fantastic day he had with Claudia, Tom decides to organize his upcoming work week with where he needs to go and who he needs to see. Since he covers most of the Detroit metro area, there's a number of potential customers, new customers and existing customers he needs to talk with covering five counties. But the first thing he needs to do is figure out a reason he needs to be in the office as much as he can this week. Will it seem obvious that now his schedule changes enough to where before he was only in the office a couple times a week to more than that? At this point, he doesn't care and just wants to see her a little more often. He turns on the tv and begins going through his company calendar setting his schedule. He's got Monday down pretty well figured out. Stop by the office, present to get things in order as if they aren't already, say hello to Claudia and then leave for the day of sales calls. It could just be that Tuesday through the rest of the week duplicates Monday. But Monday will be a good day as the first thing he'll see is that big beautiful smile. The eleven o'clock news comes on and he's just finishing up some scheduling for the week and heading to bed.

Breaking news is reporting the death of a young man found in an alley between two apartment buildings on the east side. Details currently show this to be a suicide as we are being told he may have jumped from the roof. Police aren't giving out a name at this time and investigation is under way. More details to come as the investigation continues.

Tom sits back on the couch suddenly not remembering the wonderful day he just had. His hands are shaking as he puts his beer down on the table next to the couch. The glass of beer rattles to the glass on the table, he notices how nervous he really is. Heart pounding and sinking to his stomach again, he puts his hands over his head and curls up with his knees to his chest while sitting on the edge of the couch seat. "Why is this happening? Why me? These people dying because I'm dreaming. These poor people," he sighs. "God, I wish I could tell them." Tom is losing it. He's thinking of these innocent people and the horror they must have gone through simply because he had a bad dream. He sits up, wipes his face and walks to the bathroom. He stares at the bathroom mirror and thinks. Staring himself in the eyes he says, "there's got to be something I can do. There has to be some way I can warn whoever is going to be hurt. What the fuck!" He washes his face and heads for the bedroom. Not knowing what he's going to dream about tonight and scared shitless about it, he sits in the small chair in the corner of the room positioned under a reading lamp and opens a magazine. "Fuck it, I'll just stay awake."

A kink in his neck is the least of Toms worries today. He tries to move in the chair that apparently, he fell asleep in last night while reading his magazine. He looks around to make sure he's not in a dream, but how can he really tell he's not. He checks his watch, 5:38am it reads. He scratches his head while trying to straighten out his neck that was dangled over the back of the chair for who knows how long. Stretching his legs and arms, he slowly gets out of the chair and heads for the john. He comes to the conclusion that he's not in a dream and gets ready for the day. On his way to work, all he can think about is that damn dream and how he could've either stopped the dream or stopped the guy from getting hurt. He keeps going through his mind wondering if the guy jumped simply to kill himself or if he was thrown off the building for some other reason. Regardless, it's all too coincidental and in perfect line with what happened years ago. He gets to work and heads up to the floor his company's office is on. Completely forgetting how excited he'd be when he sees Claudia, he runs into her in the lobby. "Hey good looking," she says. His smile is less than convincing and she's a little taken back by it and says, "is everything okay?" "Oh ya, everything is fine.

Just had a bad night's sleep and trying to get with it today. You look great! How was the rest of your evening?" A nice save as he's able to make her believe everything is okay and not a mess like what is in his head. "It was good, just hung around getting some things done around the place." They walk in the office together, turn and smile at each other and head to their separate cubicles. As Tom mumbles to himself, "I wonder if everyone saw that or if everyone is watching us?" He looks around the office and nobody is looking or probably cares anyway. After checking emails and doing a little administrative bullshit, he gathers his stuff from the desk and heads for the exit. Only this time, he first circles way around to the other side of the floor just so he can say goodbye to Claudia before leaving. "Oh that was sweet Tom, thanks for stopping by before you left. Have a great day." The receptionist next to Claudia glances over as if a dirty little secret was just revealed.

Chapter 12

Tom completes a couple sales calls and does his job to keep customers happy. It's early afternoon and he's still very curious about what happened with that young man who died yesterday at those east side apartments. He decides to go to the apartments just to see if there is anything he can learn. Before driving to the apartments, Tom searches his smartphone for reasons why people dream. All kinds of things pop up in his search showing different types of dreams and why people might have them. Nightmares aren't as common as one would think. They are generally in part because of personal trauma or stress or emotional problems. A less severe form of nightmare is a bad dream. These types of dreams are more common and sometimes more regular in frequency. They also aren't the types of dreams that would make you scare yourself to wake up like a nightmare would. Then there are the night terrors that generally happen with children when they are frightened suddenly by a fall or loud noise like a scream. Adults sometimes have them, but are generally more apt to not be frightened out of a dream by one of those. Recurring dreams are simply that, they happen often enough and may have some of the more frightening characteristics to them. The dream that caught Toms eye was the lucid dream type. This is the type of dream where you can actually recognize during your dream that you are actually dreaming. In other words, you're in your own dream watching and doing what you're dreaming about. Studies show many people can manipulate their dreams and influence how they unfold during the dream. Tom feels this is very much like what he's experiencing as he did the night before in the middle of his dream. Even though Tom knew he was dreaming, the dream continued as he tried really hard to not only get out of the dream, but to manipulate how it goes. Obviously Tom isn't very good at this yet, but feels he's going to have to master it in order to make all this chaos stop.

Parking down the street, Tom steps out onto the sidewalk and looks down the block to see where the building is. It's not hard to find considering there's still many police vehicles, news trucks and a small crowd staring down an alleyway blocked by yellow tape. There's no body of course, but Tom sees detectives measuring and taking pictures and doing whatever they do to solve a crime. He tries to get closer to see what others are seeing, but there really isn't anything else to see. Being sure this has to do with his dream, Tom must learn who this person was and what actually happened. Entering the apartment building, he's confronted by a security guard asking for his building pass. He says he's just here to see a friend, quickly changes the subject and asks, "what happened man? Police are everywhere." The security guard tells him there was a misfortune and that someone from the building committed suicide early Sunday morning before light and that's all he knows. Again, he asks for his building pass. "Suicide," Tom replies with a terrible look of concern on his face. "Who was he? Did he live here?" The security guard is once again drawn into the conversation and says, "Ya he did. It was this dude on the 7th floor that decided it would be better to jump off the roof than deal with whatever he was dealing with. I knew him a bit to say I said Hi to him as he would come and go. Are you a reporter or something? And what friend are you here to see?" Tom decides this is the end of this conversation and there's not much else he's going to get out of this guy without giving it away that he has no business here at all. "Oh never mind," Tom says. "I'll catch up with him another day." On his way out the door, he hears one of the police officers say, "there is no way that was a suicide. He wouldn't have looked like that if it was." Tom stops and takes note of what he heard. He's scared to know the details, but is now even more curious about what happened. "Hey Butler, come over here," yells one of the detectives. Tom nonchalantly hangs around making sure he doesn't bring attention to himself. Detective Butler walks over to see what the other detective wants. They are having one of those private, quiet discussions which makes Tom want to get closer to them. "Scratches on his arms, bodily injury that just doesn't match up well with a suicide. What are we looking at here," he says? Tom is nudged by one of the police officers while walking by as he bumps into detective Butler. Butler looks at him and says, "can I help you?" "Oh, no thanks." Tom jumps into his car and heads for home.

Chapter 13

Detective Butler has his hands full with this one. A dead young man where everyone that knew him is completely dumbfounded as to why he'd even consider suicide. They say he had everything going for himself and was liked by all. The idea he'd jump from a building is absolutely unbelievable and many of the people interviewed are wondering if there was something more to this. After gathering all the data, he can possibly get from the scene, Butler heads back to the office where he can start making phone calls and further investigate this awful tragedy. While driving to the office, he reaches out to his twin brothers James and Darius just to see how they're doing. James is finishing up grad school in order to get his law degree and practice as a corporate lawyer while Darius is hard at work for one of the local construction companies 'rebuilding Detroit' as he puts it. Both have done pretty well for themselves in making sure they keep their heads above water and they've managed to stay out of trouble. Ray is glad to hear all is going well and keeps in touch with them every so often as he's always done since they were young. But in every conversation with them, the question was always asked about how their oldest brother Charles was doing. Charles was unfortunately, on the wrong path as a young man. While his intentions were good, he just wasn't able to stay out of trouble with the law and as the saying goes, the law won. Charles is spending all of his time in the local county jail serving time for drug related crimes along with a very odd murder charge from a shooting that he continues to fight. Being involved with the types of people he was, it's hard to defend him simply because he's either guilty or guilty by association. His story was that he didn't pull the trigger and didn't even have a gun, but of course all of the criminals say the same thing. Is Charles actually telling the truth? Ray's job was to keep him from getting the book thrown at him which he was able to do, but time in jail seems to be the best way to keep Charles from adding to his problems. Ray assures the twins that Charles is doing well and that they should visit him sometime soon.

Sitting as his desk, Butler looks at the list of cases he's confronted with, (murder of a local woman at the church), (fatal dog attack on east side of a middle aged couple), (woman strangled by ropes on a swing set / possible suicide), (young man jumped off building / possible suicide / other), "and this is just the short list! What is going on around here," he asks himself aloud. He continues to shuffle through paperwork including interview notes, pictures and forms to be filled out in detail for each case when the phone rings. "Hello, detective Butler here," he answers. The phone is relatively quiet for what seems like forever only it's just a second or two, "hello detective Butler, my name is Tom. I was wondering if maybe we could talk about some of the cases you're working on." Detective Butler is of course, initially bothered. Is this a reporter? Someone looking for a story in some bullshit magazine? Butler says, "what can I do you for Tom? I don't usually discuss cases to people that call me out of the blue and ask for information on them. Why would you ask? You writing a story or something?" Tom's heart is pounding, his hands are shaking and doesn't really know how to respond to this. He's thinking that if he brings up dreams he's had and how they relate to the deaths, he'll just get hung up on. On the other hand, if he tells him about the connection to all these events and Butler decides to talk further, is he implicating himself into more trouble than he wants from this? "No sir," Tom replies. "I'm only looking to discuss why I think some or all of these murders, accidents or whatever you're calling them are happening." Detective Butler leans back in his chair and asks, "and what do you think you know about them Tom? This time, you could hear a pin drop from the silence on the other end of the phone. All of a sudden, Tom found himself in a very uncomfortable position. Not knowing what exactly to say to detective Butler, Tom stumbles through saying, "well, I don't really know much about them other than there might be a way to stop them. I'm not even too sure about how, but I think there's a way." Butler seems even more uninterested at this point and simply says, "well I'll tell ya what Tom. You come up with a concrete idea that will stop these crazy events and I'll listen. Until then, have a nice day," and hangs up.

Tom's deflated, his shoulders fall to a slouch and his head drops touching his chin to his chest. He knows in his heart this is something that has to be discussed with detective Butler or someone that might have an open mind about what's going on. But like most movies, he'd be considered crazy. He bellies up to the bar at the local dive and takes a drink of his beer contemplating on whether or not he should have made that call. His mind starts to wander about if they traced the call and are now on their way to come arrest him simply because he made that weird call. He looks around the bar and sees no suspicious activity, just the normal beer drinking crowd of seven or eight people including him. Ordering up another beer, his phone beeps with a text he probably needed right about now. "Hey you, how's it going? How was your day Mr. salesman?" A smile grows on his face as he reads the text and begins to reply. "It's going okay Miss admin lady, how are you doing? Done with work? Heading home?" He's waiting for a response and doesn't see the three little moving dots when someone on the other end is typing. Putting his phone down and taking a drink of his beer, it dings again. "Ya, done for the day and heading home to chill out. Long day today with all the normal Monday crap. How about you?" He thinks of a good response that's different from volunteering with a bunch of drug attics and begins typing. As he's typing, the softest touch of a hand gently glides along his shoulder and across his upper back to his left. He slowly glances over his left shoulder only to see a woman standing there looking at him with big beautiful eyes, lips and a fine figure to match. "Hi Mr salesman, waiting for someone special?'

Chapter 14

"I saw you walk in and thought I'd have a little fun with you. How's your day going? Lose a sale or something? You look like you're in a great deal of thought." Claudia's making small talk knowing something's bothering Tom. She reaches over and lightly places her hand on the bottom of his left arm just above the elbow. Tom laughs, "no I certainly didn't lose a sale. Just have a lot going on right now that doesn't make much sense to me." Tom is seriously thinking of changing the subject almost immediately because he just doesn't want to have Claudia thinking he's crazy or for that matter, thinking he's anything other than what she thinks now. Things are moving along so well for the beginning of whatever this is and he just doesn't want to throw anything negative in the mix. She continues to offer her light touch which is very soothing to Tom as she says, "lay it on me buddy, what's bugging ya?" Tom isn't sure where to begin. He's got has this wonderful woman sitting next to him for what could be a fantastic, long-term relationship and then he has his chaos sitting with him. He slowly introduces her to his childhood and what he dealt with in regards to his dreams. She's intrigued of course, but a little skeptical without looking as if she is. Deep in conversation, Tom sees more and more that Claudia is engaged and truly interested in what he's sharing with her. One of the dreams he recalls from when he was young was a dark day in Detroit being lost in the outskirts of the city where nobody should really be. It was a dangerous area filled with drugs, prostitution and the dirtiest of people he's ever seen. Although Tom was young at that time and didn't actually hang out on those streets, talk around town made him feel as if he knew them well. "I remember walking in the middle of the street too scared to get close to any of the parked cars or the houses surrounding me. It was late at night and down the street all I could see were one or two street lights glimmering and the full moon in the sky that lit up the area. Noises like voices, screams, whispers, banging and other weird sounds came from the homes and open fields where homes used to sit. I couldn't see very far really and had that terrible feeling something was right freakin next to me. Every time I'd turn to see what it was, nothing was there." "Holy shit Tom, you're giving me the chills and this was just a dream of yours," she claims with excitement. "Ya, no shit," Tom says. "What then," Claudia asks. "I remember having a gun for some reason. Maybe because my Dad always used to talk about having a gun or maybe because it was like the wild west when everyone got to carry a gun. Either way, there I was with a gun on my side in the middle of this awful part of Detroit. It's a little fuzzy now, but the only other thing I remember is shooting someone and running as fast as I can. Of course, the dream didn't let me run fast and it was like I was struggling so hard to run yet something was holding me back. I woke from that dream in the middle of the night and couldn't get back to sleep. That's what I remember." Now stuck to the edge of her seat, Claudia says, "So how does that dream mean anything? Wasn't it just another weird dream?" "Well, that's just it. The next day there was another shooting in Detroit that had something to do with some young kid." "Ya, but that kind of happens often you know," she says. "Okay, but this was odd. From what I remember watching the news, that kid didn't do it. The evidence wasn't there, but he was blamed anyway. It was all just too weird and coincidental for me." "Wow Tom, how often does this happen? And just so you know, I do feel this is more coincidental and not your fault, but if you truly believe in this, I will help you anyway I can." Toms eyes gloss over and he loves what he just heard. Someone that may not think he's crazy.

He opens up even more telling her more specifics about his dreams and what types of dreams he's had lately trying to connect them with the events that have also been happening in the area. The warm, gentle touch makes him feel even more confident in allowing him to fully disclose what has been going on. "Tom, do you really feel that those dreams are actually the cause of these awful things?

What's been happening lately is disturbing and terrible, but you can't really take responsibility for it can you?" Tom sits and thinks about the sensibility she's describing and certainly knows this sounds pretty crazy. But in his heart, he feels he does hold the responsibility and needs to address this now. "Yes Claudia, I actually can. This has followed me around my whole life it seems and I just can't let this continue. I have to let detective Butler know without making me look like a crazy man." Rubbing his back now with the utmost compassion she says, "how do you plan on letting him know? Are you going to simply tell him and see what he says or does?" "Well, I called him a little earlier and he basically thought I was either nuts or a reporter so he told me to have a nice day and hung up. I know I have to reach out again, but not sure how." Laughing, Tom says, "Are ya sure you don't think I'm nuts?" Her reaction to this question surprises Tom as he smiles even more while giggling about this drama filled conversation. "Of course not Tom! What you've shared with me is so personal and I'm positive, very difficult to share. I won't judge you Tom, what do we do next?" Excited and encouraged, Tom starts thinking about what his next steps are going to be and that now he's not going to be alone in this.

The evening goes on as Tom and Claudia sit at the bar sharing appetizers, more personal stories and a few drinks. Trying to come up with a plan on how to bring this to detective Butlers attention without seeming crazy or becoming a suspect is going to be tough. They brainstorm for a while until realizing it's time to get out of there. In just a short time, both of them feel they've become closer and have obviously learned so much more about each other. Tom still has some concerns about laying it all out there to her and hopes she feels the same about him tomorrow. All he can do now is wait and see. Saying goodnight, they both lean in and give each other a warm hug. As they release this embrace, there was a moment of bliss where their eyes met and they both wanted so badly to kiss. Holding each other's hand, they slowly let go and depart.

Chapter 15

I'm standing in the middle of an angry crowd being pushed around by people moving all over waving signs and yelling at the top of their lungs. It's unclear what's going on here and why I'm in the middle of this mess. I know there were protests going on and other public events in the city, but this is crazy and out of control. It's light outside, but I can't see the buildings clear enough to make out where I am exactly. I can't even tell what these people are yelling about and why they are here. Looking for something to make sense of this, I see a tall stage far from me on the other side of the street that is also unexplainably wide. There must be sixteen lanes on this road for Christ sake. There are people on the stage saying something and I can't hear them at all. It does look like there are police over there so I try to make my way to them. Bumping my way through the crowd like a running back tries to get through a defensive line, I push through what seems like hundreds of people aiming my way towards any clearing I can find. The efforts are useless and I'm stuck in this mess of people arguing and fighting amongst themselves. I certainly don't recall any news or protests that could even come close to this, but I have to get out of here. As I push further towards the stage that I can barely see now, I notice it's getting darker and night is falling. Why are these people here? What the hell? Then the crowd noise gets muffled and the light in the sky gets dimmer with a cloudy haze over the top of all of us. Am I the only one noticing this? People continue to rumble as the darkness falls even more upon us. That eerie feeling of something or someone very creepy being so close comes over me as the hair on the back of my neck stands up and shimmers down my spine. There is silence all around even with the hundreds if not thousands of people still surrounding me. I turn to see what it is behind me that's making me feel utterly frightened. Not believing my eyes, the darkness and deeply disturbing presence that stands in front of me is awesomely huge. With tremendously long arms, a hooded cape structure towers over me gleaming down on only me. Black as black can be, this demon hovers over me extending more than ten feet above while moving towards me as if a huge blanket was about to drape over me entirely. I yell as loud as I can for everyone to run and nothing comes out of my mouth. No voice, nothing. I turn to run as fast as I can and find I'm paralyzed with only the ability to slowly move away while struggling with all the energy I have to move my legs and arms. Knowing what is behind me, I struggle my way through some of the crowd with no end in sight. Pushing others out of the way and gasping for air, the fear within me is overwhelming. I come to a small clearing where one man stands staring at me as if we were the only two there. This was a large man with some sort of costume or uniform on. He stares right at me and at that moment, I know now I'm in one of my lucid dreams. Grabbing my face, I try to wake myself. Looking around and doing whatever I can to get out of this horrible dream, I look back at this man in front of me as he stands only a couple feet away. I can see his face clearer now, but have no idea who he is and why he's there. Out of the corner of my eye and from the side of this man comes what looks like a person with a knife. As I yell "NO" and "Watch out" as loud as I can, nothing is heard. The knife dives deep into his side and the grimace of pain strikes through this man's face.

Literally, Tom jumps out of bed seeing much clearer now that the dream he had might just have some relevance to something terrible in the very near future. Quickly grabbing his phone, the first person that comes to his mind is the only one right now that might just understand. "Hey, did I wake you," Tom asks softly. "No I was up, you okay? Is everyone alright?" "I had a dream that I think might be telling me something. It was the same kind of dream with that really fucked up, scary image of that demon thing I've told you about. It keeps showing up in some of my dreams as if it's trying to kill me or something. But every time it shows up, something bad happens to someone else." "Are you sure about this Tom? Could you make out what it was this time?" Tom goes on explaining the dream to her as the morning grows lighter from early morning to daytime. They both realize it's either time to get ready for work or blow off work and deal with whatever this is. "Tom, let's just see what, if anything happens today and maybe this will be nothing. I'm concerned, but what could possibly happen that would even come close to resembling that dream other than someone getting stabbed which happens pretty much all the time around here." "I get that Claudia, I do. But for some reason, I feel I need to go talk with detective Butler this morning and tell him something is going to happen. He should know." Tom struggles with this decision because he knows he's going to be looked at as a crazy speculative with nothing else to do than waste the detectives time. "Did you want me to go with you Tom?" As nice as that sounds to Tom, he doesn't feel that is going to be good for Claudia and says, "thank you for that, but no. I think I should do this on my own for now. I'll call you and let you know how it goes though if you'd like." "Absolutely Tom, call me the second you're done with him." "Will do and thanks so much. I do hope it's nothing."

Chapter 16

Standing in one of the conference rooms in this deteriorating precinct, Butler is staring him down like Tom was already a criminal. That was the scariest part of when he told detective Butler what might happen today or sometime very soon. He explained to the detective in the simplest way without going too much into detail about his recent dreams and when he was a kid. He didn't want to come off as completely crazy, just a little crazy. "So I'm supposed to do what," Butler asks. "Run around town looking for someone to get stabbed and stop it before it happens? Do you have any idea how unrealistic that is?" "Yes, I sure do," Tom responds. "I know all this sounds crazy and I know you're looking at me like I'm a nut job, but I have to say that even I didn't believe it for a long time. I've been having these experiences since I was a kid and I just brushed them off like they had nothing to do with me. Now they are so much more serious and since I've studied dreams and how they work, I'm convinced there is something to them." Tom felt even more nuts now that he heard himself describe this to Butler. You could've heard a pin drop after that and the silence was killing them. "Okay Tom, I'll tell ya what. I'll keep my eyes and ears open for anything resembling what you've told me and when something like that happens, I'll give you a call. How does that sound?" Tom, staring into space now imagining himself being locked up for a murder or stabbing or whatever was to come next simply because he shared something so important to detective Butler. His mind was going a thousand miles an hour now with thoughts that whatever did happen in the next day or so, he'd be blamed for it and hunted down by the police department. Was this a huge mistake, Tom thought. "Sounds good to me detective. I just hope nothing happens and that these are all unfortunate coincidences. Thank you for the time." After providing the detective with information on how to contact him, Tom heads for the door. While walking to the front door of the precinct, he can only imagine all the eyes on him watching his every move. All kinds of thoughts run through his head and it seemed to be the longest hallway to the door he's every walked. He gets outside, looks around behind him to check if anyone is following him then takes his phone out of his pocket. "Hey, how'd it go," she asks. "Did you find a new boyfriend in the jail cell you're calling me from?" Claudia laughs and says, "sorry, I couldn't resist. Just trying to make you laugh and lighten up the mood a little. So really, how did things go with the detective?" Tom did think that was funny and appreciated the humor as he giggles while responding. "Ya as a matter of fact, he told me he'd protect me from all the other big, bad guys in this place. Seriously though, it was weird. I did explain to detective Butler what the dream was about and what could possibly happen today. He wasn't sure what to say and honestly, didn't believe a thing I said. But what worries me now is that if something happens, are they going to come after me as if I'm playing some sort of sick game? Are they going to assume I did it and come get me? I mean shit, did I do the right thing? Holy shit!" "Okay Tom, calm down a little. You know there's the thing called evidence and proof and all that detective stuff they do to find out who did what. If it's not you, you have nothing to worry about." "Ya, I guess you're right. I'll try not to think about it too much and hopefully now that I've brought this out into the open, these things will stop happening. How's work going?" Tom is trying to change the subject for his own sanity and to get all these bad thoughts out of his head. "It's okay, just another day with the same old bullshit. What are you going to do, make some sales calls?" Tom's not sure if making some sales calls would help or if he'd seem like a guy with something else on his mind while talking with customers. "I think I'll call in sick today and head to the mall or something. I'm really not sure I can focus right now while thinking that any minute something bad is going to happen," Tom says. "Want to just give me a call later when you're off work?" "Sure Tom, I'll do that. You make sure to keep in touch too and text me whenever you want. Tom, be careful today, please!" The thought of Claudia telling him to be careful today warmed his heart a little knowing that she was worried about him and what might happen. They both are on edge all day waiting for news or some report or even worse, a phone call from detective Butler telling Tom to come into the station for some questions. But for most of the day, it's quiet, too quiet. Tom picks up some new jeans and a couple shirts while wandering around the mall. He's doing nothing but wasting time and probably stopped in every store in the mall including Big and Tall stores and because his mind is elsewhere, he probably even strolled into an Ashley Stewart or On the Plus Size for women store. "Ding," Toms phone rings. It's a text from Claudia, "hey you, how's it going?" Tom finds a bench in the middle of the mall isle, places his bags on the floor next to him and begins to type. "Well, I got some new jeans today. Can't wait to show them off, such style." Tom watches as the little someone else texting icon remains on his screen knowing she's typing back. "Oh cool, can't wait to see them. What else did you buy?" "Oh just a couple shirts is all. I think I may have noticed a couple things you'd like in the Huge and Huger for Women store." Tom's laughing as he's writing this to Claudia. "How'd you know I shop there? I get my bras there because my boobs are just so freakishly huge." They are both laughing as much as they can typing back and forth together trying so hard to keep from asking the burning question about if either of them have heard anything anywhere in the news. The mood is light and fun and brings smiles to both of their faces. Claudia types, "dinner later? Free?" Once again, Tom loves this feeling and responds quickly, "oh hell yes, where and when?" As he watches the little icon squiggle while she's typing, his phone rings.

Chapter 17

"**M**r. Chapman?" "This is, who's calling?" "This is detective Butler, we spoke earlier this morning. Are you in the area?" Tom thought that was a curious question, why wouldn't he be in the area. "Ya, I'm over at the mall. What's up? Did something happen?" Toms hands start shaking as he stands up to pace around the bench he's been sitting on. Butler responds, "I'd like to continue our discussion from earlier if that's okay with you. Can I come pick you up and bring you to the precinct?" Oh shit, Tom thinks. What the hell is going on. His heart drops to his stomach and he sits on the bench grabbing his bags by his feet. "Sure detective, what's going on? Is everything okay?" Tom is trying so hard to initiate a casual conversation between two guys trying to figure something out. But it's not working. He feels as if the detective is being particularly vague as to not give away any information. "That would be great Mr. Chapman, meet me outside the main entrance in about 10 minutes, I'll pick you up there. Thanks." Detective Butler hangs up the phone and Tom stands there for a minute frozen with what to do. Why was the detective so short and why wouldn't he want to talk more with me? Quickly, Tom dials Claudia. "Well, maybe he just wants to talk more about what you said earlier or something. I haven't heard anything on the news so I don't think something happened," Claudia says. Tom looks around to see if there is anything unusual going on or if anything is just off. He grabs his bags and starts heading for the main entrance of the mall. "Something must have happened. Why would he want to come pick me up? I mean, he asked if I was in the area like I'd be out of the area for some reason. What the hell?" Why wouldn't he just ask me to come back in? Am I a suspect now? Maybe there's another incident he's looking at me for? Maybe something from the past is coming up or maybe," Tom's interrupted by two officers standing on the inside of the mall entrance looking around as if they were trying to identify someone. "Holy shit Claudia, there are already a couple officers waiting here and they look like they are looking for me. Do they know what I look like already?" He continues to walk through the front doors and stands by a trash can out by the parking lot where detective Butler asked him to meet. "Okay, looks like those cops weren't looking for me I think," as Tom peeks behind himself just to see if they followed him out the door. Claudia quickly jumps in and says, "stop being paranoid Tom, it's just a meeting he wants and now you're letting your thoughts get the best of you. I'm sure it's nothing so just be normal and nice to the detective and figure out what he wants. Besides, if he wanted to arrest you for something, he most likely wouldn't be asking if he could come pick you up. I'm sure you're fine." "Okay, I'll do my best to be normal," he says. "Ya Tom, that will be difficult for you," as she laughs. "Let's meet for dinner after okay? Can't wait to hear what happens," she says. A dark colored Ford Crown Victoria pulls up and I know it's detective Butler. The unmarked cop car is so obvious with the black wheels with no hubcaps, large black adjustable lights above each of the side mirrors and the red and blue signal lights hidden nicely beside the rear view mirror. The passenger door window goes down, "Tom? Jump in." Climbing into the car wanting so badly to start a conversation that would be casual and friendly, Tom says, "so what's up detective? Were you able to come up with anything from what we talked about earlier this morning? I certainly hope nothing happened today. I mean, I don't want anything like what I told you about in my dreams happening to anyone. I also haven't seen anything on the news." Rambling on and on, Tom finds himself wanting now to shut the hell up. "Oh we just want to find out a little more about you and dive deeper into what we discussed earlier is all. It won't take too long and hopefully, you'll be back home soon." HOPEFULLY, Tom thinks. At first, he thought he said the word out loud and glanced over at the detective. "Well, whatever I can do to help detective." The car was sort of a mess with papers all over the back seat, by the back window and small boxes, cartons and envelopes on the back seat floor. There were even some small books laying on the dash board that looked like little journals. Maybe he used them for note taking for crimes and investigations. Oh, that would be so cool to dive into one of those and read the notes trying to figure out what the crime is. After a few minutes, the car pulls up to the precinct and parks in the reserved for detective spot. "Pretty cool having your own reserved spot for parking huh," Tom says. As soon as it came out of his mouth, Tom realized if he didn't look crazy, he most likely did now. Butler just looked at him and smiled a little saying, "ya, it's a nice perk. Come on, let's head up to my office."

The office is on the fourth floor and typical for a detective's office with a large wooden desk, a credenza behind holding his computer and shelves full of pictures, accomplishment plaques and keepsakes, two chairs in front of the desk as usual in any office and filing cabinets on the other wall. But this was much different than his car which was weird. Everything was very organized with papers stacked neatly, pens and pencils standing almost perfectly upright in the holder, a name plate positioned just right in the center of the front of his desk and folders aligned on top of his desk with one oddly out of place. This one had a name on the top of it, Chapman, Tom. Sitting in the caption's chair, detective Butler says, "so Mr. Chapman, can you tell me where you were early this afternoon?" Well, this doesn't sound good, Tom thinks. "I've been at the mall since we talked earlier, took the day off. And you can call me Tom, Mr. Chapman sounds a little weird."

"Okay Tom," Butler replies. "We talked earlier about the dreams you had and how you feel certain events are occurring because of those dreams. Is that correct?" "Um ya, that's right." Butler pauses, still staring Tom down and then takes some notes. "Is there anyone that can corroborate your story or whereabouts?" Okay, this is getting serious now and Tom is really getting nervous. "Detective Butler, will you please just tell me what's going on? I came to you remember?" Toms attitude changed considerably which made Butler take notice of his demeanor. "So I'd really like to know why I'm here." Detective Butler shifts in his chair to a more comfortable, casual position. "Tom, we did have an incident today. In fact, early this afternoon one of my officers was stabbed and is at the hospital in critical condition. What concerns me was what you told me this morning and then hours later, an actual stabbing on my team. Sounds curious don't you think?" Okay, now Tom knows for sure he's looking at him as a possible suspect. "Is the officer going to be okay," Tom asks abruptly. Butler watches Tom as he speaks as if he's looking for body movements that give him some idea of guilt or involvement at all. "We don't know at this time, but we're all praying for him. So do you have someone that can verify where you were today?" All Tom can come up with is, "I have receipts of buying stuff that might show the time on them. But I can tell you this, I didn't do it. I know this sounds as crazy as it did earlier today, but I'm being completely honest with you. Do I need a lawyer or something?" That remark made detective Butler sit up a bit and ask Tom, "I don't know, do you?" Tom thinks about that question because he's not sure where he stands with the detective. "I don't want to have to have one and I'd rather work with you than against you on something I had nothing to do with," Tom says. "So you tell me detective, should I get one or are you willing to understand I'm as deeply concerned about this as you are. I know you don't know me and I just came to you today, but I'm telling you I had nothing to do with your officer being hurt today. So what do we do now?"

Chapter 18

"As of now, Butler thinks it's just coincidence and nothing more. He also told me not to leave town and was pretty clear about that. "Where are you going to go," Claudia asks. Tom couldn't wait to get out of that office and meet up with Claudia for dinner. They picked a nice quiet pub to sit and wind down. She was really the only one right now that seemed to be on his side. "Let's just say I'll be in touch regularly with the detective because he said so. He was suspicious for sure, but I guess I can understand why." "Well, I guess you can, but he should have been more understanding," she replies. "I just know this; I'll have to make sure I can prove where I am at any given time from now on. If something else happens even if I don't have a dream about it, he'll be calling me. Maybe I shouldn't have said anything at all. This sucks!" "Tom, please don't say that. If this is something real, it's the only thing you could have done." The ice cold beer tastes even better after an afternoon like he had. Being interviewed isn't much fun especially from a detective looking to pin a crime on someone. "Let's talk about something else, how was your day?" Tom breaks up the conversation about the day and leads to something a little nicer. He forgets that he's still quite attracted to Claudia and doesn't want to lose track of what's developing. They enjoy their evening together talking about Claudia's day in the office along with many other topics not including anything to do with dreams or police.

> Breaking news is reporting an incident involving a police officer who was making a routine stop today and found himself confronted by two men resisting arrest. One of the men pulled a knife out and stabbed the officer, witnesses say. The two men are still on the run and the police are making every effort to find them. The officer is still in critical condition at the hospital.

They both stare at the tv waiting for the news to end when Tom gets up and says, "hey, let's get out of here." With no destination in mind, they slowly stroll down the sidewalk looking at the Canadian lights across the river. Brushing up against each other, they find their hands touching much more frequently than even intended. Soon and without much hesitation, they are hand in hand. This feels good, Tom thinks. The softness of each other's touch along with the tingling that runs through their bodies is overwhelming. No talk about the news or anything having to do with the drama unfolding every day, just casual conversation about each other and whatever else came up. They find themselves standing in front of the railing overlooking the river. Shoulder to shoulder, their elbows resting on the railing while they gaze out at the reflection of the moonlight glistening off the water. Claudia leans in and kisses Tom on the cheek as if to say it's going to be okay. He turns to her, looks into her eyes, gently places his hand on the lower part of her back and leans in for the kiss. As their lips touch, they slowly explore the taste and smell of each other while the pheromones fly throughout the air around them. From the small of her back, he pulls her in closer making their bodies almost as one. Her arms fall around his shoulders and her fingers tickle the back of his neck during what could be described as the most passionate kiss he's ever had. Her breasts rest against his chest and her leg moves gently to the side of his engaging even more. His hands slide down to the upper portion of her ass as he becomes even more excited. The kiss continues for what feels like forever until they hear from a distance, "get a room!" They both look over and start laughing and barely separate. It's getting late so they start walking back with their hands were swaying back and forth like a couple young kids in love. The feelings they both share at this moment is the exciting, new relationship vibe you get when you can't wait to explore even more with that person. Saying goodbye for now was not in either one of their minds. They decide to take this back to Toms apartment.

With her hand on his back as he unlocks the door, they enter Toms apartment with such anticipation of what's going to happen on the other side. Closing the door behind him, she stands only a foot or two away from him while glancing quickly over the clean and tidy apartment. Turning towards each other for a brief moment not knowing what's next, he grabs her and gently, yet forcefully pushes her up against the wall with a strong kiss. His arms are strong, stronger than she imagined. Holding her tightly, the kiss turns into hands roaming all over each other. Both very excited, all their movements are orchestrated as if they've done this before or had some chemistry in the past that made this night possible. Now barefoot, they stumble their way into the bedroom with kisses and fun physical gestures along the way. The evening is filled with exploration and excitement for both of them as they learn more about each other in an evening than most do in months. Enough time passes and they find their bodies still entangled with lots of thoughts coming to their minds. They talk about how amazing this was and that it's a shame it took so long to get to this point knowing they each had something for each other for quite some time. Regardless, they are both very pleased where this is headed and can't wait for the next time they see each other. She says her goodbyes and heads for home.

Chapter 19

Excited and relieved, Tom starts closing up for the night as he revisits all the events he just experienced again in his mind. Wishing she was here to relive all of them, he heads for bed. Brushing his teeth, cleaning up a bit and getting ready for a good night's sleep, he can't help but to notice his smile that hasn't left his face since she left his apartment. He climbs into bed, the one he just messed up with Claudia and reminisces about the evening imagining her still laying here with him. Smiling, he dozes off a bit.

Completely comfortable, I find myself lying in bed wondering when I'm going to fall asleep. My bedroom is lit up which is weird because I sleep in complete darkness. The phone rings, but I don't answer. Instead, a loud voice tells me I have a visitor in the main lobby. "It's three O'clock in the morning for Chris sake, who the hell could that be?" I get out of bed, throw on some sweatpants and a t-shirt and head for the door. Looking around my room, things seem out of place. "Why is my dresser is by the window instead of the wall where it usually is. What the fuck?" Walking to my apartment door, something is off. It's cold, dark and gray. It's never like that in my apartment. Exiting, I close the door behind me and see people, none of which I know, stumbling from one side of the hallway to the other. I get to the elevator door that is already open. It's gloomy and dark with all the lights flickering on and off. I know I need to go in there, but it does not look safe even though I've been on this elevator every day. The hairs stand up on my neck and I get a chill that runs through my entire body as I slowly enter. I'm pushed from behind forcing me to the back of the elevator as I turn to see who it was. A large dark shadow covers the door and hallway outside the elevator. I'm suddenly frozen with fear and realize at that moment, I'm in a dream. Looking around trying to wake myself up, I press a button on the elevator wall, but have no idea what button I've pushed. The doors close so slowly as I move back as far as I can avoiding the shadow or demon I've seen before. The elevator races faster than imaginable and the feeling of free falling is overwhelming. Lights continuing to flicker, the walls of the elevator look as if they've been through destruction like an old deserted building. Expecting to break my legs when the elevator stops, I brace myself for impact as if that's going to help. "Come on damnit, wake the fuck up!" I scream as loud as I can knowing and sort of not knowing I'm in one of my fucked up dreams. Without slamming into the ground, the doors open quickly and I'm faced with a dark and hazy lobby filled with people lying all over the floor except for one man standing by the desk. It's detective Butler. I yell to Butler, "hey over here! What the hell is going on?" He doesn't hear me, but stares right at me. Is my voice not carrying that far? "Butler!" I yell again walking towards him. Still staring at me, he turns towards the desk and picks some papers up off the counter. "Hey, can you hear me," I say. He looks directly at me and says something that I don't understand. "Say again!" He starts running for the door and gestures for me to follow. On the sidewalk, it's normal as normal could be. Standing next to him I yell, "did you call me down tonight? What is going on and what do you want?" Once again, he says a bunch of shit that makes no sense that I can't understand at all with the exception of one word, "dreams." He starts running for the street with no warning whatsoever. I tried to follow him, but couldn't move as my arms and legs were being held back by something. That eerie feeling came upon me and I didn't want to turn around this time to see what it was. Glancing back at the street, I see detective Butler get slammed by a car getting rolled over and over upon. It was like it happened only a few feet away from me.

Opening his eyes to the darkness of his bedroom, Tom quickly looks around to make sure things are in order. Dresser is by the wall and everything else looks right. He throws the covers off of himself and heads for the door. Down the hallway is silence, not one single person to be seen. Closing the door, he checks out the rest of his apartment just to make sure everything is normal and that he isn't in a dream anymore. Realizing how clear the dream was and knowing it's one of his lucid dreams once again, he's determined this time to prove his dreams are truly dangerous and need to be taken seriously. "Butler," he yells out loud. "Crap, I have to warn him now!" It's 3:00am and he has to warn the detective. "It was 3:00am in my dream too. Okay, that's a first," he says to himself. He sits on his couch contemplating on whether to call detective Butler so early in the morning or does he wait for morning when he might be up. The possibility of something happening could be at any time during the day or even later. Hell, it could be on his way to work! "Fuck it," he says. Dialing his number, Tom waits for the detective to answer. It goes to voicemail. Tom hangs up, thinks for a minute and dials again. "Hello," with a voice that sounds like it came out of a deep sleep. "Sorry to bother you so early detective, but this is important." "Who is this?" "Tom," he replies. "Tom Chapman, remember me?" Butler pulls his phone away from his ear, looks at it like he's trying to identify the number or name on the display and returns it to his ear. "What time is it? And why are you calling me?" Tom knows this isn't going to go well, but he continues anyway. "Detective, I know this is going to sound crazy just like the other times we talked, but I have to tell you about a dream I just had." For a few seconds, nothing. Now Tom looks at his phone just to make sure the detective didn't hang up on him. Putting it back, he says, "detective?" "Are you kidding me Chapman? It's fucking 3 O'clock in the morning and you're waking me up because of a dream?" "I know this sounds nuts and I wouldn't call unless I thought it was important. But it involves you this time," Tom explains. "I'm just going to blurt it out and tell you that you are in harm's way. It could be an accident or something worse, but you got smashed by a car in my dream," Tom says enthusiastically. With a tired raspy voice Butler says, "okay, thanks for the heads up. Call me at the office in the morning and we'll talk," and hangs up. Tom sits in his living room frustrated and wondering what he's gonna do. He knows the detective doesn't believe him and is probably even more disturbed with him after that call. He says to himself, "the only way I'm going to convince him is if I show him."

Chapter 20

The loud buzzing from his alarm wakes Tom as he's still on the couch. Getting up early enough to find the detective is extremely important. Not being sure where he lives or what area, his only chance is to get to the office early enough, find a spot to park and watch for the detective. At this point, Toms idea is to simply watch over Butler for the day and make sure whatever the event is doesn't happen. The most difficult part of this idea is that Tom has absolutely no clue on what or where something will happen. He just knows it will. Sitting in the parking lot before any other cars show up seems a little suspicious and quite obvious. So Tom decides to park down the street and sit nearby on one of the park benches by the precinct. He intensely watches over the precinct only hoping the detective will come directly to work without making one single stop. The parking lot grows crowded with more cars and trucks filling the spots, some reserved but most of them open for employees and the general public. The detectives reserved spot is still open, but it's still early so Tom continues to sit and wait. It's a slightly chilly morning with a little dew on the ground in spots and a lot of small animal activity in the trees around him. The precinct is actually quite nice with a lot of activity surrounding the area. There are fields for baseball and soccer where the local kids can play in their leagues along with just hanging around playing on the playgrounds that are relatively new and kept in very good shape. The precinct building itself is one of the old historical buildings in Detroit that has been restored by the city for the use of this police department. There are courts, many offices and even a small jail for the usual silly crimes people would stay overnight or be in and out during the same day. But overall, the building is beautiful and really shows the history of Detroit.

The Crown Victorian pulls up, parks in the reserved spot and detective Butler heads for the door with folders and paperwork under one arm against his side and coffee in hand and in the other hand holding his phone to his ear. Tom stands up not sure what his next move is going to be. The detective did tell him to call him in the morning, but Tom feels it's going to be another long conversation trying to convince him of what might happen. Tom feels if he just follows him for the day, he might be able to prevent something from happening to the detective which could help prove what Tom has been telling Butler all along. He watches the detective enter the building and disappear within. Sitting back down on the bench, he picks up his phone. "You're not going to believe the dream I had last night," he exclaims.

"Well, good morning to you Tom," Claudia says. "Are you coming into the office today?" Tom completely forgets he's got a job and disregards anything having to do with what sales calls he has to make or where he has to be for the day. He describes the dream to Claudia not missing one single detail. Claudia's deeply concerned, but not just for Tom. If something happens to the detective especially after Tom's been there talking with him, he might be in some trouble he can't explain. "No, I'm not coming in today. I'm going to make sure nothing happens to Butler. I know it sounds a little over the top, but it's what I have to do. I'm outside the precinct now and he's inside." Claudia agrees and asks Tom, "do you need me there with you?" Tom just loves that and recalls what the evening before was like with her. "Hell ya," he says. "But only if it's not going to get you in trouble with work." She tells him how she's going to get out of work for the day and will text when free to meet up with him. The thought of hanging with Claudia for the day is awesome, but the thought of being with her while trying to figure out this whole dream thing is even better.

As Tom waits outside the precinct for any movement at all from the detective, he's wondering if this is even worth it. He knows Butler has to eventually go somewhere and that's when it will be tricky. He's a cop and trying to tail a cop might be a little difficult without being spotted. And what if he is spotted, he starts to think. Is it going to look like he's following him to harm him instead of what his actual intentions are? Butler already thinks Tom is crazy so locking him up wouldn't be too far-fetched. Toms phone rings, it's detective Butler. "Hello, this is Tom," he says without trying to sound surprised or bothered. "Tom, this is detective Butler. Okay, you're going to have to clear something up for me. Did you or did you not call me at 3:00am to warn me about some bad dream you had? I woke up this morning and thought that was a dream." Now it seems, Tom has his attention. Maybe not on the level he'd like, but it's time to get the detective to engage. "Yes detective, I did. Sorry to have to wake you then, but it was important and I didn't want to take a chance not letting you know." "You mentioned me falling in the street or getting hit by a car or something right?" "Yes actually. In my dream, you got totally smashed by a car, sorry." Laughing on the other end of the phone detective says, "look, I appreciate your concern. Really I do. But you should see a therapist and talk this out. I'm sure I can recommend one if you'd like." Toms shoulders fall as he thought maybe this time the detective would be more willing to listen or just listen enough to be aware. "Ding," a text comes in while Tom is on the phone. "Detective, I wish I was making all this up. I don't like any of this either and I'm sorry to keep bugging you with it. But this time, it's serious." "Okay Tom, I'll keep my eyes open. And by the way, the officer that was stabbed the other day passed early this morning. You have a nice day," and hangs up. Frustrated and scared now, Tom looks at his phone to see who texted while he was talking. It was Claudia, "hey, I'm here. Where are you?" Tom texts back letting her know which bench he's sitting at. Claudia walks up, looking as beautiful as ever of course. "Hey," with a smile that kills. "Any action?" As she approaches, Tom stands up to greet her. They come together and kiss, a soft kiss with full lips pressed against each other. Much like last evening, tingles of excitement run through both of them as they sit on the bench. Hand in hand, Tom tells her about his phone call with Butler. "I figure I'll just stay on him today and if I have to, I'll stay on him tonight and tomorrow too. Oh and I forgot to tell ya, the officer from the other day died this morning. That was the last thing he told me before he hung up. Claudia, I'm really worried." "What? He died? That's awful," she exclaims. She takes her other hand and holds both of her hands on his tightly as if to comfort him. "Let's just make sure nothing happens, okay?" They sit for a while on the bench not sure if they should go somewhere or sit here and wait. It's mid-morning and they are both getting hungry and anxious about when Butler's going to move. Claudia makes the suggestion of her running to get some coffee and something to eat for both of them while he stays in place during this stake out. As she's disappearing around the corner behind one of the buildings, detective Butler comes out the door and walks towards his car. Without hesitation and trying not to be seen, Tom gets up and heads for his car as well. "He's on the move," Tom whispers in a low, but loud enough voice not to be heard by others in the parking lot. "Hurry up and get back here!" She comes racing around the corner while Tom starts his car.

Jumping in the car with nothing in hand and both of their stomachs growling, they follow the detective as he drives out of the lot.

Chapter 21

Following someone without being noticed is a lot harder than it looks on tv. Most of the time, there are multiple cars doing the tailing. That way they can turn off and a new car can engage. Seems much easier that way. "I'm trying to stay as far back as I can, but I don't want to lose him," Tom whispers to Claudia. "Why are you whispering," Claudia laughs. Toms starts laughing, "I have no idea." Four or five cars behind, they follow Butler through the city to a small city building on the other side of town in the business district. "Stop here," Claudia blurts out. "It looks like he's going in that parking lot so we can walk from here." "Good idea. I'll pull over here on the street and park behind this van." They get out of the car watching the detective walk from his car to the building and then enter the building and disappear from sight. Both standing looking at each other, Tom says, "what do we do now? Should we hang outside the building by the street? This is going to be so freaking obvious and I'm just going to get in trouble for stalking him." "Relax Tom, I'll go over closer to the building as watch for him. You stay here." Quickly thinking of how this is going to be difficult for Tom, she launches into action. Tom's even more turned on now with her. She makes her way over to the front of the building and hangs out by one of the taxi stands nearby. The sidewalk if filled with people going to and from work, shopping at the many stores up and down the street or just hanging around doing what they do. The streets are busy with traffic from much of the same, but buses and taxis fill most of the lanes on both sides as pedestrians cross hastily before the walking light tells them to stop. Around here, people have to be on the move as most of the buildings host business people who either commute to work or live amongst the apartments throughout the buildings. It's a very busy area for not being downtown. Claudia looks back at Tom and gives him a little wave as if to say she's found her position.

About twenty minutes go by and nothing much is happening other than the hustle and bustle of the business district. Exiting the building, detective Butler and some other guy come out of the building as Claudia quickly motions to Tom. Not sure what to do, Tom stays perfectly still until he knows if he's heading for his car or if he's going somewhere else. Walking past Claudia, Butler and this other guy head down the busy street. She picks up the phone, "hey, I think they might be going for lunch or something. He's not carrying anything and they look like they are just shooting the breeze about stuff. I'll follow them closely okay?" Tom is so nervous because at that moment, he realizes this is the best option. Not only does he not want to put Claudia in harms way, he for sure doesn't want Butler to get crushed like in his dream. Walking on the other side of the street while Claudia is close behind the detective, Tom avoids other walkers while he focuses on everything around making sure he's ready for anything that might be a threat. "Do you think we're just wasting our time with this," Tom asks. "Look, if saving someone's life is a waste of time, then shame on us. Besides Tom, this is kind of fun. I mean the following part, not the part where he gets killed." "Oh man," Tom exclaims. "Don't say that. Let's just see where this goes." Tom knows she's kidding about that and trying to make things a bit lighter. But he's also frustrated because not knowing what is going to happen or where is killing him. Butler and his buddy enter a small cafe while Claudia continues to a hot dog vendor on the opposite corner where she and Tom won't be seen. "Well, I suppose we should grab one since we're here," she says. "I'll get us a couple and you keep watching the cafe just to make sure he's staying there for a while." "Good idea Claudia, thanks."

Claudia orders up a couple of the finest, Detroit vendor hot dogs on the market. You can really add just about anything you want on one of these. She orders some up and watches as the master of hot dogs on the street throw them together. Adding items like saut ed onions, some green and red peppers, a little seasoning out of a bottle with no name, some mustard and catsup and then the final touch. He takes a small torch and burns the entire hot dog and everything he just added. It's like a secret trick or something even though he does it right in front of you. She pays the man and walks over to Tom with a couple of the most beautiful street hot dogs ever to be found. "Oh wow, these look great. Thanks you, this is going to hit the spot," Tom says. Giving Claudia a little kiss on the cheek as he turns back to dig in. They dig into their dogs while making a little bit of a mess on the street as some of the onions and peppers fall to the ground because of how much the vendor put on them. With tiny little napkins given, they wipe their mouths and focus on the cafe. "We didn't miss them did we," she asks. "Oh hell no," Tom says. "Even when I kissed you I had my eyes on that place. We are not going to lose him." Standing around for another ten minutes or so, Butler exits the cafe. Instead of heading back to where he came from, he and his buddy are headed right towards them. "Shit, shit, shit, I have to hide," Tom hurriedly says. "Stand over there behind that truck," Claudia quickly whispers. Tom bolts over to the truck where deliveries are being moved back and forth between the truck in the street and a building they're standing in front of. He walks to the front of the truck with his back to the intersection where Butler is walking from. The walking light signals to walk and a large group of people along with the detective and his buddy start to cross. Tom looks over at Claudia and looks at her with that look of what the hell do I do now, shrugging his shoulders. As Butler passes and continues on the sidewalk, Claudia immediately blends in with the crowd and follows closely behind. Tom then jumps in the crowd even further behind blending in nicely. Stopping in the middle of the block off to the side of the sidewalk, both men stop and begin talking. Pretending to look at something on the ground or in the air or on a building, Tom stops and turns in circles like he's lost or something trying hard not to be noticed. In this busy street, he's sure he won't be. Claudia continues to walk past them and stops on the other side. "Watch out," someone yells at the top of their lungs. Without warning, a large truck smashes into one of the taxis on the street hurling the car up onto the sidewalk exactly where Butler is standing. Sprinting towards Butler, Tom tackles the detective pushing him away from this out of control taxi as it smashes up against the building. With gasps and screams of people all along the sidewalk, everyone is running around and rushing to anyone else's aid during this accident. Detective Butler and Tom lay only feet away from where the taxi ended up as Tom climbs off of the detective. Tom looks down on Butler and reaches his hand out to Butler as if to help him off the ground. "I fucking told you detective," Tom yells. Butler grabs his hand and gets pulled up off the ground only to find chaos all around them. Not yet saying a word, they both turn to see the car on the sidewalk and see if anyone's hurt. Just then, the detective yells, "NO!" His buddy is crushed between the building they were standing in front of and the taxi that was thrown up onto the sidewalk.

Chapter 22

Back at the precinct once everything was figured out, cleaned up and dealt with at the scene of the accident, detective Butler and Tom sat at his desk both very confused. Detective Butler looks directly at Tom and says, "now that we have a chance to talk after all this fucking bullshit today, what the fuck is going on Mr Chapman?" Angry as hell, Butler throws all of his emotion right at Tom with that question. Without hesitation, Tom responds, "I'm sorry about your friend, I really am. But that could have been you and if it wasn't for me pushing you out of the way, it would have been. Detective, I don't know exactly what is going on and why this happens. But the very first time we met, I tried to tell you without sounding like a crazy man and you didn't believe me." The detective stares at Tom with hesitation and a little less doubt than before. He settles down a bit, sighs and looks at Tom. "I'll admit, that dream shit sounded crazy to me and yes, I thought you were setting me up. Figured you were letting me know of a crime you were going to commit or knew about so I considered you either a nut job or a possible suspect I'd have to interrogate one day. That was it, nothing personal." "Well, it is personal me detective," Tom abruptly replies. "I've been dealing with this for years, since I was a child. I didn't know half as much about this as I do now and what I experience during these dreams is in fact, real. Well, most of it." "What do you mean, most of it," Butler says. "I have lots of dreams, everybody does and I have plenty of pretty normal dreams too. The dreams I'm talking about include something so scary it makes my skin crawl. There's something in those dreams. All I know is when I see whatever that thing is, I do whatever I can to wake up and get out of there." "So you're telling me there's something about your dream that makes these things happen? You do understand how unrealistic and completely impossible that is right? I mean, let's be real here. I have lots of dreams, some I don't like and others I do. But none of them make people die." This conversation goes on for some time. "Ding," Toms phone gets a text. Looking down at his phone while the detective is still talking, "sweetie, how are things down there? I'm worried." After the accident and all the craziness earlier, Claudia stuck around as long as she could before Tom and the detective left together. She also needed to grab Toms car for him. "Just wanted to see how you are and your car is in your spot at the apartment. I'm heading home so call when you can okay?" Tom picks up his phone and texts Claudia that things are going as well as could be and he'll give her a call soon. The final text Tom gets is a heart symbol. He looks back up to the detective with a little smile trying not to show it due to the circumstances and continues to listen to Butler. Spending all afternoon talking with the detective about the dreams he's had lately and what's been happening on the news, Butler is intrigued especially after what occurred earlier today. He admits to Tom that if it wasn't for him, he'd be the one pinned between the car and building. They discuss the conversation from late last night and why Tom was following him all day today. The thought of Tom following him all day to make sure he's not harmed makes Butler feel a little different about this man. Butler's still a little suspicious and tells Tom exactly that. But he's willing to give this some attention and will work with Tom to see where this goes. It's getting late in the day and Tom departs back to his apartment. On his way, he calls Claudia. "Hey, what's up gorgeous?" Toms voice sounds much better to Claudia even after what seems like a really long and disastrous day. "Gorgeous, well Mr, Chapman, are we feeling a little better given the day you've had?" "Ya, it's been a tough one. Butler knows now that I was only there to help him and he appreciates it. I mean, he's got some shit to deal with. He just had one of his friends get killed so he's pretty beat up about it. But he did seem grateful and we are now going to talk more often, especially when I have something to tell him. I mean the dreams." "That's good to hear. Where are you now? Heading home or do you want to stop by?" Oh fuck ya, Tom thinks. His heart is pounding and excitement takes over, but his voice remains calm, "sure, that would be nice. Did you want me to pick anything up for dinner or did you eat already?” “No, I’ve got something for you here.” Oh he’s thinking of what she might have. “I figured you might not eat so I went ahead and made something for you hoping you’d want to come over.” Toms mind is going nuts. Oh there is something I’d like to eat, that’s for sure, he thinks. He pulls his phone slightly away from his ear making sure he didn’t just say that out loud. “Oh my god, that is so sweet, thank you. I’ll be over in a few.”

Candles sporadically placed throughout her apartment, lights dimmed just right and dinner waiting on the island along side the kitchen area, Claudia is almost ready for Tom. She goes to the bedroom and puts something on that is both appropriate and sexy for the evening. Yoga pants that show off her taught ass and a decorative tank top showing enough cleavage to bother any normal man. Her hair is down and she’s looking her best considering it’s an evening in. Figures she’ll play this outfit as something comfortable that she likes to wear when bumming around the house, but she knows better. Maybe Tom does too. Entering the apartment, Tom pretends not to notice how freakin hot she is and what just might be in store for him tonight. “Hey, thanks again for having me,” he says. “Oh I haven’t had you, yet anyway,” she responds with that sarcastic, sexy tone. They laugh, get a nice welcoming kiss in and head for the kitchen. “Cold beer?” She doesn’t just ask, she offers it to him like one of Bob Barkers beauties on the Price is Right shows off one of the prizes behind one of the doors. "Door number one it is, yes and thank you," he says. The flirtatious banter continues throughout dinner and finally they find themselves sitting on the couch talking about the wild day they had. Tom gives her the low down on the day at the precinct with the detective and where they feel it goes from here. Feeling better about the whole situation, Toms voice sounds much lighter and explains to Claudia how he feels as if there's been a huge weight lifted off his chest. Facing Tom as she sits with one leg folded on the couch and the other up with her elbow resting on her knee she says, "I'm really glad the detective is listening to you now. And by the way, I hope you can move as fast as you did for him today if I'm ever in trouble." The tone of her voice and the way she says it while sipping on her glass of wine excites Tom more than he already is at the moment. "Are you in trouble now," he asks as he leans in for a kiss. The first kiss was a short, soft kiss. "As a matter of fact, you're the one in trouble mister," she quietly whispers in his ear. The drinks rest upon the glass table by the side of the couch and they slowly engage in more kissing, touching and gently tickling. Laying sideways on the couch, his hand glides along her legs and slide up her ass noticing no evidence of undies or a thong. Pulling her in tightly, their bodies are snug up against each other so much they can feel each other's excitement and warmth from the heat. Sliding his shirt off, pulling his pants down, he's now laying there in only a pair of light colored boxer briefs. She begins kissing his chest and slowly moves further down teasing him with little moaning sounds. Once she's there, he puts his head back on the top of the couch, closes his eyes and settles in for the ride. What seems like a lifetime of pleasure, he moves her body so she's laying on the couch as he kneels on the floor. With her clothes off, he takes a figurative step back and admires the beauty lying in front of him. She's playing the shy type by curving her body ever so slightly to one side. Tom forms his body against hers and caresses every inch of here body. After what seems to be an eternity, he looks up at her with a shit filled grin he says, "how's it going?" She sighs and says, "Who the hell do you think you are anyway?"

Chapter 23

ooking through his files and going over the notes he at Tom talked about yesterday, Butler tries to make sense of all this madness. The recent dreams that have caused or were similar to recent events is what really bothers the detective. One of the dreams Tom mentioned that has Butler a little perplexed is the one about some young kid in Detroit getting blamed for a murder by gunshot he didn't commit. Because of what happened with his brother Charles, it just sits with him like a pit in his stomach. Butler highly doubts it, but maybe his dream has something to do with that. But for now, he's got a lot of work to do and trying to dig up information on that isn't going to happen right now. Many feelings keep running through Butler as he continues to recall the scary and awful events from yesterday along with what happened to his friend instead of him. He finds himself closing his eyes from time to time thanking God for not chosen yet to stand in front of the pearly gates. But he also thinks of Tom often now which bother him. This is a man that comes to him with crazy ideas about dreams, continues to bother him and then saves his life based on a dream he had. It's all just too much for the detective, but he's going to make sure he gets to the bottom of this. He refocuses on his desk and starts hammering through all the paperwork in front of him.

"Dinner was nice babe, thanks so much," Tom says. "Babe huh?" Claudia actually liked being called babe. "I have to say, that sounds pretty nice buddy," she exclaims with a quiet voice. She's in the office now with nosy neighbor listening in on every word since the last time Tom left the office saying goodbye to her. "So you actually working today." "Ya, on my way to a few of the calls I was supposed to make yesterday while we were saving the world. I figure, I'll just keep busy doing my thing and you," he mumbles under his breath just enough so she can maybe hear it or maybe not. "Hey, I heard that young man," she says. "Oh, sorry I thought I just thought that." Laughing as these two do usually, they continue their conversations until they hang up and go to work. Without even wondering or asking, they both kind of know they'll be seeing each other after work.

Sitting on the bar stools facing the windows overlooking the city, they share a pizza provided by one of the local pizzerias. For Tom, it's pepperoni, mushrooms and either green olives or in this case, pineapple. For Claudia, it's a cheese pizza! She lovers her a good cheese only pizza. "I'm sorry babe, but how boring is that pizza. I mean, these are really good and honestly, he's got the best pizza in town. But for christ sake, put something on it," he laughs as he insults Claudias pizza choice. "Hey," she says loudly. "It has cheese on it!" "All pizzas have cheese on them," Tom says as pizza comes out of his mouth from the laughter. They finish up their pizza, puts whatever is left over in foil and throws it in the fridge adjourning to the couch for a little scary movie watching night. All cuddled up on the couch in front of his awesome big screen tv, they dive into one of the latest supposedly scary movies. In Toms mind, this couldn't be better. He's holding this beautiful woman snuggly in his arms while they sip their drinks and simply enjoy the city lights through the window while watching tv. The only way this was better is if there was an NFL game on instead. But who's complaining. After another awesome evening with this new found love, the kiss at his door, hands holding while his thumb rubs her fingers and they say goodnight. "Make sure you text me when you get back okay?" Tom can't believe what just came out of his mouth. He actually cares enough to start the old ritual people have where they have to communicate each time there's a travel destination just to make sure they get there safely. "Oh look at you watching over me now. I like it, thank you," she says with that sexy little voice. He watches her walk to the elevator, gets in and disappears from view. Closing the door, he sits back down on the couch flipping channels.

On my way to work this morning, I find myself taking detours outside of the downtown area and through many of the residential streets of Detroit. I never go this way, but I'm sure this is the way to one of my sales calls. For a second I stop and think, which sales call am I going to? A school bus filled with young children drives by me and I realize I'm in the middle of a school zone with lots of kids, parents dropping their kids off and school buses coming and going. The school buses are a weird, darkish yellow color, one I've never seen before. Maybe they changed the colors of their buses lately or something. I mean it's been a while since I've spent any time in the residential streets let alone spent any time near a school during the day. I'm following one of the school buses closely because they are going so freaking slow. I almost want to lay on the horn, but don't want to be THAT asshole honking at a school bus full of children. The rear of the bus is one big window instead of the usual windows, door and safety stuff. Okay, I've never seen this before. Moving even slower, I look around and realize I can't see much except for some of the children staring at me through the window. Around the bus is gray like there was a storm or fog or just a really cloudy day. I see the kids standing not moving much at all, hands by their sides with virtually no expression on their faces. There must have been five or six kids standing there staring at me. Creepy as hell. Still behind the bus not moving at all now, a chill runs up and down my spine. I look behind and around me unable to see much of anything due to the fog or whatever this was floating around all of us. I look forward again only to see many more expressionless little faces pushed up against the window as if something was forcing them to stay there. They are literally right in front of me, so close it seems I could reach out and touch the glass they're standing behind. Peering out my window and into their little faces, I SEE IT! From behind them, the growing darkness floods the bus compressing their faces even more into this large window that is in fact, the back of the bus. My hair is standing up on end and paralyzing fear is running through my body. This is it, I'm dreaming again and can't get out of it. I slap myself on the face a few times, but nothing happens. Looking back at the bus, It's suddenly taking off at a speed unlike no other bus. I jam on the gas and follow as closely as I can still watching the motionless children's faces being squashed by the blackness surrounding them. The bus turns violently to the right then back again heading directly at what looks a giant tanker truck. The bus moves even faster as I lay on my horn with only little spurts of noise coming from the car. "I know my fucking horn works damnit," I scream! Stepping on the gas even harder, I catch back up to the bus where now there are hundreds of little terrified faces smashed up against the glass with nothing but blackness around them. I jerk to the back of my seat when something terrifying appears above their faces. What I thought were two little faces is not that at all. They are dark gray eyes staring down directly at me. Once again, the bus races much further ahead of me and with a moment of pause, it slams into the side of this tanker exploding the second it hits. A large pile of flames come flying up in the air followed by a dark cloud like none I've ever seen before. The cloud rose in the sky as if to fly away like a large bat or black crow when spreading their wings.

Chapter 24

Opening his eyes, Tom lays in bed trying to grasp what just happened. Being in a hazy stage of waking up, he finally snaps out of it and comes to grip with what he just dreamt about. Rushing to the bathroom, he brushes his hair, his teeth and gargles some mouth wash before bolting for the door. "Shit," he yells. "Might be nice if I got dressed first." After throwing on some jeans and a t-shirt, he takes off and heads directly for the precinct. "Detective Butler, this is Tom. I'm on my way to the precinct right now. I have to let you know what happened in my dream last night, kids are involved. Call me back as soon as you can," Tom says with one of those worried, yet aggressive voices. It's early so there's plenty of time before school buses or children get ready and head for school. The only advantage they have to find this before anything happens is that the number of buses for Detroit schools is limited and only a few of the schools use them. Because children are involved, it's even more important they find whatever it is they're looking for before something terrible happens. "Good morning sweetie, how'd ya sleep," Claudia answers with that sexy morning voice that's so damn welcoming. "Hi babe, well I had one of those dreams and I'm heading to the precinct right now to see Butler," Tom exclaims with an excited tone in his voice. He tells Claudia all about the dream, "holy shit, Tom. That's awful. That thing appeared again? Did you get a better look at it?" "Oh, I forgot to tell you that I saw it's eyes. They were huge and were looking right down on me this time." "Oh my God Tom, chills just ran through me. What are you going to do?" Tom focuses on driving and still has a few minutes before he gets to the precinct not even knowing if the detective is there yet. "I have no idea Claudia, not a clue. All I know is that I left a message for Butler and hopefully he'll call me back real soon. Or I'll just have to wait until I can find him. Do I go to the schools where buses are being used? Is there way to find out which ones use buses?" "Calm down Tom, let's figure this out," she says in a soothing voice. Tom breathes as he realizes he's thinking way too much instead of deducting how to solve this. The first thing he needs to do is get to Butler. "Tom, what can I do," she asks. "Do me favor, the police will probably know where buses go and stuff like that. But can you search for which schools use them? Maybe we'll have a head start on this because there will be some time between now and when I get with Butler to explain what's going on. Can you do that?" "I'm on it right now babe, relax and I'll shoot you whatever I can find," her administrative voice says. "Let me know how it goes when you get with Butler, okay hun," she says. They hang up the phone and he continues on his way to the precinct feeling a little better that someone is at work right now trying to solve this mystery.

Arriving at the precinct, Tom sees Butlers car in the reserved spot right in front of the building. Sighing with a little relief, he parks his car and hurries towards the door. On his way in, his phone rings. "Tom," Butler asks. "Ya, this is," Tom says. "I'm returning your call from earlier. You said something about a dream and kids being involved this time. What's up," the detective inquires. Tom tells the detective he's heading in the building right now and needs to see him. Sitting at his desk, Butler listens as Tom tells him about the whole dream not leaving out one single detail that he can remember. With Butler taking notes, he quickly picks up the phone and calls someone within his office. The way Tom could tell it was an internal call was because Butler only hit a couple numbers on the keypad using the phone that sat on his desk. It was like being at an office desk from the eighties or something. Maybe they should upgrade, Tom thinks. The detective asks this person for a list of all the schools in the area and a list of all the schools in the area that use buses for transporting children. He also gets a list of the special needs buses. "Oh good one," Tom says. He hadn't thought of that. Butler hangs up the phone, grabs some paperwork from his desk and the note pad he was using and says to Tom, "let's go!" They jump up and head for the detectives car. On the way out of the precinct, detective Butler makes a couple stops to let other know to be on the lookout for something having to do with a runaway bus full of children. Not being able to explain why wasn't a problem for him seeing as most of the department respects and listens to him because of his position. In the parking lot, many other cars are rushing out into the streets in all different directions. Jumping in Butlers car, we scream out of the parking lot heading to one of the schools on his list. Flying down one of the residential streets, you can hear all the chatter from the police radio in the detectives car. Most of the noise coming from the radio is just that, noise. "Do you honestly understand what everyone is saying," Tom says with the look of confusion on his face. "Ya, every word. It takes some time to get used to and I asked the same question years ago when I came to the force," Butler says. Tom sits wondering how on earth they even get half of what is said. Turning into one of the schools parking lots, detective Butler drives right up to the transportation building where many buses are still sitting. Some are idling while waiting for the drivers to get in them and head out to pick up the children. From what Butler says, many of the other police cars have arrived at some of the other schools where much of the same is going on. "So what do we do now," I ask. He looks over at Tom with a questionable look and says, "I thought you would know what to do. This was your dream man," he exclaims. "Shit," Toms says. "I have no idea what to do. It's not like there was one bus in particular and remember, it was a dream. I suppose it could be any of these or any of the ones at another school." All the buses begin heading out of the holding area and in route to pick up children. Both the detective and Tom look at each other at the same time. "Okay," Butler says. "I guess we'll get out there and see about following as many of them as we can. We have another car with us so we'll send them in another direction for now." He gets on the radio and directs all other cars to do the same not knowing exactly what is going to work or if they'll find or see anything. But after Tom saved his life, Butler isn't taking any chances. Slowly, they drive off and start following bus number one.

Chapter 25

alls are coming in from all the other police cars and the radio in detective Butlers car is going nuts. All of which Tom doesn't understand, but nothing too important yet. Just information on buses that are driving their usual routes and picking up kids all over town. the bus Tom and the detective are following picks up the last child and begins heading for school. Slowly, it turns down the main street where the elementary school is located and heads into the parking lot. Butler keeps on going to find another to follow as many of the buses are still out on route. A call comes over the radio that even Tom understands. The officer is talking without using all the abbreviations or code numbers they usually use when they call something in. "Sir, I have no idea where this bus is going, but it isn't towards the school," the officer says at it comes across the radio in static fashion. "It's making sharp turns swerving from side to side." The radio goes silent for a moment as Tom and detective Butler are literally on the edge of their seats waiting for confirmation of anything with that bus. "Sir, we are now heading further away from the school and the bus is increasing speed. I'm going to initiate a stop just to see that everything's okay," the officer says. Butler responds, "that's a 10-4," as he looks right at Tom. The both sit and wait for the officer to come back with information about the stop. Some of the officers that are done following buses from other schools head in that direction just in case the officer pulling the bus over needs assistance. "Sir, the bus is refusing to stop at this time," the officer states clearly. "The bus is now accelerating." The officer sounds his sirens many times and lights are blazing. Detective Butler begins racing towards them as they are approximately three minutes from their location. The officer loudly calls out on the radio, "all units, all units. I am in pursuit now of bus #09 heading down Main Street at speed upwards of 80 miles per hour. Bus refuses to stop." Main Street is one of those roads that has three lanes on each side, a turning lane in the middle and is usually pretty busy heading in and out of the city. Office buildings, store fronts, churches and pedestrians line each side of the street with gas stations on almost every corner. It ends at the city, but continues far out into the suburbs of Detroit. Butler turns on his lights and siren and heads in that direction. Fortunately, they are in the direction the bus is heading so they will reach them quicker depending on how fast each of them are traveling. They are only one minute or so from their current location, but that may be much shorter now. The officer yells out on the radio, "bus is disregarding intersections and traffic signals." Driving even faster, the officer speeds up alongside the bus to see if he can get the drivers attention or see what is going on. From the side of the bus inching his way to the front, he can see all the children with their faces pressed against the windows crying, yelling and screaming. As he moves closer to the driver's window and now can see the woman driving the bus. She has both hands on the wheel only looking forward as she's completely focused on the road ahead. With sirens as loud as they can go and three police cars now in pursuit, this has become a very dangerous situation. Changing the tone of the sirens, the officer tries even harder to get the driver to look over or get her attention. "Driver, pull over," yells the officer over his speaker system. "Driver, pull over," again yelling with no reaction at all. Racing towards another intersection at a high rate of speed, other officers have blocked the cross streets to avoid possible collisions. "The driver is unresponsive to commands either ignoring me or can't hear me" the officer blurts over the radio.

About a mile or so ahead, Tom can see lights from the police cars and the bus coming in their direction. Detective Butler slows to a stop while blocking all lanes on their side of the road so cars behind him won't interfere or get hit. Tom looks at the detective and says, "are we going to just sit here? What if it comes right for us?" "Why do you think it's still in drive and I've got one foot on the brake and one on the gas," he exclaims. "Was this in your dream," Butler asks. "No, I mean yes. I mean I was the one tailing the bus and it surely didn't look like any of this," Tom says. The bus is now about a half mile away and veering off to the right a little. "We are at 90 miles an hour," the officer says over the radio. There were now several police officers in pursuit of this bus. Each of them reported sights of children crying and waving their arms for help. Suddenly, the bus veers off to the right heading directly for one of the corner gas stations. Only a few hundred yards in front of Tom and detective Butler, the bus crashes up and over the street side curb taking out a light pole as it heads into the main area of the gas station. Crushing gas pumps, attended cars filing up and pedestrians running for their lives, the gas station ignites with a huge explosion rocking the ground around them. The bus continues through into the gas stations convenience store and comes to rest totally destroying everything in its path. The fire out by the gas pumps is burning hot as another explosion rocks the other side of the gas stations parking lot along side the building. "All units, fire and EMS," comes across the radio as Tom and Butler race towards the scene. Screeching to halt, Butler stops the car far enough away to avoid the fire and to allow the fire department enough room to fight these incredible flames. "Stay here," detective Butler yells at Tom as he bolts from the car and runs for the school bus. Tom can't believe his eyes and can't believe this is all happening in real time as he just got done describing something like this to Butler earlier this morning. Not standing the thought of sitting there being totally useless, Tom gets out of the car and runs for the bus.

Fire and destruction all around, police run in the store from all angles trying desperately to get to the children. The bus itself is not on fire, but damage is evident as they worry even more about the passengers. Broken side windows, a smashed front windshield with blood smeared across and many yells, screams and crying come bellowing from the inside. One of the officers pries open the side door where the driver lays motionless on the steps going down. Checking her pulse, he looks up at detective Butler and slowly shakes his head. Climbing up and over the driver, detective Butler sees the little ones all over the bus like they were thrown around on some carnival ride gone bad. Crying and screaming, the children call out for help as Butler makes his way further onto the bus. Other officers also make their way on and assist the children. As EMS and the fire department pull up, many officers are now on the bus attending to the injured while the fire department engages the fire along with the injured that were filling up their cars or in the convenience store area. Butler quickly assesses the bus looking for children needing the most attention. While cruising down the middle aisle as quickly as he can to see which of them need more attention than others, he's stricken with sadness. Hastily attending to those with care and delicate movements, the ones he focuses on are the ones that didn't make it. By now, a full fleet of police, EMS and others help get the children off the bus with the exception of the few that weren't as lucky. With bruises, cuts and some broken bones most of the children will be fine. Gently holding underneath the head of one of the deceased children, Butler can't believe what he's witnessing. With a lump in his throat, he looks around at the chaos that has ensued. The only ones left on the bus are Butler and the sadness of the few motionless children that remain. With this young boy in his arms, he raises his head and looks out the broken side window only to see Tom looking in. With tears in his eyes, Butler looks back down at the child.

Chapter 26

Toms phone rings, "Hello," answering in a low, sad voice. "Tom? What's wrong? Were you able to talk with the detective this morning," Claudia asks with a concerned voice. The time it took between the last conversation with Claudia and now was only an hour or so and she has no clue what has transpired. "Oh my God Claudia," Tom exclaims. "I am so sorry I didn't get back in touch with you. All kinds of shit happened since we talked." Claudia changes hands holding the phone as if she's going to hear better with the other, "What Tom? Where are you right now? I can hear all kinds of noise in the background. Are you still at the precinct?" Tom, looking at the bus where Butler still is, "Oh Claudia, you're not going to believe what happened, where I am or what I'm looking at right now," he says. Claudia sit's quietly as Tom goes through every detail from sitting at Butlers desk to standing in what's left of a gas station convenience store staring at a half destroyed bus with dead children. On the other side of the phone, Tom hears Claudia crying as he's telling this terrible story. She even left her cubical to a more private area in the office so she doesn't bring attention to herself. Wiping her eyes with a tissue she says, "Oh Tom, I am so sorry this is happening. Are you okay?" Tom is still standing outside the bus and has been for some time. The fires are extinguished and others that were involved or injured in the crash have been attended to and are either on their way to the hospital, dealing with their damaged vehicles or heading home. A large crowd gathers around from all over as Quaker's stop to see the excitement. Tow trucks now on site clearing up car wreckage and debris from the accident while other emergency crews get ready for the investigation and delivery of the few dead children. "No, actually I'm not," Tom says. "I can't even imagine what the detective is going through right now. I can see him through the windows, but he disappears from view now and again taking care of the children that didn't make it. I'm not sure how many there are, but he hasn't come out yet. This is so terrible Claudia!" Crying on the other end of the phone, "What can I do? Do you need me to come pick you up," she says. "I don't know exactly, I haven't been able to talk with the detective since he's been in the bus the whole time," Tom says. "Can you stay with me on the phone until I can find out," he asks Claudia in one of those desperate needy voices. "Absolutely Tom. In fact, I'm going to pack my shit up and get out of here. But I'll stay on the phone okay," she says in a supportive tone. Standing in front of the bus where the drivers seat is, Butler is talking with one or two of the other officers occasionally looking up at Tom. The conversation continues for a few minutes as the detective exits the bus. "Hey Claudia, let me call you back, Butler's coming," he says and hangs up the phone.

Heading towards Tom and wiping his eyes, he stops a couple feet in front of him not looking directly at him yet. Tom puts the phone in his pocket and stands perfectly still until the detective is ready to talk. Slowly looking up at Tom he says, "so this is the stuff you dream about huh? We need to talk some more, but right now I have to deal with all of this. Are you okay getting back," the detective asks. Tom watches Butler as he talks and realizes it's so hard for him to even say those words. Trying to show no emotion, the detective was struggling a little talking with the man who brought all of this to their attention. Tom's sure this is one of the most difficult and confusing times for Butler. "Ya, I'll be fine," Toms says. "Is there anything you need me to do," Tom asks. "No," the detective says. "I'll be in touch when I can and we'll have to go over this again if that's okay with you. I need as much information about this as possible before I even think of bringing in more of our team in case we have more of this coming. It's going to be difficult to explain this one for sure." Butler nods and begins walking towards one of the ambulances standing by. "Hey," Tom says to Claudia. Can you come get me.? Looks like Butler is going to be busy with this whole mess." "I sure can Tom," says Claudia. "I'm already on my way. What did he say?" While walking away from all the madness, Tom explains what the detective and him briefly said and then told her where to pick him up. Not being able to get terribly close to the accident, he's guiding her to another spot down the road. Tom continues, "if there's one positive thing to get out of this, it's the fact that now detective Butler believes me. I can't tell you how much a relief it is not to be looked at as a crazy man," Tom says with excitement in his voice. "I'll bet," Claudia says. "I'm not too far away so keep a look out for me okay?"

Driving away with Tom in the passenger seat, Claudia gawks behind her in amazement while Tom looks out the side window in a daze. She places her hand on his resting on his leg and says, "How ya holding up babe? You doing okay?" He looks over at her, looks into her eyes and says, "actually, I'm doing okay. I know this sounds weird, but I feel pretty good. What happened back there was awful to watch and I watched the entire incident unfold right before my eyes," he exclaims. Watching the road Claudia says, "was it anything like your dream or was it more like a clue of what's going to happen?" "That's just it, I could've told you what was going to happen as it was happening. I just knew when it was coming right at me and the detective that it was going to crash into that gas station. We watched the whole thing. But I feel good Claudia," Tom says again. "I feel as if something I've been burying within me for so long can finally come out and it's such a relief. It's like a huge weight is being lifted off of me," he says. "I can understand that, I really can. Do you think maybe this will be the end of the dreams," Claudia says with some enthusiasm. Tom didn't think about that before. What if all these bad dreams or this curse that has haunted him for so long went away? Is it possible for all this to stop? "Shit," Tom says. "I suppose anything's possible. Who knows, maybe if I can finally stop one of these from happening, I'll break the curse," Tom says. "Now I DO sound crazy!"

Chapter 27

Sitting in the cafe, Tom and Claudia place their orders for lunch and settle in. It's early afternoon following the tragic accident. Toms car is back at his apartment building lot and the cafe is only walking distance from there. Staring across from one another with each other's hands touching in the middle of the table, their booth faces the busy street outside where people go busily to and from places with no idea what's really been happening. "What's really important? Look at all these people walking around as if nothing happened today. They go about their lives until something bad happens to them. Do you think any of these people are parents of the children on the bus today," Tom asks. "Wow Tom," Claudia says with surprise in her voice. "I guess I never thought of that until just now. Has it been on the news? I'm positive the parents of all children at the school know by now. It had to be announced at the school and I'm sure there are plenty of police there too," she claims. "Wait, what was your first question," she asks. "What's really important," he says again. "What I mean is there are a few young kids dead now because of a dream I had. There is also a young couple attacked by dogs, dead. A young man taking a nose dive off a building, dead. An older woman simply going to church, dead. Some lady playing in her backyard by the swings, dead. Even an officer stabbed and now, dead. Oh ya, and let's not forget about Butler, he's not dead but his good friend is because I pushed him out of the way. But that didn't stop it did it," Tom says with a weird look on his face. "There was still today. An awful day because of a damn dream I had. So I'm just wondering what's really important." Tom sits quietly for a bit while Claudia doesn't dare say a word. She's curious what's going through his mind and he's got a look about him as if he's figuring something out. Tom continues, "and what about the ones when I was a kid," he blurts out as she looks around a bit to make sure nobody notices the conversation. "What about the ones that died when I was a kid and didn't even know they died. Do you suppose there are dead people because of me way back then?" "Hey Tom," she says quickly. "You can't possibly blame yourself for any of this or the ones way back when. This is something odd for sure, but not your fault." He doesn't have the appearance of being upset or mad or even disturbed. Rather, he has the accomplished look like he just got done putting one of those 1000 piece puzzles together. "The image I have in each of those dreams. The one that keeps showing up in all of them. You know, the dark shadowy thing that scares the living shit out of me? That is what I have to figure out. Why is it showing up and why is it showing up in some dreams and not others? You know, I do have other dreams Claudia, other dreams with no image of that thing. Nice dreams. Nothing goes wrong after THOSE dreams." Tom thinks he's on to something even though he's thought like this before. "Tom," Claudia interrupts. "You told me before that the dreams you have that you feel are bad ones involved something like a demon or thing or whatever it is that makes you scared and makes your skin crawl. Is that what you're talking about?" Claudia's voice is encouraging and she tries hard to keep Tom focused while figuring this out as he talks it through. Their lunches come and they begin to eat while they continue to mull this over and over trying to make any sense of it. Club sandwich, the usual for Tom. He's a pretty easy guy when it comes to sandwiches. As a kid, he used to make grilled cheeses almost every day and dip them in tomato soup. One of his favorites, but a good club sandwich is a close second. For Claudia, the chicken caesar salad is a winner. She does eat like shit from time to time, but generally watches what she eats. Of course, there are times her and Tom have shared a not so healthy meal together and there will be more.

Finishing up lunch and paying the bill, they head back for Toms apartment. Spending a couple hours in a cafe in the middle of the afternoon is sometimes refreshing depending on what the circumstances are. "So how do you feel now," she asks. They are walking slowly on the outside of the sidewalk to avoid the busy worker bees making their way through the city with what they feel are their very important jobs. Holding hands, Tom and Claudia feel even closer together with all they've been through in such a short time. "I think I feel clear. Well, clearer than I did before. If I'm to confront this phantom shadow thing that keeps showing up in my dreams, maybe I can make it go away somehow and stop these horrific accidents. I can't believe I'm saying this, but maybe instead of being afraid of it, I should engage it and see if it says anything to me," Tom says with a total disbelief in even himself. "I don't know Tom, I just don't know," she says. They stop in the middle of the block right in front of his apartment building. Looking at each other, they embrace and kiss. Not giving two shits who's around or even if it's in the daylight, they kiss like it's their first passionate one. Holding her hands, he stands back just a little and looks deeply into her big, beautiful eyes. With a confident stance and a low toned voice, Tom says, "I'm gonna do it. Once that fucking thing shows up in my mind, I'm going to stop running babe. It's time I see what it's made of and what it wants. I'm going to confront it!"

Chapter 28

While wondering how and when he'll be confronting this monster in his dreams, Tom heads up to his apartment after leaving Claudia for the day. He's also thinking of her very much lately. With all the drama, confusion and terrible incidents going on, he still finds time to keep her in his thoughts. She's capturing his heart little by little each day and he's loving it. This afternoon was great, time with her really grounds him and keeps his mind clear from all the other nonsense. She's like his comfort zone and he is loving this relationship they're building. Those thoughts and more continue in his mind as he cracks a beer standing in his kitchen. Staring out the large window overlooking the city, he sees people all over walking the streets, driving through rush hour traffic and catching buses and taxis everywhere they can. Soon it will be dark and the city lights will shine through the window lighting up the walls with a colorful glow. Turning on the tv, Tom tunes in to the local news to see what the latest is on the crash from this morning. The news reports all of what Tom already knows with the exception of the fine details only he and Butler know about. The news is sad stating information about the children that were injured and killed on the bus. Tom thinks of how he could've helped avoid such a tragedy. Could he have found the bus earlier? Could he have identified which it was sooner? How is he going to prevent something like this next time? All these thoughts go through his mind as he finishes his beer and heads for the kitchen for another. Switching channels to watch a little sports or whatever else is on tv, he gets comfortable on the couch while it gets darker and later in the evening. Texting with Claudia throughout the night was the highlight of his evening by himself. Finally after three beers and a bunch of time wasted, Tom heads for bed. One final peek at the city lights, he closes the blinds slowly wondering if this will be the night his dreams take a wicked turn.

Lying in bed trying to fall asleep, he stares at the ceiling thinking of all the things going on in his life. He thinks about all the different types of dreams he's had and even the ones when he was a kid. It bothers him that he's never had the chance or even thought of how to deal with them. What bothers him now is how he's going to stop them. How is he going to put an end to these dreams and what they end up doing to people. So much time has gone by and he's still laying there trying to fall asleep. It's 11:53pm and he can't believe he's still up. Picking up his phone and typing, "hey beautiful, you still up," he texts Claudia. Toms phone rings, "what are you still doing up," she responds. "Don't you usually go to bed around now?" Sitting up in bed Tom says, "ya I do. I have no idea why I can't fall asleep. I've been laying here for about an hour or so and nothing. My mind isn't shutting off and I'm just not that tired." In a quiet sexy voice, she says, "would you like some company?" Tom practically sits straight up with excitement at the thought of her being with him right now. Trying to calm himself a bit not to give away his excitement, "seriously? You'd want to come over this late?" She's delighted and says, "of course, I'm already on my way." Claudia already packing a small bag of a few essentials just in case this is an all nighter, grabs her keys and heads out the door.

Running around the apartment straightening up a bit, Tom prepares for the arrival of this woman who has stolen his heart. She's is close by and it won't take her long to get here. He opens the blinds enough to see the city lights and creates a little romance within the apartment. Leaving the tv off, he lights some candles and low dimmed lights just enough to see, but not enough to be seen. Of course, one of the hazards of having such a nice apartment is that others across the street do too. So at night, it's always best to know there can be others looking into the apartment if things are lit up brightly. Wanting some privacy while still enjoying the beauty of the city at night, Tom arranges things accordingly. A light knock at the door, Tom opens the door to a warm and beautiful smile. They get comfortable on the couch and without turning on the tv, watch the city lights flicker in the night while talking about the day. The conversation doesn't get too involved in the earlier events because they've already beat that dead horse. It turns into a conversation about them and how they've become so close in such a short time. "Ya, you kind of had me when you grabbed that Snickers bar in the fridge," he says jokingly. "I can't believe someone didn't take that. It happened before where I put two of those on that shelf and one of them was gone when I went to grab one. I have to admit Tom, I keep a bunch of them at my place. You never know when you're gonna need a pick me up candy bar," she smirks. Tom looks at her as they both are laughing and says, "Oh I saw them there and actually considered taking one. I figured who's gonna miss one right?" "Watch it buddy," she says playfully while tickling his sides. "I would have missed it, that's who!" They banter on as the night grows darker and later. The bantering and flirting go on for a while until she leans in for the long kiss. Moving this kiss into the bedroom, he smacks her on her ass as she jumps onto the bed trying avoid a second. Playfully, they roll around the bed kissing, touching and exultantly enjoying each other's bodies as they slowly begin to lose one piece of clothing after another. Without skipping a beat, they are now skin on skin with virtually no space between them at all. Allowing just enough room between them, Tom glides his hands up her stomach and across her breasts exciting her nipples to their fullest. Her breasts are firm, but have a soft and smooth feel to them. He kisses and plays with them while she lays her head back to enjoy. "Holy shit Tom," she says heavy breathed. His hand wanders down to feel the wetness between her legs and finds a gloriously welcoming state. Moving his body over top of hers while pressing down on her with his chest just enough for her to feel controlled yet loved, he moves in place while sliding his chest softly against hers and gets in position. With strong, muscular arms in place beside her, he pushes her legs apart with his and begins to make love to her. Pinning her hands to the bed by holding her wrists, he gracefully leans in to kiss her on her lips, neck and anywhere else he can reach while he slowly slides in and out. Looking deep into each other's eyes for a moment, she closes hers and begins to orgasm. Turning him on so much at the sight of her coming, he tightens his grip on her wrists and begins orgasming. Low toned growls come from him as he closes his eyes and finishes inside of her. Opening her eyes, she watches as he comes feeling every bit of him. Finished and resting on top of her, Tom leans next to her on one arm and gently tickles her body while they look at each other in awe. "You know, I could get pretty used to this," Tom says quietly. They continue holding each other while talking as the conversation continues on until the middle of the night. "I can't believe how comfortable I am with you," she says. "You gonna be okay with someone else lying next to you all night?" Tom gives her that quirky look at says, "oh I'm sure I will. You're not going to fart all night are ya?" She elbows him and they both laugh as they get more comfortable with each other. His chest to her back as he wraps his arms tightly around her. They fall asleep.

Chapter 29

Six hours later, "Detective," Tom exclaims. "We need to talk. Are you in? We have to meet right away." Detective Butler doesn't like these calls from Tom, but hears the urgency in his voice. "What is it Tom," Butler asks. "I know you're exhausted from what happened the other day, but it happened again. For some reason, it's happening more often. I mean, I've had many dreams in between these nightmares and have never had consecutive nights with them. But this one is bad detective, we have to act now," Tom explains in a hurried voice. Butler tells Tom that he is at the precinct but leaving in just a couple minutes. They decide to meet at the Northern Mall since that's possibly where the dream took place. Tom jams his phone in his pocket shaking his wrist from the weird sensations he's feeling in his left hand. Disobeying many of the traffic laws, Claudia and Tom race to the mall. On their way, they brainstorm trying to figure out which one of the malls is the one from his dream. Making some sharp turns and speeding down streets where there's little to no traffic, they bounce up into the mall parking lot aiming for the middle where Butlers car is sitting. Screeching to a halt, they jump out of the car and run up to the detective where he's leaning his ass up against the hood of his. Walking back and forth, still rubbing and shaking his left hand, Tom can't stand still as he explains the entire dream to Butler. This goes on for five or ten minutes with questions and answers from the detective, Tom and even Claudia jumping in from time to time. Butler leans in his window grabbing the police radio, "All units, all units," he blares out with directions and orders for the police force. All over the city, there are now police vehicles racing to all the known area malls. Looking at Tom, detective Butler says, "you better be right about this one Tom. I'm not doubting you, but we've got the entire force scattered all over the city right now." "I know detective, I know. I wish I had more information so we could narrow it down, but I don't. This is what I recall and it's possible we are in the right place. But like I said, it could be any of these malls detective. Dreams are like that," Tom exclaims. They move the cars closer to the mall, get out and walk around the parking lot. Each of them head in a different direction with phone in hand just in case. It's still pretty early with little to no action going on at the malls. The morning progresses as the parking lots begin to fill up with retail and mall employees, maintenance personnel and straggling in patrons who begin to walk the mall. Lots of older people show up when the mall doors open, but most of the retail stores are still closed as they walk the length of the mall over and over again for exercise. Detective

Butler enters one side of the mall, Tom another side and Claudia enters on the opposite side slowly wandering the halls. Walking in circles around them, the older people become scarce as the morning moves on and retail stores get busier with patrons from the surrounding communities. More officers show up and join in the walk around the hallways of the mall trying not to bring attention to themselves. Business as usual here at the Northern Mall for quite some time as Butler gets restless wondering if any of this is worth the time.

Noon comes rather quickly and all of them are growing tired of walking the entire mall occasionally passing one another with a gentle nod. Meeting up in the middle by some of the hallway retailers, Tom and Butler stop to discuss what's going on. "Have you heard from any of the other malls detective," Tom asks anxiously. Butler shakes his head no and says, "I've talked with some of the other officers and even the police caption who is at the Southland Mall and nobody sees anything out of the ordinary. It's been couple hours Tom, what do you think we should do," Butler asks in a way that isn't a question. He continues, "I can't have all my officers wandering malls right now, they need to be out on the street in their coverage areas." Tom looks down with his hands on his waste thinking if he's missed something in his dream that might help them. "I just don't know detective," he says to the detective. "Like I said, all I can remember is what I told you. If there was some sort of sign or road or recognizable feature in the dream, I might be able to identify which it was easier. Just based on what I recall, this was the one that made sense. I'm sorry, but it could be any of them detective," Tom says with a sigh in his voice. Just then, Claudia nonchalantly walks up and says, "well boys, anything?" Both Butler and Tom look at her shaking their heads no. "Tom, I'll stay with you for a while, but I'm also going to have to call this in and allow some of the officers go back to their regular duties. If something happens, I'm sure they'll be ready to act as they always do," Butler says. As he steps away to make a few calls, Claudia puts her arm around Toms lower back, "it's going to be okay honey, it will. I'm with you all day and we'll find this son of a bitch," she says. Tom looks at her, shakes his left hand again while rubbing his wrist and gives her a kiss. "I hope so babe," he says. "I hope so."

Seven hours earlier. Walking hand in hand, I look over at Claudia with a huge smile on my face knowing I've finally found a wonderful woman who thinks I'm pretty great too. "You're so beautiful," I say out of the blue. Claudia looks over at me, but doesn't say anything, just smiles. "Did you color your hair," I ask. For some reason I don't recall her hair being so dark. Looks like she must have gone to the stylist recently and I just didn't notice. Shame on me, I think to myself. Those are the things chicks love for us dudes to notice. "No silly," she says. "I got my hair done a while ago and really need to get it done again soon." She continues, "it's so long, my hair. I really need to get it done again soon." I look at her with a confused look on my face like she just repeated herself for no reason. It just sounded weird is all. Then as we continue walking, I notice her hair is back to the normal color. Maybe I'm imagining things, but I swear I just saw a darker color. Man, I must be losing it. We continue walking hand in hand and she says to me, "we should really get out of here Billy." "Billy," I say with a shocked look on my face. Did she just call me an old boyfriends name or something? "Why did you call me Billy," I laugh. She looks at me with that great smile, but again doesn't say anything. We continue walking as I look around at all the stores in the mall not really being able to make out some of the names on the store fronts. The mall is huge with hallways that seem never ending. Different levels to the mall extend way above us with hundreds of stores. I mean, who the hell is going to need all of this anyway? People are walking around, but it's dark and I can't really make out who they are or what they look like. "We should really get out of here you know," she says again. "Why do you keep saying that," I ask her with a concerned look on my face. We stop in the middle of the hallway and turn towards each other, "we really need to leave now," she states. "Claudia," I say with a raised voice. "Why do you keep saying that?" Just then, it was almost like the lights were turned off at one end of the mall. I'm standing still looking around trying to figure out what is going on. I turn back to Claudia and she's gone. "What the hell," I yell. "Claudia!" Shit, I'm frantic and can't see her anywhere. I thought maybe she went into one of the stores close by, but all of them are now closed with gates down. What the hell, I think. Did we come at closing time? I'm turning in circles watching many people walk the mall as if nothing is wrong and business as usual. Then it appears! Way down at the end of the mall, it was like a cold dark shadow filling the hallway from side to side and top to bottom. In the middle of this gruesome shape are two blood filled eyes staring right at me. "Shit," I yell out. "I'm fucking dreaming again." Just as I turn to run, Claudia bumps into me knocking us over and we land on the hallway floor looking at each other.

"I see it, I see it," she says pointing down the hallway and with the most frightened sounding voice I've ever heard. She shimmies backwards on her hands and feet trying to stand up to run. "Get up Claudia," I yell. "Get up and run babe!" All of a sudden, people are running all over the mall frantically trying to get away from loud noises coming from the other direction down the hallway. Claudia runs away from me as I try to catch up with her while yelling for her the entire way. My feet feel so heavy and my arms are trying so hard to gain momentum to run, it's just not working. "Come on damnit," I yell. "Move your fucking ass," I yell again making every attempt to get my body to move as it should. I gain some speed, move across to the other side of the hallway where I think Claudia is hiding and come to a sliding halt. Still not being able to see where Claudia is, I see a man down the hallway picking anyone and everyone off with some type of automatic weapon.

Kids are dropping, women, men and virtually anyone that is in the hallway is being fired upon. That includes me! Yelling for Claudia, I scramble for cover. "Tom," Claudia screams out from what seems to be a mile away. "Tom, where are you?" I jump up to see Claudia on the other side of the hallway hiding behind one of the large potting plants in front of one of the stores. "I'm here Claudia," I yell. But my voice is too quiet for her to hear me. "Claudia," I try again. There is no way she's going hear me and I have to get to her before she moves. Shots continue to blaze through the hallway dropping anyone in sight. The sound of shattering glass is everywhere. For a few seconds, it's silent. I think maybe he's reloading or something so I jump up and bolt over to where Claudia is hiding. Sliding towards her like a baseball player sliding into third base, I slam against the wall right by her. "Are you okay," I ask while getting my balance and looking back at the shooter. "Ya, we have to get the hell out of here babe," she yells. Just then, shots ring out blasting out the glass right behind us. I get up and make it so Claudia is behind me before we start running. Hand in hand, I pull her as we sprint across the hallway trying to get out of the way of the raining bullets. Still watching other people drop in all directions around us, I yank Claudia around me and push her behind one of the solid walls leading down another hallway. Just then, it rips through my left hand. One of the bullets tears my hand apart as I dart behind the wall next to Claudia. Grabbing my torn apart left hand with my right, I scream from the intense pain I'm feeling. Looking down the hallway where the dark shadow appeared earlier, I see nothing but dead people laying all over the mall floor. I turn back towards Claudia as she's turned facing the other way completely frightened and perfectly still. Behind her, it appears again. Only this time, it's ten feet tall maybe more. Arms resembling a giant skeleton stretch entirely across the hallway. Looking down on both of us with those huge white eyes, we freeze in our tracks staring right back at it. What seemed like forever, Claudia turns to me and screams at the top of her lungs. I turn to see what it is and come face to face with the end of a long gun. Everything goes dark.

Jumping out of his dream, Tom finds himself holding his left hand. The pain in his hand is minimal, but very uncomfortable like the tingling of an arm or leg that fell asleep. Claudia is sitting up looking at Tom with a concerned look. He looks at her and says, "I had one again. I had another one of those dreams babe." "I know," she exclaims. "I could tell by the way you've been moving all over the place. I kept trying to wake you up thinking that would help." "Did you see it," Tom asks while sitting up with a hopeful look on his face. "Did you see it?" She looks at Tom with the crooked eyed look as if she's missed something. "What do you mean," she asks. "In my dream, you said you saw it," he tells her. "No babe," she says. "I'm not sure what you're talking about." Tom tells her all about the dream not missing one single detail. She jumps out of bed and says, "we better get in touch with the detective babe!"

Throwing clothes on and running out the door, Tom dials Butlers number.

Chapter 30

Still wandering the hallways of the Northern Mall, Tom and Claudia are getting tired and hungry since they haven't eaten anything since last night. Detective Butler left just a short time ago since there was no activity here or at any other mall in the city. Officers have gone back to their normal duties and things seem quite normal as of now. They finally decide it's time to get something to eat, but don't want to stop keeping a watch out. So they grab some to-go food and eat at one of the benches inside the mall. There are still many people around and will probably be getting busier as the day moves on. "Remember when I said that I'd confront that thing in my dreams to see what it wants with me," Tom says to Claudia. Wiping her mouth she says, "ya, I remember. Didn't you say you faced it last night in the dream?" "I did, but I didn't really confront it. I only came face to face with it and then turned to run along with you," Tom says. "But that's also when I thought you saw it too. In my dream you saw it twice. I started thinking you were in my dream and were able to see this thing with me." She looks up at him from taking a small bite of her sandwich and says, "no, I had some really weird dreams, but nothing like what you're having." Tom continues looking around for anyone suspicious occasionally taking a few bites of his lunch. For the middle of the afternoon, the mall is surprisingly busier than they would've imagined. Kids don't get out of school for another hour and it just seems all to busy this time of day. After eating, they decide it would be better if they split up and wander the mall separately for a while. "Let's stay on the phone just in case," Tom says with a concerned tone. Claudia looks at Tom, gently holds his face with both hands and says, "hey, it's gonna be okay. I love that you're worried about me. We can stay on the phone if that makes you feel better. But I wouldn't want to be anywhere else babe. If either of us see anything out of the ordinary, we'll just have to hang up with each other and call 911. Sound good," she says with such a warm and calming voice. Tom nods his head yes and they start off in opposite directions.

Passing each other now and again, they wave or wink or gesture in a way that makes both of them giggle as they continue down the hallway. The mall is now packed with kids, teenagers and adults going in and out of stores, shopping at the center isle retailers or just walking around like they are doing nothing more than people watching. "POP, POP!" A loud crack is heard from off in the distance down one of the other hallways. "POP, POP, POP!" There is goes again. She turns quickly and says, "Tom, did you hear that?" Changing hands while holding the phone,

"Ya, where was that?" A few people come running around the corner of the hallway looking back quickly as if something was chasing them. "Tom," she yells. "People are running right at me!" "POP, POP!" The sound is even louder than before with people scattering all over the hallways darting into stores, bathrooms and where ever else they can hide. "Claudia," Tom yells into the phone. "Where are you?" Claudia takes off towards the other direction not looking back and holding her phone in her hand, but not up to her ear. Hearing the noise through the phone, Tom yells, "Claudia!" He starts running in the direction of the noise and notices people beginning to run in his direction now. He's clear across the other side of the mall and running towards Claudia as fast as he can. "Claudia," he tries again with no response. He quickly hangs up the phone and calls Butler. "Get your ass over here detective, he's here," Tom yells. "I'm already on my way Tom. The call came in a minute ago and police are on their way. Get out of there," he exclaims to Tom. "I have to find Claudia," Tom yells and hangs up the phone. Flying around the corner, Tom sees a large crowd of people running in all different directions. He comes to a sliding stop and presses his back up against the wall right by the corner of the hallway so he can see in several directions. His phone rings, "Tom, where are you," Claudia screams. "I'm down by the footlocker," Tom says. "Where are you?" Just then, Tom notices something. Laying in one of the hallways are a few people motionless. His heart drops as he regains his focus on the phone, "Damnit, where are you," he says even louder and with some anger towards this whole situation. "I'm stuck in the small bathroom area by the food court. I can hear loud shots so he's got to be close to us," she says while shoving and pushing others hiding from this monster. "I'm right around the corner," he says. "I'll be there in a minute!" "No," she yells back at him. "Stay where you are and stay out of the way. He's picking off people left and right and I don't want you getting shot." Claudia doesn't get a response on the phone and when she pulls the phone away from her ear, she notices he hung up. She tries to call back, but there's no answer.

Tom's watching as people are dropping now and again from the gunfire sporadically covering the hallway. He sees the man now. He's a white male maybe six feet tall wearing a dark baseball cap, blue jeans and a black sweatshirt. He gets back on the phone with the detective, "he's in the food court area," Tom exclaims. "I'm pulling in now Tom, hang tight," Butler says. Police are running down the hallway from other directions heading right for the murdering bastard. About fifty yards away from this asshole, Tom sprints towards the opening where Claudia might be stuck by the bathrooms. Watching to his left as he runs, he clearly sees the gunman now picking off people like he's shooting clay pigeons. Just then, the man turns down the hallway in Toms direction to see police positioning themselves to take him out. He makes some minor adjustments and starts firing directly at them. Just as

Tom's about to reach the others, "Mother fucker," Toms yells out as loud as he can. One of the bullets blazed right through Toms left hand just above his pinky finger and tearing some of the flesh off from the side of his hand. Holding his hand tightly, he enters the bathroom area where Claudia and others are hiding out. The police quickly rain fire upon this man dropping him to the floor quickly and efficiently. For a moment, the silence was incredible. You couldn't hear anything other than the moans and groans of the injured and footsteps of police covering every inch of the mall. Tom crouches down in agony as blood pours from the embraced hands. Claudia quickly grabs Tom and wraps her arms around his back and shoulder as she recalls watching his arm swing backwards when he got shot. "Tom," she screams. "What the hell were you thinking, you maniac?" She holds him even tighter trying her best to calm him down and relieve some of the pain. Tom calms down a bit, looks up at her and says, "there was no way I was going to let him get to you." Claudia starts to cry as they walk out of the bathroom area and into the hallway. What they see is disastrous. People are being attended to from different areas of the mall and food court. Claudia grabs one of the towels from the nearby stores and wraps Toms hand with it. Many people are crying and frightened of what just happened as they are directed from police to head for the exits. Tom and Claudia stand right in the middle of the hallway looking around them in awe of what just happened. One of the police officers comes up along side of them holding one arm out as if to direct Tom to one of the standing by EMS teams. Without saying a word, they walk slowly wrapped around each other towards the exit where fire, EMS and other police vehicles and teams are gathering. Almost to the door, Butler quickly approaches them looking at Toms bloodied up hand and towel and says, "we should have been here Tom! I won't doubt you again."

Chapter 31

Sitting up in the hospital bed with bandages wrapped around Toms hand and up his arm, he's wondering how many people were killed and how many are in the hospital rooms around him. For Tom, going home tonight is a luxury and he's lucky it wasn't worse. Because of the tear where the bullet passed through, he'll be in some pain and shouldn't lose any movement in his hand. "You're lucky as hell Tom," says Claudia. "I can't tell you how much I appreciate you coming after me and doing whatever it takes to get to me, but that was crazy." He looks over at her and says, "I just wanted to make sure you'd be okay babe. He wasn't facing me when I started to run so I thought for sure I'd get there with no problem." She reaches for his good hand and holds it tightly as if to tell him she loves him without actually saying it. A while passes and Tom is cleared to go home. Even a torn hand from a bullet doesn't get the overnight stay in the hospital where you get to enjoy some of the best food and personal attention anywhere. Well, that's Toms joke on the way out anyway. Resting on Toms couch, late night news is all over this story with gruesome details about families that were torn apart because of this whack job that decided to go out and kill a bunch of innocent strangers with no regard to how old they were or who they were. It was just a senseless bloody massacre, they said on the news. Claudia walking back to Tom with a glass of water and a couple pain killers, "hey, why don't we turn off the news babe? Unless you need to watch for some reason, I just think we've seen enough of this don't you," she says with a completely sympathetic voice. "Ya, I agree. I don't know how much more I can watch. I would like to know how many people were killed and who was injured though, but I can check on that tomorrow when I talk with Butler," he says. "I'm sure during your conversation with him, he'll let you know," she says. "Here, take these. You're gonna need them for sleep and hopefully, they'll keep you asleep," she giggles. Tom takes the pills and washes them down with the glass of water. He looks up at Claudia for a long moment as if he's deep in thought. "What if I have another one tonight babe," he says with an exhausted tone to his voice. "No babe, you can only have these and then more in the morning when you get up," she responds. Tom gives her his quirky look while angling his head a little, "no dork. I mean what if I have another one of those dreams?" Sitting down next to him, she doesn't respond right away and let's Tom continue to think about this because of the look on his face where he's going to start talking again, "Ya, what if I do? There is no doubt that people are going to wonder either why things are so crazy or what is causing all of this don't you think," Tom says concerned. "What if people find out that it's me that's causing all of this? What if they figure hey, let's just take that guy out and all this nonsense will stop," Tom says. Claudia puts her hand up a little and says, "okay dork, that's not going to happen. Besides, we don't know that you're causing all of this. Just because it's a dream you're having don'ts mean you have the dream and then it happens. Maybe you've got one of those premonition abilities. Maybe you're psychic," she says with a little laughter. Looking at her again with the sideways smirk on his face he says, "I don't think I have that. But I am a little confused on what to do now. Seriously, what do I do," he says with a sort of depressed tone.

Late in the evening, Claudia gets comfortable in her sweatpants and t-shirt then sits by Tom again on the couch as he's slowly dozing off. "You're staying," he asks. "Of course I am. That is if it's okay with you," she says with raised eyebrows. Instead of responding verbally, he puts his one arm around her and pulls her in close. They stay on the couch for a while talking about everything going on. The topic of just them comes up and they start to talk about how starting a relationship like they have done can make them so much stronger due to all they've gone through so early on together. They feel even closer after all of this and can't wait to continue this wonderful and exciting adventure. After some time, they decide to move to the bedroom where he can get more comfortable and properly get some rest.

Claudia turns on the tv in the bedroom and channel surfs until she come to one of her favorite late night shows. Tom watches for a few minutes and starts to doze as his eyes grow heavy while leaning up against her more comfortable than he's ever been in his own bed. After just a few minutes, he falls asleep in Claudias arms.

Chapter 32

Waking up to a ringing phone, Tom slowly and somewhat painfully reaches over to see who's calling. "It's Butler," he says to Claudia who's stretching and yawning next to Tom. "Hello," Tom answers. "Tom, this is detective Butler, sorry to bother you this early but I wanted to check on you to see how you were doing," he says. "Well, I'm soar and have been taking some pain killers to sleep, but I'm okay. I'm much better than most of the other people at the mall aren't I," Tom responds. "Yes, I suppose you are," the detective responds humbly. "I need to know if you'd be up for some questions later today. I have a bunch of stuff I have to attend to early, but have some ideas I'd like to pass by you regarding your dreams and why this is all happening," Butler says. "You have some ideas," Tom asks surprisingly. "What kind of ideas?" Tom perks up a bit wondering where the detective is even going with this. But it sure sounds like he's maybe shedding some light on the subject and might just start to figure this shit out. "I can't tell you right now Tom," he says. "But I'd like to sit down with you later if you're up for it. I can even come to your place if that's better for you." Tom doesn't hesitate too much because it's either that or wait even more to try to figure this whole mess out. "Sure detective, I'll be free. Just give me a call whenever and I'm sure I'll be around since I'm really not doing much today but resting," Tom says. After hanging up the phone, Tom tells Claudia about the short conversation he had with the detective as she's again, walking in the bedroom with a glass of water and a pain killer for his pain. Downing the pill and water, Tom says, "what if we could actually figure this out?" His face lights up as if he's just had the best idea in his life. "What if this could finally go away," Tom says with the look of optimism on his face. Claudia climbs back in bed watching the excitement on Toms face, "that would be awesome Tom," she exclaims. "The scariest part about all this is that all of your dreams have been pretty accurate to the event. Think about this Tom! From when you and I started talking, the dreams have become more specific on what is happening hasn't it," she asks. "I suppose so," Tom says confused. "Where are you going with this," he asks. "Some of the dreams you've had were more in general of what was going to happen. You didn't know where or even if or when it was going to happen. But lately, these have been more specific to the result. Do you think that means anything," she asks with excitement of just figuring out something. Tom stops to think about all the dreams he's had and what happened after them. Not sure if it means anything, they brush it off a little and decide what they're going to do for breakfast.

Later that afternoon, Tom gets a phone call from detective Butler. "Hi Tom, how are you feeling so far," the detective starts off. "I'm good," Tom responds. "The pain isn't as much as I thought it would be or the pain killers are really doing their job." "Great to hear," Butler says. "Hey, would you be up for some brainstorming in a bit? I have some things I need to finish up, but could be by your place around 7ish if that's okay with you," the detective says. "Ya, that would be fine detective," Tom says. "Claudia went home a little while ago to get some things and freshen up a bit, but will be back soon. Is it okay that she's here too?" Tom wanted nothing more than to have Claudia there with him. Not only for the support through this whole thing, but to have her ideas as well. She was so excited earlier this morning that Tom feels it would be disrespectful not to have her with them. "Of course Tom, she'll probably have some pretty good input as well," Butler says. After hanging up the phone, Tom puts a plastic bag around his hand with a wrap provided by the hospital and jumps in the shower. Feeling much better from the shower, Tom dries off from the shower, runs his hand through his hair to make it look presentable, puts some jeans and a t-shirt on and heads for the living room. "Ding," a text comes in from Claudia. "Hey babe, I'll be there in just a bit. Butler get there yet?" Tom smiles as he always does when a text from her comes in. He texts back, "nope, not here yet. Just got out of shower." Toms phone rings, "God I hate texting," she says with a sigh. "Should I pick up anything to eat? Are you hungry, I am," she exclaims. "Hey that would be great babe. How about a pizza just to keep it simple. Plus if the detective is hungry, that's an easy one. Who doesn't like pizza right," Tom says laughing. Claudia gets to Toms place just minutes before the detective. Pizza sitting on the counter and fresh ice cold beer in the fridge, Tom says, "hey before we get going on this, you hungry? We got pizza," Tom exclaims. The detective looks at Tom and says, "thank you, but no. I don't like pizza." Both Tom and Claudia look at each other and at the exact same time say, "you have to be fucking kidding me," as they both start to laugh about it. "What," Butler says in a higher pitched voice. "It's not really that I don't like pizza, it's that it doesn't like me," he says. They all giggle a little bit and begin their conversation the detective requested.

Feeling guilty about eating pizza in front of the detective, it sits on the counter getting cold. But cold pizza is sometimes the best. "Look you two," the detective starts. "I've been looking over the notes I've taken since the first conversation we had. I read them over and over again even reading the details about the dreams you had when you were a kid trying to see if there was any connection at all with what really happens." Claudia and Tom are sitting on the edge of their seats just waiting to see where this goes. "Okay," Tom says. "If I were to believe that you're dreams were causing these catastrophes, I'd have to say you were either psychic or have the ability to make people do things," Butler says. "Okay," again Tom says with a long ending to the word and the look of anticipation on his face. "So here's what I've come up with," as he looks back and forth at both Tom and Claudia. "I don't believe you're making this shit happen. I don't believe for a second that you have any ability to possess people to do these things in any way. I don't believe you have any of that at all. What I do believe is different than this and you do have something to do with these events," the detective says with convincing tone. At this moment, Tom feels like the police are going to come crashing into the apartment and arrest him for all the deaths that have been happening lately. In a second, all of what the detective said runs through Toms mind as he tries to understand where Butler is going with this. "So detective, if you feel I have no abilities whatsoever and can't make anyone do these terrible things, what is your idea or is that it? Because if that's it, we've already been down this road before," Tom snaps in a non-confrontational way. Tom and Claudia wait for a few seconds for Butler to respond, "here's what I do believe. Have you ever thought of being a messenger Tom," the detective asks. "A messenger," Tom asks while looking at Claudia. "Yes, a messenger," Butler says again. "What I mean by that is you might be delivering a message from a higher power in order to stop a particular event that will happen in the future. In your case, the immediate future. Did you ever think about that," Butler asks. "Not really," Tom says. "But the only dreams where the events like yesterday actually happen is when I see that dark shadowy thing or whatever it is. And that thing is scary as shit! I can't imagine it's trying to communicate with me because every time I look at it, it looks like it's going to kill me or attack me. So how the fuck am I a messenger," Tom says. Claudia is watching as these two guys go back and forth about all this and decides to speak up, "Tom," she says calming him down a little. "I think what the detective is saying is that whatever that scary thing in your dreams is might not be that scary after all. Maybe it's trying to tell you something," she says putting her hand on Toms leg. "Hey look you two," Tom says sitting back in his chair. "I know what I saw and that thing scares the shit out of me and has no intention of trying to sit and have coffee with me while it tells me all about an event that is going to happen!" Tom has a look of disgust on his face and feels he's right back to where people wouldn't believe him when he was a kid. Because he's older now and more educated, he refocuses and realizes these people are here to help and for once in his life, they believe there actually is something here. Tom sits and thinks for a moment while looking out the window at the city filled with lights. "Okay," Tom says quietly. "What if it is trying to communicate with me? Each time I've seen it, it doesn't say anything and for sure doesn't show me it's friendly. So how the hell am I supposed to talk with this thing," Tom asks in a helpless tone. "That's just it Tom," Butler replies. "I just said I have some ideas is all. I didn't say I have the answers and thought it would be helpful to share them with you. If there's a way we can stop some of this, I'm up for anything," Butler says. "Let's just say you're right detective," Claudia jumps in. "If you're right, this might be something Tom has to live with for who knows how long," she says. Looking right at Tom, she says, "you would be like, a savior."

The ideas go back and forth for quite some time and finally, the detective leaves for home. Knowing what Tom needs to do now is totally out of his comfort zone. The fact that Claudia is here comforts Tom, but this new adventure he's about to go on is a very scary one. With Butler gone, the two of them mull it over as they heat up the pizza in the microwaved and have a couple drinks. Tom knows that he has to not only confront this thing, but figure out a way to communicate with it. He recalls that in every one of his dreams with this thing, it seems it was about to either kill him or dismember him and he's just not ready for that just yet. They finish up their pizza, get comfortable in bed and decide to watch some tv while still thinking of the task at hand. Claudias hands are tied simply because she's not in the dreams with Tom and can't help him with this. She can only help when he's awake and hopefully, that will be enough.

Chapter 33

In the office, Tom has some explaining to do. First of all, he's been spending so much time out of the office instead of his usual visits to check on things and say hi to his coworkers. The second thing is that he has a huge bandage on his left hand and nobody saw this before. So how the hell is going to explain this one? The truth shall set you free, he thinks. Everybody Tom passes in the hallway or in the main office area stop and ask him what happened. He simply tells the truth in that he was at the mall when the crazy whack job started shooting up the place and was unfortunate enough to take one to the hand. The look on everyones face when he tells the story is just priceless. Asking all kinds of questions and digging to get the dirt on exact details of the tragedy seems to be normal lately. All the time Tom is wandering around the office having to repeat the story over and over again, Claudia sits in her little cubical quiet as can be enjoying the fact that she's not telling the story. In fact, she took a personal day that day and it would be even more drama around the office if people knew she was with Tom during that nightmare. Once Tom is able to make it around the office and tell that damn story only one hundred times, he settles in at his desk and tries to focus on work. It's still early in the morning and he doesn't have any sales calls scheduled at this time today. However, because it is sales, that could change at a moments notice. At this time, there really is nothing else he can do until something like another dream occurs or he hears from detective Butler for whatever reason. And the fact that he DOES have a job where people count on him, he's got to make an effort on keeping aligned with his responsibilities for this company. "Ding," a text comes in from the detective. "Everything okay today?" Tom looks at his phone reading the text and understands why the detective sent that text and probably will each morning until all of this is figured out. "All good detective," Tom responds. Continuing to work at his desk, Claudia walks by and winks at him as she passes. He winks back, but his wink is really terrible. Tom has never really been able to wink properly and for some reason, both of his eyes close instead of just one. She giggles at that and keeps on walking.

Before you know it, it's after one in the afternoon and Tom has finished up all his paperwork and has caught up scheduling sales calls for the next couple weeks. Knowing how the company feels about sales people being in the office instead of out on the street selling, he begins packing up his shit. On his way out, he stops by Claudias desk and says, "dinner later?" Out of the corner of his eyes, he sees Cheryl, one of the other clerks listening in on what they say and motions to Claudia that she's listening. Cheryl is one of those drama filled people that feels she needs to know everything about everyone. In fact, she's leaning over so much to hear what they say that if she leans anymore, she'll fall right off her chair. "Dinner would be great," Claudia says quietly. "The usual place, same time," she says knowing Cheryl is listening and wanting this to be more dramatic. "You know it baby," Tom says with another screwed up wink and walks away. Tom glances over at Cheryl to see the expression on her face and like the rest of the morning, it's just priceless. Claudia goes back to work at her computer pretending to not notice Cheryl sliding her chair over to the edge of her cubical with eyes the size of saucers. "Psst," Cheryl sounds. Claudia looks up and around a bit knowing it's her, but trying to make it look like she heard something different. "Psst," again from Cheryl. Claudia turns to Cheryl and says, "hey, what's up?" Cheryl grins from ear to ear practically falling out of her chair in anticipation of the answer she's going to get from the question she's about to ask. "Are you guys, like dating or something," she asks. With one hand on a filing cabinet and the other holding herself up while sitting on her chair, Cheryl leans in even further into Claudias work area. "What makes you think that," Claudia says trying to muster up some additional drama. Because Cheryl has no shame she says, "well I overheard you guys talking about dinner and thought maybe you were like dating or something. He's so cute by the way. So, are you," she asks again practically drooling all over herself. "As a matter of fact, we are," Claudia says. "But it's purely sexual. I mean, it's amazing and we just get together now and again for dinner and sex. It's fantastic," she exclaims and then turns back to her computer. Leaving Cheryl with just that little bit of information is exactly what Claudia wanted. Before you know it, there will be rumors all over the office about the two of them and knowing the source, not much of it will be taken seriously.

Not knowing what the usual place is and what time Claudia would be available, Tom texts her just to see, "so what IS our usual place anyhow LOL?" Claudia responds, "I have no idea, but it was too funny when you left." Claudia and Tom continue texting and cracking up at the story she told Cheryl about the two of them. They decide to meet at one of the newer places not far from her apartment for a nice dinner and a couple drinks. Tom still has some things to do before then and Claudia will probably be fielding some more questions from Cheryl by the end of the work day. During his time downtown before meeting up with Claudia, Tom has to make a few stops for some things he needs back home. "POP, POP, POP!" Tom ducks as he hears gunshots and sees some guy running out of the corner bank at the end of the block. Only twenty yards or so away from this idiot, Tom hides behind one of the parked cars on the street hoping this guy doesn't see him and feel the need to fire at him. Everyone in the streets and on the sidewalks are running for cover. The security guard comes running out after him and fires a shot dropping the man on the edge of the street along the curbside. Not dead, the man turns his weapon on himself as many people around watch him take his own life. Laying there in the gutter not moving, the man is dead while blood runs down the curbside gutter and into one of the local drains. "Holy shit," Tom yells out. Not really talking to anyone, he feels like everyone heard him it was so quiet. Police cars come racing to the scene only seconds after this happens probably because they were alerted while this dude was still in the bank. The security guard stands over the man and uses his foot to drag the gun away from the criminal just in case. As police crowd the bank and the suspect, people in the street do too. Before you know it, a large crowd is taking pictures and videos of the incident with no regard for anyone's safety or confidentiality. It's a sick sight as Tom sits back and watches all of this happen and begins to wonder why he didn't know about it. Why wasn't this one of my dreams, Tom thinks.

The new place is quite lovely with romantic booths up against the wall covered with mirror images and pictures from historical painters along with little sconces that are dimly lit to set the mood. It's not an expensive place where you're only getting the best steaks, fish, seafood and other dishes only for high class restaurants. Instead, it's a nice romantic place for casual dining with a nice menu to serve just about anyone including a partial kids menu. With a beer in front of Tom and a glass of wine in Claudia's hand, Tom says quietly, "can you believe that shit? I was right by him when he put a bullet in his own head." "I can't believe you were right there Tom," she says holding his hand on the table. "You didn't dream about this did you," she asks. "No," Tom exclaims. "That's the weird thing. I didn't have any dream about this which bothers me a lot. Why wouldn't I?" Tom takes a drink of his beer, sets the beer mug back down on the table and stares at it. The mug has the name of the restaurant on it in a font that is totally cool and it has some graphics to match. He looks at the mug and says, "hey, I need this mug. It would go well in my apartment," he says giggling a bit. Toms phone rings and once again, it's Butler. "Hey, are you holding back on me for some reason," the detective asks. Butler continues, "why didn't you tell me about this?" Tom and Butler continue discussing this for a few minutes while Claudia intently listens on as she continues to sip her wine. After hanging up, he says to her, "this is so screwed up. Detective Butler thinks there's something more to this than we think. He's wondering the same thing we are, why am I dreaming about some of these and not others," Tom questions himself. Ordering dinner and a couple more drinks, they keep trying to figure out what is going on with these dreams. Done with dinner which was very good, they decide to take a short walk before heading home. Both will stay in their own places since they've spent the last couple nights together with all that's going on. Saying goodnight, they kiss for a few minutes and head for home.

Chapter 34

Sitting on a plane high above the earth, I'm in coach somewhere back in the middle of the plane. Coach isn't so bad as long as you get an exit row seat if nobody sits next to you. Soaring along to who knows where, the cabin is dark and I can only see a few rows in front of me and a couple behind. Suddenly I feel myself sinking in the seat like it wasn't even there and I get further and further down to the bottom of the plane. I'm falling through the plane! There is no way this can happen. How can anyone fall right through the seats and bottom of a major airline? Once I get to the bottom of the plane, I can see the ground from what looks like miles below me. "Awesome," I yell out loud. "I haven't had one of these dreams in a very long time," I put my arms out like I'm some super hero and begin to fly below the jet. Losing sight of the large plane, I'm on my own. Flying at speeds beyond my imagination, I'm able to twist and turn in any direction, fly down towards the ground and the water hovering just inches away. Then swooping back up high in the sky leveling off at unbelievable speeds. Suddenly I see the Detroit river and make my way towards the opening between Detroit and Windsor, Ontario. Blazing past tall buildings on the right that look like the Renaissance Center and other office buildings, I stay tight to the side of the river wondering if anyone sees me above. All of a sudden, an air force jet goes screaming by me on my left. Knowing the radar capabilities on that thing, I just know he's going to turn and follow me since now I'm an unidentified flying object. I look behind me and see him turning as sharply and quickly as the river is wide. Because of my awesome speed, I look back forward and up to the sky. My speed is intense as I climb with the pressure against my face and body while feeling the air force jet on my tail. I quickly dart downwards knowing this fighter jet isn't going to be able to keep up with my incredibly quick turning capabilities and lose him somewhere behind. I'm sure he's still on me, but I don't see him anywhere. For now, I look straight ahead of me shooting back by the downtown area and down the river. My flying powers always seem to fade during these types of dreams and it starts happening now. I'm high over some of the suburbs in the metro Detroit area and falling fast. It's like my power is only for a short time so I have to make the best of it. Falling towards the ground, I fade out of the dream.

"Holy shit that was fun," Tom says lying in bed with a smile on his face. It's not the first time Tom has had this dream. In fact, this particular dream Tom has had several times as a young adult and hasn't had it for quite a while. Most people that have lucid dreams simply recognize they are dreaming and wake themselves up before anything bad happens. Well Tom has been able to not only recognize he's dreaming, but he's been able to determine some of the outcomes of the dream. He has a lot of fun with this and looks forward to having these dreams as often as he can. They are usually fun dreams that start out in a weird way like falling through a plane. There's another reoccurring dream he has where he's walking down a pathway or sidewalk in a park that is lit up on both sides. Once he realizes he's in the dream, he starts running, dives forward and takes off like a plane off a runway. In his lucid dreams, there are times when he's flying and he'll try to find his actual home to see if he can see himself sleeping or maybe a friend's house to see what's going on there. Every time he has this type of dream, he never gets close enough to the house or can't find it, but then starts to fade out of the dream altogether. After this dream, he lays in bed wondering where those fun types of dreams have been for so long. Because of the drinks from earlier with Claudia, he gets up from bed and goes to the bathroom. Still tired as hell, he keeps the lights off, takes a leak and goes back to bed. Looking at the clock, he mumbles to himself, "oh sweet, still three hours before I have to get up."

I'm looking right at it. Its gray, bloodshot eyes are staring back at me. Only this time, it stands towering over me like a seven-foot man. Glaring down at me, all I can see is the blackness surrounding its head from a cape like hoodie wrinkled and tattered. It's so close to my face I can feel the warmth of its breath and body. Its mouth is something I've never noticed before with jagged teeth and a smirk that only allows a few of the teeth to be noticed. The lips on this thing are wrinkled and crooked as it continues to breath on my face. I know now, I have not only confronted this thing, but am about to get eaten by it. I am paralyzed not with fear, but with utter immobilization as I try to turn and run. Just then, a strength like no other grabs my entire body as forces me to look to my side. My head moves slowly to the right as my eyes are still stuck on the face of this thing. I am completely aware that I am dreaming and if this is one of those lucid dreams where I can determine the outcome, I need to get the hell out of here. I have virtually no power and no control whatsoever. This dream is as clear as day and I see no evidence of fading out of it anytime soon. Focusing in on where my head has landed with my body still contorted towards the creature, I'm looking into a black sky with a large faded billboard far out in the distance. Fading visions appear one after another. Flashes of fire. Flashes of children and flashes of numbers. Each of these fade in and out several times before I begin to notice my feet being lifted off the ground with a feeling of complete weightlessness. It's like being in space where there is no gravity at all. I turn to see this thing and how it's controlling me when it slowly fades and disappears. Still hovering in the air, I look down and see nothing below me, only darkness. At that moment, the speed and force of free falling from twelve thousand feet comes over my entire body.

Waking up, Tom feels himself sinking in his bed when it dawns on him he's back in his bedroom. Sitting up quickly, he holds his head in his hands trying desperately to remember what he saw. "Damnit," he yells. "What did I see? Think damnit, think," he yells again. Keeping his eyes closed he feels if he concentrates enough, it will pop back into his memory. But as a few minutes go by, the dream fades even more. "Shit," he mumbles. Releasing his head from his hands, he gets out of bed and knows he needs to get in touch with the detective to possibly figure this one out. Standing up to stretch, Tom walks towards the bathroom. Just then, something catches his eyes. Glancing back at the mirror above the dresser, he sees them. Scared out of his mind and stumbling backwards over the bedside table, he reaches for his phone.

Chapter 35

Tom, Claudia and Butler are now staring at the mirror in Toms room. On the mirror written horribly, almost scribbled in large black magic marker, it reads, "27 and 107." "No, I didn't write that," Tom barks at Claudia. Both Butler and Claudia study what's on the mirror questioning how it got there. After a couple questions from Claudia and Butler making Tom feel defensive, Claudia says, "well, what if you did it in your sleep honey? What if you got up while you were sleeping and wrote it down or something," she says calmly, yet doubtful. "I don't even have a fucking marker," Tom yells. "Look, this is freaking me out and I called you both over here to figure this out. I didn't write anything and explained what I saw in the dream with the kids and the fire too," he exclaims. Tom continues, "detective, you even told me that maybe I'm some weird messenger or something. What if this is one of those fucking messages?" Tom sits in his chair in the corner of the room and sighs with exhaustion. Claudia isn't saying much. In fact, she's wandered into the other room and out of view. Detective Butler says, "she was only trying to help Tom." Tom looks out the window not looking at Butler and says, "ya I know, I know. But fuck this. Nobody believes me, not even my fucking girlfriend." Butler takes an even closer look at the writing while Tom gets up to apologize to Claudia. Looking around in the living room and then the kitchen, Tom can't find her. He sees the apartment door cracked open and runs for the hallway. Down the hall, he watches as she gets on the elevator and disappears from view. Running down the hall yelling her name, he gets there just as the elevator door shuts. He knows he didn't react to her questions or suggestions properly, but knows what he saw in his dream and knows he didn't write what is on the mirror. He walks back into the apartment as Butler is walking out. "So, what do we do now," Tom asks the detective. "Look Tom, I'm not sure what it means. Unless it means something to you, I really have no idea," Butler says. He continues, "I've written it down and will think about it to see what I can come up with. If you hear or see anything, you let me know," Butler says and walks towards the elevator.

Tom closes the door and heads for the bedroom. Staring at it again, "27 and 107," he's putting together in combination after combination trying to make any sense of this. Tom begins talking to himself, "is there going to be a fire somewhere? Is 107 the address to the fire? Are there 27 kids involved with this? Fuck," he yells out loud. After calming down for a few minutes, he grabs his phone and shoots a text to Claudia. "Hey," he types. A few minutes pass with no response. Another text, "I'm really sorry hun." Finally, after a couple minutes, "please babe." Still early in the morning, Tom heads for the office thinking maybe he'll see her there. He's not sure what to say now that she hasn't even responded to his texts, but he has to try. They've only begun to fall in love and Tom can't let her slip away without giving every chance possible. Plus, Tom doesn't think this is even something two people falling in love should fight over or even think of not speaking over. As he walks into the office, he sees her quietly sitting at her desk working or pretending to work at her desk. He places his stuff on his desk and begins walking towards her. "Hey Tom," one of the guys yells from across the room. Tom waves his hand low to his body as he's totally caught in trying to sneak up to her. "Hey," he says to her softly. She turns to him and says, "hey." Not knowing if that was a good hey or a bad hey, Tom says, "can we talk for a minute?" Cheryl of course, is leaning way over once again to hear what the drama is today. "Sure," she says while motioning to the kitchen. Grabbing a water and a Snickers bar out of the fridge, Claudia says, "I know you're bothered Tom, I really do. But I was only trying to make suggestions about what could've happened and you weren't very nice. I don't take being barked at very well at all," she exclaims. "I didn't mean what I said babe," Tom says with an apologetic voice. "I woke up this morning worried I wasn't going to be able to remember what I saw in the dream. It freaked me out because of Butler saying

I was gonna be some sort of communication thing or messenger and here I am screwing that up by not remembering. Then I saw what was on the mirror and totally freaked out. Babe, I'm sorry. I didn't mean to yell," he says while trying to keep his voice down. "Hey, I've supported you through all of this right," she asks. "Yes, of course," Tom replies. "Then just because I question what is going on doesn't mean I don't support you now," she says with a little edge to her. Tom looks down realizing he's made a mistake, but is still a little hot about her not believing him. Forever, that has been the story. Not believing him is something he's used to and has a very short fuse when it comes up. "I get it Tom, it's freaky if you truly didn't write that on your mirror and somehow it just appeared. It's scary I'm sure, but you have to be open to other ideas. Sometimes we sleep walk or do things in our sleep that just don't make sense. Look at your dreams," she exclaims. Embarrassed, Tom says, "I know. Do you really think I wrote that on the mirror babe?" "I kind of think you did Tom, but that has nothing to do with it. All of this is just too weird," she says. Tom sets his water down on the counter and says with a sarcastic laugh, "thanks for your support. Fine." He walks out of the kitchen shaking his head and back to his desk. Without making a scene, Claudia slowly makes her way back to her desk. By the time Claudia sits in her chair and sets her water and Snickers bar down on her desk, she turns just in time to see Tom leaving the building.

Chapter 36

All morning, Tom can't stop thinking 27 and 107 and the flashes of some type of fire and children around has to mean something. It's around ten in the morning now as he's sitting at a local cafe trying to figure this out. "Why would that thing show me this," he mumbles to himself while writing the visions on his napkin. Tom goes over and over in his head all the obvious clues. Children in a fire? Twenty seven kids somewhere in a fire? "It has to do something with a fire and kids, but what is the 107 for," he says to himself. Just then, Butler sits on the other side of the booth and looks across at Tom. "I saw you walk in here and thought I'd see what you were up to," the detective says. "I see you're taking notes," Butler giggles as he's looking at Toms napkins. "Detective, this isn't a joke. You know from first hand experience that my visions or dreams or whatever the fuck they are truly affect people," Tom says. "Okay," Butler says. "What do we have so far? We have 107 which could mean what? I number of people, an address, a time or maybe room number," the detective says. "How about 27 or the combination of 27 and 107," Tom says. Tom and Butler sit and go through every possible scenario, 107 schools in the area, 27 fire trucks, 27 fire stations, kid's ages 10 or 7, or what has to do with the visions of fire and kids. "What were the visions of fire Tom," Butler asks. "Were the kids being burned or were they even in the fire," he says. "No detective, it was like two separate things altogether. I saw visions of a blazing fire, but in the fire was nothing. And it was so faded and far away it would've been hard to see kids inside of it. But the kids have to mean something," Tom says. "What did the kids look like? Were they scared, playing, what were they doing," the detective asks. "Running! They were running," Tom says as he looks up at the detective. "I couldn't see why they were running, but they were. And the vision following the kids was the fire," Tom says as he's moving his arms around at the table as if demonstrating the visions. Tom looks at Butler and asks, "how many daycare places are there around here. Let's just say in the downtown area?" They both get on their smart phones and start researching. After a few moments of typing and scrolling, Butler looks up at Tom and says, "Twenty seven!" They both look at each other as if they've just solved a piece of this puzzle and dig in even further trying to figure the rest out. Unsure if they are even right, they continue to check on the daycare facilities to double and triple check just to make sure. "Okay, 107. What is that going to mean," the detective says. "What are the addresses for each of the daycare facilities," Tom asks quickly. They both start scrolling looking for any connection to the daycare and see nothing in regards to the 107. Still baffled and throwing ideas around for the number 107, their smart phones are burning up from the usage they're putting them through. The waitress comes by asking them if they'd like something to eat. they order up a couple sandwiches and drinks and continue to think. Both frustrated they can't come up with anything for the 107, Butler looks at his watch, "It's twelve fifty eight man," he says to Tom. "Ya, good thing we can eat while we think," Tom says sarcastically. "WAIT," Tom exclaims. "What time did you say it was?" The detective looks up at Tom and has the same idea pop into his mind. "Shit," they both say getting up and running out the door. "It has to be right detective, it just has to be," Tom says. The detective gets on the radio in his car which is parked in the parking lot right next to the diner. He directs officers to each of the daycare facilities in the downtown area immediately. It's one o'clock now and they have to move. "Where do we go," Tom yells to the detective. "Which one is closest Tom," he says. Quickly, Tom looks at his phone and finds one of the daycare places around the corner a couple blocks. "Let's go, it will be quicker on foot," Butler yells and they begin running through the streets. Racing past people as they bump into many apologizing and excusing themselves as they go, "It's 1:04 detective," Tom yells from slightly behind Butler. "Then move your ass," Butler responds. Arriving at the daycare located at the bottom of one of the tall high-rises downtown with a minute to spare, all is quiet. They enter the daycare with the detective casually showing his badge to the woman at the counter and motioning to her that all is okay. Wandering through and watching the children play, they catch their breath knowing they got there in time. The detective looks at his watch and looks at Tom, "1:07".

On the phone, detective touches base with one of the other officers to see if there is any activity. After a few phone calls in just a minute or so, his phone dings from an emergency text message alert, "Fire at the Uptown Kinder-care facility," it shows. They race back to Butlers car and head for towards the scene. Pulling up to the small office building just off Mack Avenue in smaller area of downtown Detroit, they find police and fire trucks everywhere. Firemen are in the building fighting a fire that has been almost entirely put out as smoke billows through the building and out the windows on the fourth floor. On the other side of the building and across the street, Tom sees officers, people from the office building and what looks to be an amazing sight, children standing behind them. News crews are also on the scene capturing footage of the fire, survivors and the fire crews at work. The detective talks with the fire chief briefly and comes back to Tom, "everybody got out and the fire is under control. Look Tom," as Butler smiles and points over to the children. "Ya, I saw them," Tom says. The detective starts laughing, punches Tom in the shoulder and say, "you have to be fucking kidding me!" Looking at each other with relief and disbelief that this is even happening, "All is good here right? All is good," saying to Butler trying to hold back some of his emotions. "Ya Tom, all is good," the detective says reaffirming his confidence. They start walking towards the children across the street and Butler says, "you know what the really sad part about this is Tom?" Stopping in the street, Tom looks at the detective with a puzzled look on his face. The detective continues, "there are two really great sandwiches sitting at our booth right now being wasted."

Chapter 37

ater that evening, Tom is in his apartment sitting at the kitchen island thinking back on the day. What he should be feeling right now is utter relief and excitement about the positive outcome from the dream. Instead, he can't get Claudia out of his mind. His heart is heavy wondering what she's doing and if she's thinking of him. It didn't seem like a big deal at the time, but maybe to her it was. Grabbing some food from the fridge and cracking a beer, Tom settles in for a long, lonely night. Wanting so badly to text Claudia, he holds back knowing it may not be the right time. As much as he wants to, he feels he's justified in being upset about it and after all, she wasn't even there to experience the successful day he had.

The local news comes on and the top story of the evening is the fire at the childcare facility. This is the first time in a long time where Tom wanted to watch. Reporters are everywhere happily conveying no deaths or injuries due to this fire and that there was ample time for all tenants along with all the children to get out of the building thanks to the Detroit police department. The news continues talking about how the cause of the fire has not yet been determined, but that there was a break-in the night before and further investigation is under way. Tom is overjoyed with this and wishes so much that Claudia was here to celebrate it with him. Just then, he sees himself on tv. One of the news crews captured him and detective Butler standing in the middle of the street laughing about something. "Holy shit, there I am," Tom says laughing. "Damn," his smile fades as he starts thinking of her again. "Ding," a text comes in. "Saw you on tv, way to go," Claudia texts. The biggest relief comes over Tom as he almost drops his phone trying to position it to text back. "You saw that," he texts. Toms phone rings. Looking up at the ceiling, he silently says, "thank you." "Hello," says Tom. "Hi, did I catch you at an okay time," Claudia asks. "Ya, just sitting here watching me on the news is all," he laughs. "I saw that and had to say, wow. Did everything work out the way you hoped for? Obviously, you were able to figure out this puzzle right," she asks. "Ya, we figured it out at the cafe. It was one of those last minute kind of things," he says. The conversation is weird and not like it usually is with them. Tom doesn't go into much detail and her questions are basically for yes or no answers. Finally, she says, "hey Tom, sorry about earlier and not believing you. I need to tell you something about myself that I haven't shared with you yet," she says. "Really? I thought I knew absolutely everything," Tom says laughing.

"When we can get together again, that is if you'd still like to, I'd love to share more with you Tom," she says getting Toms heart beating faster. "Is it too late to see each other tonight," Tom asks optimistically. "I was hoping you'd say that," as she hangs up the phone. Suddenly, there's a soft knock at the door. Opening the door to a beautiful, warm smile, Claudia comes in and stands just inside the door. "So what if I said I didn't want to see you, huh," Tom says trying to be serious. "Oh, I would've just busted the door down is all. I could do it you know," she says clinching her fist towards in front of her. Tom leans in pushing her slightly up against the wall and kisses her gently on her lips. Only inches from her face he says, "I really am sorry for raising my voice to you, hope you know that." She puts her hand on the back of his neck and pulls him in for another. "It's me who should be sorry," she says after releasing from the warm, wet kiss. They grab a couple drinks and sit on the couch talking about the day. Tom is excited during the whole conversation almost like he's started a new chapter in his own life. Claudia is thrilled with his achievement and asks him, "do you think that's the beginning of your communication with this thing in your dreams? Were you able to say anything," she asks. "That's the thing, like I said earlier I didn't even get a chance to say anything or try to communicate at all. It was like it controlled me from the beginning and showed me those visions. So I guess that's the way it communicates. I mean it's not like I'm going to sit and talk with this thing. I'm telling ya, it scares the shit out of me," Tom says.

After getting a couple more beers and sharing more of the day, Claudia says, "I'd like to tell you a little more about me if that's okay," she says. "Of course sweetie," Tom says confidently making her feel as comfortable. Claudia goes into her past telling Tom everything about growing up with her father. During many parts of the story, Tom holds her hand comforting her and showing his love and understanding. She goes pretty deep into her childhood and why she couldn't wait to grow up and leave the IA. It wasn't just because of her father, but because she wanted to have a new life and a new beginning of her own. Being held back as she explains to Tom, was only one of the many reasons she needed to move on. She then explains to Tom why she was so upset earlier this morning when he raised his voice to her. After hearing all she said tonight, he fully understood and said, "it makes more sense babe. I know there will be disagreements from time to time with any couple that is together for any amount of time. Maybe just understanding that will help," Tom says. They both feel relieved after this discussion and continue to joke a bit and talk more about the day, the success and the new feeling they have while falling more in love after such a deep conversation. Not realizing they've been talking for hours, Tom looks at the clock and asks with a smirk on his face, "spending the night?" For a second, Tom thought she was getting up to leave. But as she gets up she says, "not before this," she says in her sexy voice. She starts unbuttoning her blouse to show off a new laced bra. Tom sits back on the couch enjoying this private strip show as she undoes her pants and they fall to the floor. She turns showing off the matching thong with her sexy legs running up to that fantastic firm ass. Straddling Tom, she places her hands behind Toms head on both sides of the couch and leans in extremely close. Without touching him with her hands or lips, she moves her hips feeling his excitement and ever so softly rubs on him until he can't stand it anymore. Moving his hands onto her ass, he pulls her in close making her waste rest against his lower chest. He begins sliding his hands up her lower back to her bra strap. With one flick of his good hand, her bra comes off and those wonderful breasts fall upon his lips. Continuing to play with her body like his own little playground, his clothes also start coming off little by little. Because she knows he loves it on the bottom, she slides his final piece of clothing off and climbs back on top of Tom. For what seems to be forever, Tom enjoys the 'hands free zone' and thoroughly enjoys her body. Once done making love, they hold each other staying in the same position kissing and bantering a little back and forth. "It's late babe, wanna climb in bed," Tom says. They make it to the bedroom, once again cuddle up closely and fall asleep.

Chapter 38

With their heads laying on their pillows facing each other, they look into their eyes as the sun begins to rise. Today is a day they are going to make for themselves. "Anything," she asks laying there with her hand rubbing his arm. "No, I slept great," he says. "I don't recall one single dream last night. Normally, even if they're short dreams, I remember something." "You don't think this is over do you? I mean what if you don't have any more dreams," she asks. Tom sits up in bed and says, "well, we can only hope that's the case but I don't think so. I have had many thoughts of this going away and for such a long time, I thought I was causing these events. This is all new babe. If it goes away, great! But if this is only the beginning of something different, then I might be," Tom's interrupted by Claudia, "WE," She says. He sighs and smiles. "Then WE," he pauses, "might be in for a totally new ride." She smiles bashfully accepting his warm welcome into this mess he's been living. "So what are we going to do on our day off babe," she asks. "Well, I don't know about you, but I'm thinking a nice hot shower, breakfast at one of the best breakfast places in town, maybe a ride out to the country and then we'll see from there. Sound good," Tom asks with enthusiasm. Throwing a pillow at Claudia's head, Tom jumps up out of bed still totally naked and runs for the bathroom. Turning on the shower and reaching in to check the temperature, he feels two warm hands gently gliding along his stomach as her wonderful naked body presses up against his back. He takes her hand and steps into the shower. The water is a perfect temperature as they stand under the falling streams skin to skin. Their bodies become drenched with water all over them as they passionately kiss under the water running down their faces and past their lips. He turns her around placing her hands eye level on the gray and white tile wall as he soaps her body up, not missing a spot. With care she's never felt before, he fills his hands with shampoo and runs his fingers around her scalp lathering up her long brown hair. The suds from the lather run down her naked body and into the drain. He then disconnects the shower head and gently pulls her hair back to rinse all the shampoo out. Slowly finishing the rinse, she turns to him wiping her eyes from the remaining water and pulls him close. Returning the favor, she lathers him up and massages his head until his legs are like jello. With his eyes closed, his hands still exploring her body while she finishes up rinsing the shampoo out. She then soaps his body watching his every move and twitch learning more and more about this man.

Drying off and blow drying each other's hair, they laugh and banter the entire time. Heading out for breakfast holding hands, they can't believe the giddiness they feel for each other. Breakfast is at one of the favorite downtown spots called The Dime Store. Known for their spectacular breakfast specials and unique dishes, Tom and Claudia grab a table by the window and look over the menu. From chef specials like kung pow chicken hash to cinnamon and apple french toast and even biscuits and gravy, there are plenty of dishes here for anyone. Only open until the middle of the afternoon, their specialty breakfast and lunch menus are spectacular. Claudia orders up a malted Belgian waffle special while Tom picks out an avocado bacon omelette special. To go with these dishes, they both order up a spicy bloody and a glass of water to replenish hydration lost from last night and this morning. Watching the folks walk past them on the sidewalk downtown and looking around the restaurant, they find themselves in their own little world. With so many things going on around them and so many people running back and forth from work or where ever they're going, it seems as if this metaphorical place was meant for just them. Finishing up breakfast amazed at what they just ate, they head for the his car safely parked in his lot. Hand in hand, they stop on their way to the car at one of the local coffee shops for her to grab her everyday morning coffee. Even though it's mid-morning, she still loves the taste of coffee and has one or two daily. Tom on the other hand, doesn't like coffee and has never been able to get used to the taste. His choice of caffeine is in one of the popular energy drinks that he might have once or less a day.

Driving to the country is pretty easy around here. Anything outside of an hour or so pretty much in any direction will get you there. As they reminisce about how they're are doing together and the excitement both have in their hearts, they continue driving out West to some of the small towns. Driving on one of the two-lane roads in the country, they love the sights of horses, little ponies, cows and even the occasional field of sheep and goats running around. To them, that's home. Stopping in the middle of this small town, they get out and walk around like a couple of tourists from the big city. Stepping away from Claudia so she can't hear him, Tom wanders off a bit to make a couple quick phone calls. She asks, "who was that?" "Damn telemarketers," he responds and then changes the subject. The local shopping is funny compared to bigger cities or even a downtown area like Detroit. You know you're in a small town when the local hardware store is closed on Sunday. They both laugh at that sign. People around are extremely friendly and welcoming. It's just the way Claudia and Tom like it. Wandering through almost all the stores and getting a little hungry as the afternoon continues, they decide to head North to one of Toms favorite places in Michigan. Muskegon has always been one of those places Tom has been while growing up as a kid. His parents used to take his family there for many years and it's become one of the staples for him and his family. Now being on his own and older, it's been some time since he's been there and thought Claudia would love the short trip. Never being there before, Claudia loves what she sees so far and can't wait to get further into the area. Pulling up and parking down one of the streets by many stores and small shops, they get out once again and start their tour. It's a beautiful Fall day and you can feel the breeze coming in from Lake Michigan. It's not the smallest town with a population of approximately 38,000 people, but it's small enough. Busy with tourists and folks that live in the area, Tom and Claudia feel as if they are in an entirely different world than back home in Detroit. The fact is, they are. This small town is an escape for a lot of people and families. Such a great place to hide from the hustle and bustle of the city life.

After wandering the city for a while doing some shopping and sight-seeing, Tom decides to take her to a special place for a nice romantic dinner and some drinks. Pulling into the parking lot, Claudia is delighted at the views she's noticing and the style of the restaurant. It's beautiful out here at the Lake House Waterfront Grille with fantastic views inside and out. Walking in to the restaurant lobby, the hostess asks, "do you have a reservation?" Claudia looks at Tom with an 'uh oh' look like we didn't know we needed one. As busy as it is, she thinks they're not going to be able to even get a table. "Yes," Tom says and gives his name. The hostess has them follow her and leads them to a somewhat private table by the window and next to a large glass fireplace. They say thank you to the hostess and sit down gawking out the window and the beautiful view of the great lake. Claudia turns to Tom and says, "telemarketer my ass!" They laugh, grab the menus and soak in the atmosphere. They start by ordering a sharable plate of bruschetta and a couple of the local brewed beers. The menu consists of choices ranging from seafood to filets and even burgers and sandwiches. All the food there is considered top of the line and Claudia is amazed by not only the selection, but that the prices aren't going to kill your average family. Finishing up dinner, they sip the last of their drinks and watch the sunset just before leaving. "I really don't want to leave babe, this was just wonderful," she says to Tom. "I know, it's great up here isn't it," Tom says. "How long of a drive back," she asks. Tom makes it look like he's thinking about this and trying to get an accurate time on how long it would take for them to get back to the Detroit area. In reality, it is about a 3 ½ hour drive to get back. But Tom has a different idea. "Oh, I think it's about five minutes, maybe less," he says with a smart ass smirk on his face. "Huh? What does that mean," she says smiling. Tom gets up from the table as Claudia follows. Out in the parking lot, Tom says, "would you be okay if we stayed the night here and left in the morning?" She gleams with happiness and smiles from ear to ear. "Where do you plan on staying," she asks. Tom tells Claudia that down the street is one of the really nice hotels facing the water that he's already made a reservation for them. She grabs his hand, pulls him close and says, "telemarketer MY ASS," she screams joyfully.

The hotel is gorgeous with a room to match. The views on the 8th floor are stunning and would have been more stunning if they got there before the sun finally set. Regardless, they settle in with some wine and a fire and enjoy the view of the lights coming in from nearby hotels and the small city and the remarkable view of Lake Michigan. Because they are having such a great time together, time flies by as it usually does. Heading off to bed, they both laugh about not having anything to wear in bed or having any of their bathroom necessities. Laughing Tom says, "I'll be right back babe." He runs down to the hotel convenience store and picks up a couple tooth brushes and some other essentials he thinks she might need. When he gets back to the room and enters the bedroom saying, "I got some stuff for," he's interrupted by her seductive posture on the bed. "Holy moly," he says as his jaw drops wide open. Lying naked on the bed with the sheets barely covering her body, she says, "I'm pretty sure we're going to have everything we need right here!" Not taking his eyes off of her, he drops everything including his clothes and goes in for the kill.

Chapter 39

Once again, it appears. Only this time, it's standing at the end of a dark lit alley somewhere in the downtown area. A streetlight behind it in the intersection shows its massive size and hooded shape and the glow of its white eyes, even visible from here. The two buildings I'm between aren't recognizable at all. Dark brown, large gray brick and very tall with lots of windows extending as high as I can see. I look behind me only to see I'm in the middle of this alley as the buildings extend far down in both directions. Looking back, it hasn't moved. In fact, it's taking up much of the space between the buildings like a permanent fixture between the two. I have no idea what to do. Looking around me at my hands and arms, my feet and legs, and everything else surrounding me right now, nothing seems right. I look back up and down the alley, it's still there. I know now, I'm dreaming. "Tom, wake up," Claudia says. I'm in the middle of a dream and need to decide quickly what to do. Usually at this time, I'm slapping my face or doing something to snap out of the dream. But now with a better understanding of what's expected of me, I stay put. Not sure if I should be moving towards it or waiting for some type of signal to let me know what to do, I slowly walk backwards just to see what it's going to do. Keeping my eyes on it, I've moved two or three car lengths, maybe more and it's still not moving. "Come on babe, you're dreaming," Claudia says raising her voice this time. The feeling of this thing watching me is making my skin crawl. I know those eyes are focused only on me. One of the lights in front of it is flickering and with every flash of brightness, I can see the definition in its teeth and eyes. Not being physically held back like in other dreams, I turn and run as fast as I can. As I'm running, I can feel the sensation of warm, moist air on my neck. Stopping in my tracks, I hear raspy, deep breathing right behind me. "Tom," Claudia yells. Not wanting to turn back, I cringe with my arms to my side and my head as low to my body as I can trying to hide any visible areas of the back of my neck. Slowly I turn expecting to come face to face with this thing staring at me with its jagged ass teeth and smoky white eyes. There it is, still standing in the same place it was before. With a short lived sigh of relief, I look around me noticing I'm in the same spot as when I started. "What do you want," I try to yell but no sound is heard. It's as if I'm in a vacuum where no sound can be heard no matter how loud you yell. But I can hear things, little things. The sound of cans tumbling down the alleyway on cement, papers shuffling as if blowing in the wind and I can even hear voices other than mine coming from everywhere. Why can't they hear me, but I can hear them? Looking back down to the end of the alley, it's still just standing there. The only option for me now is to walk towards it. Scared out of my mind, I slowly begin walking in its direction. "Let's go Tom," Claudia says while shaking his shoulder a bit. In the buildings on each side of me, there are closed garage doors, broken windows covered by boards, dumpsters every so often and trash slightly blowing around by the wind. The ground beneath me is dark like a blacktop paved street with large cracks I'm avoiding in every step. Trying not to step in one of these large cracks, I look back up to keep my eyes on it. It seems I've been walking for longer than it appears because I haven't moved from the original spot I was in. Even though I've passed several windows, doors and the occasional dumpster, I'm literally in the same place. "What the hell is going on," I yell angrily. This time, I heard that! Now knowing I can hear myself I yell, "What do you want damnit?" Hearing that as loud as I yelled it, I immediately hear another loud and disturbing sound. From behind me like a huge freight train, the noise of this super large semi truck is barreling down on me. Slamming against both buildings on either side as if it's out of control, it continues coming right at me. Turning to run as fast as I can, I see that thing is no longer standing at the end of the alley. It's gone! The deafening sound of this semi truck forces me to turn back to see how far it is when suddenly, the feeling of being brutally destroyed comes over me.

"Tom," Claudia yells louder watching him come out of the dream. Waking up in a panic, Toms arms are flailing as Claudia is trying to grab hold of them to secure him during this nightmare. "Holy shit babe," Tom says widening his eyes. Leaning up against the headboard, Tom wipes the sweat from his forehead and looks at Claudia. "Babe, I've been trying to wake you for a while," she says. Looking at his hands and around the room just to make sure he's awake, Tom gathers himself. Claudia asks, "What kind of dream was that babe?" Struggling to get off the bed quickly, Tom says, "We need to get back home, now!"

Chapter 40

Shooting across I-96E towards Grand Rapids, then Lansing and down to the Detroit area disobeying all the speed limit signs, they talk about the conversation Tom just had with detective Butler and try to figure out more about the dream. "Did it give you any other clues," Claudia asks. "Nothing really," he says. "Just an alley and a truck crashing through it, apparently running me over. And it just stood there at the end of the alley in the intersection the whole time," he continues. "Or running SOMEONE over," she exclaims. "Well yes, that's apparently the idea of these dreams, but usually I have more to work with. In most of them, I'm able to decipher details which bring us closer to the result, sort of like the fire at the daycare," he says. "And you said you didn't know which buildings they were right," she asks. With a disappointed look, Tom says, "not a clue!" They drive on passing through Grand Rapids and heading towards Lansing with only a couple hours to go before getting into the Detroit area. They left the hotel sometime after eight so rush hour has come and gone. Detroit is busy as usual with people all over the place, taxis picking up and dropping off, buses making their usual stops and many tractor trailer trucks of all sizes making deliveries and pickups throughout the city. "Do you think we can stop for a potty break and a coffee babe," Claudia asks. Tom doesn't hesitate for a second and responds, "of course we can. There's a couple good places up ahead we can stop at." They drive another 10 minutes and get off at one of the more popular exits with coffee shops, gas stations and other amenities for travelers. Heading for a Starbucks, they kill three birds with one stone and pick up coffee, something to eat and hit the john all at once. Getting back on the road in no time, Claudia asks, "I wonder how the detective is doing?"

A couple hours away, detective Butler is scrambling just on the information that was provided by Tom. With little to go on, Butler has officers in every alley possible considering the size of the city and how many alleys are actually in the city. He's even narrowed it down to ones that would be getting might be able to get deliveries from large semitrailer trucks and still isn't covering all the alleys. Officers checking in from time to time informing headquarters of any activity. So far, business as usual. One of the main problems in Detroit is the homeless situation and the number of them living in the alleyways and other spots throughout the city. Determining even that makes it more difficult to pinpoint where something might happen. To make matters worse, the only thing they've determined that will happen is someone getting run over by a truck. That is it. At this point, the detective has covered all he can and all he can do now is wait. Picking up the phone, he calls Tom. "How's your drive going Tom," he asks. "Pretty good detective. We are now passing Lansing and should be in the area in about an hour or so," Tom responds. Hitting the gas just a little from the anxiety of being on the phone with the detective, Toms speeds are upwards of eighty. "Look Tom, there is no reason for you to hurry and not much you could do here anyway so please drive safely okay," Butler says calmly. His foot slowly letting off the gas with a little relief, Tom resets the cruise control at around seventy five setting a pretty good pace. "Thanks detective," Tom says. "We really wanted to be there as quickly as we can just to help in any possible way," Tom continues. "Ask him if there's anything we can do when we get there," Claudia says motioning to Tom. "Hey, Claudia asked if there's anything we can do when we get there? Do you want us to head to you," Tom asks. With police interruptions in the background from Butlers radio, the detective says, "just give me a call when you get in town Tom. We'll figure it out from there okay?" "Sounds good detective. Talk with you soon," and Tom hangs up.

With only twenty minutes to go, Tom and Claudia are anxious as hell from not hearing from the detective. "I should call him," Tom says. Tom reaches for the phone on the seat as Claudia softly grabs his hand and says, "just wait hun. I'm sure if something happened, he would've called already. We still have fifteen minutes or so and we'll be able to get there and see how we can help." Holding her hand and putting his bad hand that works rather well now considering it was blown apart by a bullet, they cruise at a comfortable speed getting to the edge of the city limits. Approaching a couple intersections that will determine where they end up in the city, Tom makes the call, "Detective? Are you there," Tom asks while looking over at Claudia. The phone call didn't go to voicemail and was certainly answered, but Butler hasn't said anything yet. On speaker, all Tom and Claudia can hear is noise in the background with sirens and people yelling. "Detective," Tom yells louder. Just then a voice comes on the phone, "Tom, is that you," Butler says quickly. "Yes, what's going on," Tom says. "We have a situation here Tom. There are several people killed and even more injured. I have to let ya go, but I am in the intersection at the professional buildings in the new center area," as the detective hangs up. They both are staring at each other with their mouths hanging open. "There's nothing you could've done Tom," Claudia exclaims right away noticing the guilt Tom shows on his face. Without saying a word, Tom drives and parks as close to the scene as possible. Running to find Butler, they are confronted with yellow caution tape being put up as they approach. Trying to sneak underneath, they are stopped by an officer, "I'm the one," Tom stops, "I mean I know what happened here and," Tom stops again knowing they aren't going to know what the hell he's talking about. Just then Claudia yells out, "where the hell is detective Butler?" "Ya, what she said," Tom states. The officer is too busy putting up tape and trying to get things in order and calmed down. "Ya, it's me," Tom exclaims with his phone to his ear. "We're on the other side by some of the caution tape. They won't let us in here," Tom continues. "Tom, you're gonna have to wait until I get cleared up here. It's a mess. Come around to the other side of the building and you'll be able to see what's really going on. I have to go," Butler says and hangs up. As Tom and Claudia make their way around to the other side of the building, they see fire trucks, ambulances and police all over the place. Making their way through the crowds, they are held back approximately a block or more from a scene that is utterly terrifying. Because most of the fire trucks and other emergency vehicles are parked strategically blocking most of the destruction, they are only able to see an occasional blue tarp covering what could possibly be a victim of whatever happened. They scan the area for Butler only to see more and more of these blue tarps. Just then, Butler walks up from the left of them and says, "hey guys." He's taking off a pair of rubber gloves and throws them in a trash can nearby. Going under the caution tape, he makes his was right to Tom. "From what you told me, there was no way in hell we would've figured this out," he says. "What was it? What happened," Claudia asks. Detective Butler explains how one of the food delivery trucks went crashing through an intersection and into an alley destroying everything in its path along with many people. "Turns out the driver was drunk and we have him in custody now," Butler says. He continues, "you guys go back to your apartment and I'll touch base later. Tom, don't let this get to you. It's not your fault," the detective says while placing his hand on his arm. "Doesn't make it much better, but thanks," Tom replies with his head down.

Chapter 41

"I had no possible clues with the exception of the obvious in that dream," Tom says. "What am I supposed to do, ask for more clues? The second I started moving towards that thing is when the truck came out of nowhere. What the fuck else am I supposed to do," Tom continues getting upset. Sitting at a small restaurant trying to choke down something to eat, Tom and Claudia are beside themselves after what happened today. It's not so much the dream and that they couldn't do anything about it. It was more the idea that Tom thought he was making progress by understanding this thing and his responsibility to it. "They daycare fire, that was great," Tom says. "But then this? What the fuck Claudia," Tom exclaims. Not saying much to Tom while he battles this back and forth with himself, Claudia is patiently waiting for him to finish venting to put her two cents in. "Maybe I waited to long or something? I did run away first you know! I told you that right," he looks at Claudia. "Right," he asks again. Waiting for Claudia to respond, he sips his Cherry Coke enough to take a breather from his vent session. Still waiting for her to respond she finally says, "okay Tom, are you done being hard on yourself for all this? I understand your grief and certainly get the frustration. But you can't possibly have given detective Butler any more information and there was absolutely no way to stop what happened today," she claims. "Yes, you did tell me you ran away at first, but you also told me you decided to walk towards it. That alone, no matter how scared you were, is a big step in figuring this out while in one of those dreams," she continues. They order some fries and a couple club sandwiches just because they feel guilty for sitting there without ordering food. Not necessarily hungry after all this crap, they pick as they talk. "Think about this for a second Claudia. What if I walked to it right away? What if it was waiting for me? Maybe it couldn't come to me and I had to go to it," Tom continues as he chokes down a fry or two. "Hey, that could be true Tom," she says. "Think about this Tom," she continues. "The next time you are able to confront this thing, make every effort to do it right away no matter how scary that might be," she says while grabbing his hands on the table. "You know you're gonna wake up and you know this is something that has to happen. Hey," she laughs, "maybe use your super powers of flying when you do confront it." Claudia does her best to cheer him up a little with some fun facts from the previous dreams he's shared with her. Laughing a little Tom says, "that would be pretty funny wouldn't it. Standing in front of that thing and all of a sudden, I get to take off in the air leaving it way behind." They both sit for a while mulling over what was discussed and wondering if there actually is some truth to it. Not the part of Tom flying away in one of his dreams, but the ideas that he needs to begin being more aggressive in finding out what this thing is trying to tell him and how to get more information from it.

Just about to finish up lunch which isn't saying much considering they barely touched their food, Toms phone rings, "Tom, Butler here. Are you near by," he asks. "Claudia and I are at the restaurant across the street, what's up," Tom responds. After waiting for Butler to respond to one of the officers who just came in to ask him something, he says, "I'm not sure if you thought of something yet, but I'd like to run a couple things by you if that's okay," Butler says. "I don't think it's going to hurt, that's for sure," Tom says. "What did you have in mind," Tom asks. "Sit tight for a minute, I'll be right there okay," Butler says. "Sure thing detective," and Tom hangs up. Claudia is hopeful that the detective will give Tom some good ideas or will have him try something new, something we haven't thought of. A few minutes later, Butler walks in the small restaurant and sits down. "How are you feeling," he asks Tom. "I'm doing okay I guess," he says. "What's up," he asks the detective. Claudia is more enthusiastic about what Butler has to say than Tom is right now. It's not because Tom isn't curious about what he's going to say, it's just that he's frustrated with the way this is going backwards after the success they had the other day. "You mentioned earlier that each time you looked at this thing that is supposed to be telling you something, it was in the same spot," Butler says. He continues, "what did that look like to you?" Tom isn't sure where he's going with this and says, "well, it was in the same spot. I'm not sure what your asking for. Every time I saw it no matter what I did whether it was running away or walking to it, it was right there and never moved," Tom says. "Did you notice where this accident happened Tom," the detective asks. Tom looks out the window as if he's going to be able to see exactly where it happened and describe it to Butler. "No, I guess not. I just figured it was in the alley," Tom says. "The way you described it to me was that it was standing at the end of the alley as if it was a permanent fixture. Am I remembering that right," he asks Tom. "Ya, that's what I said," Tom says. "Do you know what is at the end of that alley?" Tom looks at the detective waiting for him to answer his own question because he's getting a little tired of this puzzle. "It's an intersection Tom, just like you told me earlier," he exclaims. "So what," Tom says trying to figure out where Butler is going with this. "Tom, maybe the message was the intersection. That thing standing there and not moving. It was there that something bad was going to happen. Are you sure, absolutely sure there weren't other clues that you may have missed," detective Butler asks as if he's interrogating Tom. "No," Tom says and stops to think for a second, "no, I don't think so." Butler places his hand on his shoulder and says, "I just thought that might help a little. Paying attention to detail is one of the things I better be good at or I'm not a very good detective," he giggles. "Either way, there are so many intersections around here that it wouldn't have mattered. I just thought it was something you may or may not have thought about," the detective says while grabbing a few of the lukewarm fries. "So what do I do detective," Tom asks. Talking with fries in his mouth he says, "pay attention to detail. It may not say anything or show you anything like it did before with the visions. Maybe what's around it and what it's doing is where you need to focus." Claudia and Tom agree with Butler as they all look at each other like they know what the next step is. Before leaving, the detective says, "Hey, are you gonna eat that?" Tom shakes his head no. Butler grabs the sandwich and heads back to the scene. They both look at each other with a funny smile and get up to leave. On their way out, Tom looks at Claudia shaking his head and says, "I hope I'm up for this babe."

Chapter 42

Several days go by and nothing, not one single dream. In fact, Tom has been enjoying the solid sleep he's been getting lately. With work back to normal and his dates with Claudia better than ever, he feels like there's been a break or a stoppage in bad news. The bad news seems to be told to Tom through his dreams before the actual news stations deliver the news to everyone else. Things have been pretty quiet around the city also. Sure, the occasional purse snatching, shoplifting and other small misdemeanors have occurred in the city, but they do anyway. For the most part, it's been calm allowing Tom and Claudia to enjoy themselves as a normal couple. Their days have been less stressful and their nights have been even better and more passionate. Out for dinner, they're having a little fun at one of the local sports bars where they can play some Club Keno and watch their favorite teams on the many TVs. The brews come from around the state of Michigan with a number of beers on tap to quench anyone's thirst. Located in the Mid-town area, it's an easy walk to both of their apartments. The fact that they haven't talked about dreams in what seems like so long feels wonderful to both of them. The evening goes by quickly as all of them seem to do when the two of them are together. Bantering the whole night and feeling it's time to get going, they tip their waitress well and head for the door.

Hand in hand, they meander down the street with no hurry to say goodbye. This will be the first evening this week they haven't spent the night together and they're going to miss each other terribly. Kissing goodnight, their hands slowly glide from one another's as they say goodbye and head in opposite directions. Coming up to the corner, Tom stops and waits for the light to change so he can cross. Suddenly from a distance behind him, he hears the loudest scream for help he's ever heard. A few seconds later, a gunshot. "Claudia," he yells as he turns around and sprints back in her direction. Flying down the street, Tom comes to the corner where they said goodnight to each other. Not sure exactly where the scream came from, he looks both ways before sprinting towards where Claudia would've headed. The only thing on his mind right now is the safety of this girl he's falling in love with more and more each day. Watching people run down to the end of the block and in the middle of the street, Tom bolts towards the crowd. More and more people are now gathering around as on-lookers congregate on the sidewalk and in the street. Pushing his way through the crowd with the feeling of complete and utter helplessness, he can barely see two people in the street with one holding the other. As he makes his way through, he sees a young woman bent over, assisting the person laying beneath her. Moving in closer to see better, he sees that the young woman on the ground is Claudia. "Claudia," he yells again shoving people out of the way. He kneels down beside her, across from the other young woman assisting any way she can. "Police are on their way," the young woman says to Tom. Tom grabs Claudia's hand, looks into her eyes and says, "babe, it's gonna be okay. What happened?" In a lot of pain, she's only able to cry her response, "fucking idiots tried to rob me," then winces in pain again. With a gunshot just below her chest on her left side, Tom gets even more worried. Holding tightly to the area where the bullet went in, the young woman seems to know what she's doing. Tom looks up at the crowd and yells, "what happened? Did anyone see what happened?" Nobody answers. With sirens in the background getting closer, Tom tries to keep Claudia talking until the medics get here and take care of her.

With police and emergency rescue teams handling the situation, Claudia is rushed to the local medical center for care. Arriving at the hospital, a team of doctors and nurses are outside waiting for her as they rush her out of the ambulance and take her away. Trying to force his way into the surgical room, one of the nurses stop him and tell him he's going to have to wait outside the room. "I can't believe this," Tom mumbles to himself as he grabs one of the chairs against the wall in the hallway.

From down the hall, he hears his name being called, "Tom, hey Tom," detective Butler calls out. Rushing down to Tom, the detective immediately asks how she's doing. Elbows on his knees and head in hands, Tom says, "I don't know yet, they just took her back there." Not knowing what else to say, Butler puts his hand on Toms back and says, "It's gonna be alright Tom." Tom looks up at the detective and says quietly, "where's the fucking dream to stop something like that?" Both Tom and Butler look down at the floor thinking exactly that. Butler knows that was a rhetorical question and doesn't say anything back to Tom just yet. Waiting for what seems like forever, "I'm going to go check on a couple things Tom, I'll be right back okay," Butler says patting him on the leg. "Sure," Tom replies as he continues to look in the direction Claudia is getting operated on. A few minutes go by and one of the doctors come walking down the hallway, "are you Tom," he asks. "Yes," Tom stands quickly, "is she okay?" As the doctor starts telling Tom what the injuries were and how she's doing, Butler walks up to listen in. "She's in recovery now and you'll be able to see her shortly," the doctor continues. After answering a few questions from Butler, the doctor goes back in the direction he came and disappears from view. Butler sits down next to Tom and says, "we've got the two guys that tried to rob her in custody, Tom." He looks at Butler shaking his head and says, "this is so messed up detective! She doesn't deserve this at all." He gets up to begin pacing back and forth in front of the detective still talking, "this isn't making any sense. I haven't had a dream for about a week now and then this happens. Why the fuck wouldn't that stupid ass thing warn me about this? If it's really here to tell me something that going to help someone or stop some kind of tragedy, where the hell was it this time," he says. Detective Butler doesn't have answers for him because he's still trying to wrap his brain around the reality of these dreams. But trying to comfort Tom, Butler says, "hey man, I don't know. But something tells me you're gonna find out." A short time goes by with little conversation between the two of them when one of the nurses comes out of the room, "Tom," she asks. "Yes, that's me. Is she awake," Tom jumps up asking anxiously. In a calm voice, she replies, "yes, she's awake now and you can come see her. But she'll be a little groggy for a bit so please keep the conversation to a minimum okay dear." "Of course, thank you," Tom says. The nurse leads Tom to her private room where she is recovering from the surgery. Slowly turning her head on the pillow, a small smile comes to her face, "hey babe," she whispers. Tears come to his eyes when he sees her this way. "Babe," he takes her hand leaning over her to kiss her on the cheek, "I'm here. Doc says you're gonna be fine. How do you feel?" Still half smiling at Tom, she mumbles, "fantastic my love, just fantastic." With tears on both cheeks, Tom laughs a little with relief to see she's exactly as she would be any other time and kisses her forehead softly. She whispers something else, but Tom can't hear it. Just then, Butler walks in the room, "okay if I say Hi," he asks. Again, Claudia whispers something and Tom says, "babe, I can't hear you." With Butler on the other side of the bed, she tries again, "did you dream this," she asks. Tom looks up at Butler and back down to her, "no babe, I didn't." Claudia starts to cry and asks, "why?" Choking on what she just asked, Tom wipes the tears from his face and says, "I don't know babe. But I'm going to fucking find out!"

Chapter 43

After spending most of the night with Claudia, Tom gets back to his apartment early in the morning to catch a quick nap and head back to the hospital. Taking a quick shower and jumping in bed, Toms mind is all over this thing he's hoping he dreams about. In fact, over and over again while laying in bed he asks for it to show up in his dream. At four thirty in the morning, he figures he's got a few hours to meet up with it. He lays his head on the pillow still wide awake and closes his eyes.

Standing with my back against a wall, I'm looking around at a huge warehouse or some sort of convention center that is totally empty. Bright lights shine down on the empty, cold cement floor with large white pillars aligned perfectly holding up this giant structure. The other side of the room looks to be a mile away with the same cold, bright look I'm standing in now. Turning around, I'm faced with a white cinder block wall extending as high as I can see. No doors, no windows. Nothing that looks like there's a way in or out of this massive room. So what the hell am I doing here? If I walk to the middle of the building, maybe I can get a better view of where I am and how to get outa here. Slowly walking towards the middle passing by giant pillars, I'm noticing how white everything is. I yell loudly, "Hey. Anyone here?" Nothing but an echo. "Do I have a convention I need to setup for," I think to myself. "Was I already at the convention and now everyone is gone?" It seems I've walked enough to take a look around and view the entire place. Scanning the room slowly turning in circles, I still see nothing but bright lights and pillars all over the place. Suddenly far from my right, I see a dark figure slide past one of the pillars and disappear. I jump to my left to see if it continues and it's gone. "Is someone there," I yell as loud as I can with my voice carrying throughout the area. "Who's there," I yell again. No answer and no sign of anyone. Speeding up my walk a bit, I see it again to my left. "Who's there," I yell again side stepping towards one of the pillars. With my hands on the pillar, I lean around as if I'm playing hide and seek with someone to get a peek on the other side. Just then, I feel it. The warm, moist air on the back of my neck like something is breathing down on me. I'm frozen, unable to move. Scared shitless, I find I'm unable to even turn my head to see what it is. The brightness of the lights is hurting my eyes and things are getting fuzzier by the second. Just when I feel I'm able to turn and look, everything goes black. The darkness is terrifying. I can't even see my hands in front of my face. Holding my hands in front of me as if I was blind, I feel my way through this giant place. Every so often, there is a small flash of light coming from across the building. Following that direct the best I can, I keep running into a pillar now and again feeling the cold cement each time with my finger-tips. This goes on for some time as the flash of light gets closer and closer letting me know I'm heading in the same direction. Getting used to the pattern, I anticipate the touch of each pillar as I keep moving forward sliding my hand across each one with the other in the direction of the next. As I'm leaving one of the pillars with my right hand and left extended outward, what I touch next is no pillar. I jerk my hand back and freeze in my tracks. A soft, silky feeling of something brushed against my fingers. "What is that," I yell. "Who's there," I can hear it breathing. This is no human, but something entirely different. Once again, there is a flash of light much closer to me only this time, the silhouette of a giant figure covers most of it. Startling me, I fall backwards landing on the cement floor and up against one of the pillars. Pitch black again, I see nothing but can feel its presence very close to me. The flash of light comes again only to see this giant figure hovering over the top of me. As the flash disappears, the darkness doesn't become so dark. As if a small light shines down on me, I look up only to see two large grayish white eyes staring down. "It's you," I exclaim instantly knowing I'm in one of my dreams. Still scared to death with fear running through me like a fire through my veins I yell, "what the fuck do you want?" Its eyes get closer as the warmth from its body wraps around me. Once more, there is a flash of light that I can barely see from only the small cracks near the floor and spaces on the side of me. I am completely covered by this thing. It's eyes are only inches from mine and closing in slowly. Unable to close my eyes with the feeling they are being forced open, I see in its eyes more than I could ever forget. Like being in a movie theatre where the only thing you can see is the production screen, I watch everything from children dying on a bus, gunshots at people in crowds, blood splattering as body parts fly, many visions of people hanging, being stabbed or getting run over by cars and trucks, people diving off buildings and bridges and even visions of cemeteries flash before me. I have to make this stop as I'm horrified at what I see. Trying to push this thing away from me to stop this madness, its strength is overwhelming. Its eyes back away only for a second as it comes in for another round of movies. With all my strength I try to hold it at arms-length, but with no resolve it presses its eyes against mine. This time, it's a different type of movie. More realistic than ever, I'm horror struck and breathless from what I see. I push myself backwards as hard as I can trying to catch my breath.

Jerking right out of this dream, Tom almost falls off his bed trying to balance himself as he gains control of his body. "Holy shit," he says rubbing his head and face. He looks at the clock only to see it's half past seven. Grabbing his phone and getting out of bed, he heads for the bathroom to splash some water on his face and runs a brush through his thick brown hair. Still shaking from what he saw in the dream, he throws some clothes on, gathers up some stuff Claudia might like to have sitting around the hospital room and leaves his apartment. Immediately getting on the phone with Butler, "you're not going to believe this shit detective," he says with fear in his voice. He explains the dream to the detective on his way to the hospital telling him all about the events he saw in this things eyes especially the one that woke him up. Watching everything closely on his way to Claudia, Tom is extra careful of every step and every move anyone else makes. He begins to wonder if anyone sees how paranoid he is on his way to the hospital. "I'm here at the hospital detective," Tom says. Responding, Butler says, "say Hi to Claudia for me and call me when you get a break. And Tom, don't worry about anything. I'll be watching and won't let anything happen to you. I owe you one, remember?" Grabbing a couple cups of coffee from the lobby mini Starbucks, he enters Claudias room only to find her sound asleep. Quietly, he sets his stuff down and sits next to her. Very softly putting his hand on top of hers, she wakes. "Hey sunshine," Tom says leaning in closely. Claudia adjusts in her bed and says, "hey you, been there long?" "No babe," Tom says. "I just got there a few minutes ago, sleep well?" "Na, they woke me up a hundred times during the night to make sure I was alive or something," they giggle. The nurse comes in to assist Claudia in getting to the bathroom and back as she clumsily climbs back into bed to get comfortable. Thanking Tom for the coffee, she takes a sip as if it's the best coffee she's had in years. "You look tired babe," she says. "You didn't sleep much at all did you," she continues grabbing his hand. Tom struggles a bit to answer that question especially after what she's been through. The fact is, he did sleep. His dream from earlier this morning was horrifying and he's not quite sure how to tell her or even if he should. With the relationship they've built together and the support she's given through all this, he doesn't feel she needs to worry about anything other than getting better. "I got a little sleep when I got home earlier babe, no worries," he responds. "You're sweet for saying that, but I think we both know the truth," she says and smiles. Claudia is still having a hard time moving around and quite sore from the surgery. "Did you know they caught the guys that did this? Butler told me while you were in surgery," Tom informs her. "I didn't know that, that's good," she says. For the rest of morning and into the afternoon, Tom spends most of his time by Claudias side even when she's sleeping from time to time. They talk about what happened and how scary it was for her being confronted by a couple thugs. She describes the feeling of being shot as getting hit by a baseball at a thousand miles an hour. The pain was so intense so quickly, but she didn't remember much after that other than waking up after surgery only to find Tom right there by her side. "It's amazing how our bodies survive and put us in another state of mind when something like this happens," she says. "It was like slow motion babe," she continues. It's getting close to dinner time and she's going to order from the menu soon. She tells Tom to go get some real food for himself so they can eat together when her food shows up. Kissing her on the lips, he leaves the room.

With dinner ordered and a trip to the bathroom with one of the nurses, detective Butler knocks gently on the door, "hello, you up for a little company?" Butler comes in to see how she's doing and asks if she's up for a couple questions. "Sorry, but I didn't get a chance to ask you anything until now," he says. Agreeing to answer whatever he needs to know, they dive into the investigation with simple questions that only take a few minutes. "Is that all detective," she asks. "Ya, I don't really need much at all. I'm just glad you're gonna be okay," he says. "You know what's odd detective? Tom didn't have his usual dream about this. Do you think that's a little weird," she asks. She seems a little suspicious when she asks the question and Butler picks up on that right away, "it is a little odd as a matter of fact. But I'm not sure we've even gotten close to understanding much about his dreams," he exclaims. "Ya, I guess so," she says. "Especially the ones he had this morning that were so disturbing," Butler says. He puts his hand on her bedside, "but don't worry, I'll be watching over the two of you, I promise," he continues. Claudia sits up a little in bed and says, "excuse me detective? What do you mean his dreams this morning?" Just then, Tom enters the room, stops and looks at them both staring at him and says, "What?"

Chapter 44

Detective Butler says goodbye to Claudia and excuses himself. On his way out, he whispers to Tom, "good luck," and leaves the room. Turning towards Claudia with a look of fear, Tom says, "babe, what's up?" Setting his carryout dinner down on the table, he takes a seat next to her placing his hand on hers. "Why didn't you tell me about the dreams you had this morning Tom," Claudia asks disappointed. Without giving Tom a chance to answer, she says, "and what is with the detective telling me he's not going to let anything happen to us? What's going on Tom." The fact that she used Toms name instead of babe or honey immediately concerns him. "Look hun, you have enough to worry about right now with just being shot and having to recover. I didn't want you to worry especially now," Tom exclaims. Adjusting herself in bed as her dinner arrives she says, "babe I appreciate that, I really do. But we've been fighting this together and I don't want to be left in the dark no matter what. I would expect you to fill me in on what's going on." Unwrapping his dinner at the same time she's taking the tops off hers, he knows she's right. "I'm sorry babe, I just didn't want to worry you right now. I was going to tell you about it, just not when you're recovering from something like this," he says. Claudia gives Tom an understanding smile and begins to eat dinner. Since last night at dinner, this is the only thing she's had to eat so far. For dinner, Claudia ordered cream of potato soup, a Cobb salad and a turkey, bacon, avocado sandwich off the hospital menu. Hospital food has improved over the years and it's practically a hospital built strategically around a nice restaurant. The hours of ordering food are pretty much all day and the selection is not half bad. Tom quickly grabbed a Wendy's burger, fries and a coke which isn't the healthiest, but the quickest as he wanted to get back in time for them to have dinner together.

Sipping her soup from the spoon she says, "so what about this dream this morning? Why is it such a big deal with Butler?" Shoving fries in his mouth just to delay the reply, Tom wipes his mouth and takes a sip of his coke. "Babe, remember when we talked about me confronting that thing and finding out what it wants and why it chose me? "Ya," she says. "Remember last night when you asked me why I didn't dream about what happened to you," he says. "I don't remember saying that, but if you say I did, then I did," she says with the glazed over look. "Last night, you asked me if I had dreamt about what happened and I said no. You then just asked me why," he carefully reminds her. "Okay," she says. "What does that have to do with your dreams this morning," she asks. Finishing up his burger and crumpling up the wrapper, he throws it in the trash can way over in the corner of the room. "Nice shot! Now tell me about those dreams," she says jokingly. Diving deep into the dream and describing everything to her in detail, he lets her know of all the visions of either past events or events to come. "Nothing in the visions were specific enough for me to do anything with right now. But I think it was just a way for that thing to let me know this is what it sees or this is what it needs to tell me," Tom says with a question to his tone. He continues, "I really don't know what all of that was for other than to scare the shit out of me." Pushing her food tray to the side now that she's done with dinner she says, "so what's with the detective? Why was he so adamant about watching over you," she asks. Tom readjusts himself in his chair to get a little more comfortable before answering that question. "I haven't told you about that yet babe," he says with a concerned look on his face. "What is it babe? What happened," she says. "Like I said before, I have no time frame of when or where any of these events are going to happen if they do. So please remember that okay," Tom prefaces before he tells her. "I get it Tom, what did you see," she exclaims. "It was as real as anything I've ever dreamt about," he says. Claudia gripping on to his hand even harder, "babe, you're scaring me." Tom has his head down and trying to figure out how to tell her what he saw without making it sound as bad as it appeared. But all he could come up with was, "I saw myself dead." Claudia gasps as she grabs her chest with her other hand. "What do you mean dead? Were you looking in a mirror or something," she asks. "No babe, I was dead. I saw myself laying on the ground deader than dead could be. I still don't know how, but I was gone," he says. "Are you sure it was you honey? You know how dreams play tricks on us and everything isn't so clear," she says in a calming voice. Tom looks at her and stares into her beautiful eyes. The thought of him not being around at some point in time to enjoy this wonderful woman, makes him clam up for a minute and not say a word. Claudia, understanding the thoughts running through his mind, simply holds his hand until he's ready to talk. Choking back some emotions, Tom says, "I've seen a lot of things in my dreams and in real life. This was all too clear babe. There was no mistaken the fact that it was me. It was as clear as I am looking at you right now," he says. "Honey, I'm scared," she says. "Ya, me too," he responds. "The worst thing is I have no idea when or where this might happen. Will I be warned or is it just going to happen," he says holding her hand even tighter. "So that's why the detective said what he said. You saved his life and now he's going to watch your back and return the favor," she says as the cloud lifts from earlier confusion. "Maybe you just have to put some faith in that Tom. You're a pretty alert guy so I'm not worried about it," she says. Her confidence is warming to Tom as he puts a fake smile on to show his appreciation. "I don't think you have anything to worry about Tom. Besides, you have to stay alive," she exclaims excitedly. Tom turns to her as if she's made a point he's missed. She looks deep into his eyes and says, "besides mister, you have a lot of TLC to be giving me when I get out of here in a couple days. You aren't going anywhere!"

Chapter 45

Compared to the comforts and food selections, being home is bliss for Claudia. Recovering well, she's up on her feet and moving around her apartment just fine. Still a little sore with the occasional pain, medication is there to take the edge off. Flowers, candy and all kinds of other treats lay around the apartment from all the people at work and neighbors in the building. She mulls through the cards and treats enjoying the attention just a little. Three days later and still no dreams, Tom will be heading over later with something to eat for both of them. Claudia is amazed at how he's taking care of her. His love for her is shining through every wonderful act of kindness and care he's giving her. However, it's almost as if he feels guilty for the incident she's gone through and she continues to convince him that he had nothing to do with it. In fact, she knows he would be acting the same way if there were no dreams at all. She's totally smitten for him. Tom on the other side of town, continues his day with sales calls and paranoia as he's watching his back everywhere he goes. After that terrible dream, he's been very careful about pretty much everything from crossing the street to entering his apartment. It was much worse the first couple days while Claudia was in the hospital, but has calmed down a bit lately. Once done with his work day, Tom stops by the precinct at the request of Butler. "So what's up detective," Tom asks. "Well first of all, I wanted to make sure you were doing okay. Anything out of the ordinary going on? No close calls with death lately," Butler asks. "No, nothing," Tom says almost disappointed. "What? Are you looking forward to it or something? You sound upset about it," Butler laughs. "No," Tom chuckles. "Seriously though, it's just that I'd like to know is all. I can't get that image of me laying there out of my head." "Come with me Tom," Butler says directing him to his office. They walk down the hall and enter the detectives office only to find a woman sitting in one of the chairs opposite Butlers desk. The woman is beautiful, striking as a matter of fact. Tom is caught off guard as she stands and says, "Hello Tom, my name is Angela Adelson. How are you today," she asks. Tom immediately wonders who this woman is and how she knows his name. What's going through his mind now isn't the dreams and worries from them, but who the hell is this and what does she want with him. With long brown hair tied up in a pony tail, she's tall and slender with a pair of legs to kill. She's wearing high heels and a professional, yet sexy dress suit that fits her rather well. Oh and no ring. "Hello. I'm doing fine," Tom pauses with a confused look on his face. "Is there something I should know about," Tom says.

Detective Butler walks around to the other side of his desk, sits down invites Tom and Angela to sit. "Why I've asked you here today Tom is because I've had an opportunity to share with Angela all that has been going on. Angela is our precinct psychologist and she also dabbles in something I thought you might find interesting," Butler says. "Angela, would you please explain to Tom what we've talked about?" Tom looks back and forth between the two of them like he's just been blind-sided by Butler. "Yes detective, I'd be happy to. Tom, I am not only the psychologist for the police department, but I've studies dreams for many years. As a matter of fact, I'm also referred to as a dream reader or dream therapist," she explains. "Okay," Tom says with an utter tone of what the fuck. "I know, it sounds a little silly. But this truly does exist and I have many references to show from my work if you'd like to see them. For now, I'd like to dive in a little if that's okay with you," she asks. Tom looks at Butler and says, "Are you sure about this detective? You and I know how crazy this is and what it sounded like to you when I first told you. No disrespect Ms Adelson," he's interrupted by Angela saying, "Please! Call me Angela." "Okay Angela. No disrespect at all, but this isn't necessarily something I've believed in myself for a long time and honestly, it took a lot to convince him that I wasn't crazy," Tom says motioning towards Butler. "I'm not here to judge you Tom. I'm simply here because I do believe in what affect dreams can have on people. Studying dreams for as long as I have has given me some insights on how people react and live their daily lives because of them," Angela says. "Umm, I'm not sure you understand Angela," Tom says with a little sarcasm. Detective Butler jumps in and says, "Hey Tom, I've already talked with Angela all about what's going on and in detail. I didn't mean to surprise you with this, but you have to understand from my position I needed to have another opinion and some additional input from someone other than us." Tom understands completely what Butler's going through and why he needed to confide in Angela. "You sure you're ready for this," Tom says to Angela. "This is precisely what I've been learning about for so long. Dreams have so many effects on people and other things. From what the detective has told me, your dreams are very unique. I'd like to understand them better so I can possibly assist with what you two have in front of you," she says convincingly. Actually, this is sitting with Tom a little better now after understanding that he's not going to be trying to convince her of these things as he did with the detective. The fact that Butler has already shared the dreams along with the experiences following the dreams is a bit of a relief for Tom. "Did you want to start now," Tom asks. Laughing, Angela says, "No, not now. I'd like to setup some time very soon with you though. Would that be okay," she asks. "Ya, I guess so," Tom responds. "Oh," he says. "I'd like if my girlfriend Claudia could also be included in this somehow. She's been really supportive since I met her and I don't want to leave her out of this." Adjusting in her seat and crossing her other leg over to switch sides, Angela says, "Oh

I've heard about Claudia. How is she? She's out of the hospital right," she asks as if to show too much interest. "She's doing well and recovering quickly," Tom says. "So can we include her in this," Tom asks again. Angela says, "I'd like to start with you first and if we need her input, we'll certainly include her. Sound good?" Butler stands up and thanks both of them for coming in. "It's getting a little late and I have some things to finish up before I take off for the day. Tom, did you need me for anything before we go," he asks. Tom says, "Nope." "Angela," Butler says. "Nope," she says. Angela and Tom leave the detectives office with Angela leading the way. Tom looks at her ass and then back and Butler. Butler raises his eyebrows and shrugs his shoulders a bit and laughs as they both exit the room.

Out in the hallway, Angela says, "So when are you available Tom," she asks. Tom almost blushed because of the way she asked him. Not only is she beautiful, but her voice matches her looks. "Well, I'm usually working during the day with some flexibility. Is your office here at the precinct," Tom asks. "Yes," Angela responds. "I'm right down the hall in the corner office. Do afternoons work for you then?" Tom wonders how good she is at psychology. Is it worth his time? Is she going to bring any insights at all? Does she know he thinks she's hot? "I guess that would work," Tom says with a smile. "Wonderful," she exclaims. "Let's start tomorrow afternoon around two okay?" Tom agrees and heads out the door.

Leaving the precinct office, Toms phone rings and without looking at it, he answers, "Angela?"

Chapter 45

"I'm sorry babe, I meant to say Claudia," Tom says cringing. "Who the hell is Angela," Claudia says in a fun, but serious way. Tom goes on explaining who Butler introduced him to today and tells her he just got done talking with her which is why he said her name. He goes on and on about the meeting they had and what she'll be doing for them and that sometime soon she'll be including Claudia because he said he'd like to include his girlfriend and that his girlfriend has been so supportive. Tom was making sure he not only changed the subject, but made sure Claudia knew he's the one that brought her up and wanted to include Claudia so there was no misinterpretation in any way that he would be interested in this hot ass chick. "Oh, that sounds interesting. When do you start that," she asks. "Tomorrow afternoon. Should be an interesting conversation," Tom jokes. "Is she cute," Claudia asks with a little jealousy tone. "Oh babe," Tom says quickly. "You are what I see when I see a hot chick," Tom stops, "I mean not a hot chick, but when I see any woman, I see you who is a hot chick," Tom laughs. "Sorry, I'm making a mess of that aren't I," Tom asks laughing. Claudia laughing says, "You sure are young man!" They talk about their day and decide on what Tom will be picking up for dinner. Still a bit paranoid, Tom continues to grab some carryout and heads over to her place.

With food in one hand and a bottle of wine barely held in the other, Tom enters her apartment. "Oh honey, let me take that," Claudia says as she takes the wine from his still bandaged hand. "So what, is the wine because you feel guilty or something buddy," she asks. Tom laughs and says, "Oh hell no. It's just thought you might like some wine, that's all," he exclaims. Laughing and walking to the kitchen with the wine, she says, "ya right." They sit and enjoy the Italian carryout Tom picked up and talk about how she's been feeling. Still a little difficult getting around, standing and laying down, she says she's still doing very well with the healing process. "Not too many pain killers lately at all babe," she exclaims. "That's good. I hate taking those things even when I feel a little pain after my previous surgeries. But of course, I didn't get shot! They were just for appendicitis which wasn't really that bad," Tom says. After dinner, Tom insists on cleaning up while Claudia refills her wine and heads for the living room. Sitting on the couch together, she says, "You know Tom, I don't know what I would've done without you during this. You've been great!" Tom blushes and says, "I'm not gonna let you struggle with this. I know you say it's not my fault and you're probably right. But I still feel as if I should've known or had some type of clue given to me by that thing." Sipping his beer, Claudia says, "Hey by the way, how long has it been since you've had one of those dreams? And I don't mean the one a few mornings ago that scared the shit out of you. I mean the ones where you actually get to see something happen. One of those," she asks. Tom starts thinking of how long it's been and says, "it has to be more than a week for sure. Your accident was five days ago and I haven't had one for what seems like days before that even. I think the last one was the accident with the truck." They both sit in silence thinking of the inevitable and that it really has been more time between those types of dreams than before. Holding each other a little tighter as they cuddle on the couch, Claudia looks at Tom with a sad face and says, "I hope you don't have any of them again." Claudia was serious. Her emotions showed it through and through and Tom knew it. "If I could control when they happen or if they happen babe, I would," he says trying to reassure her that all will be okay. Even Tom knows it's not all okay. He's walking around town each day wondering when his time is coming. With no warning or clues whatsoever, he's worried as hell.

Another night with no dreams and Tom is getting more concerned. Waking with Claudia was nice. Tom got up early and went to the small restaurant just down at the end of the block and picked up some breakfast to go. Serving Claudia in bed, he was able to make her day cheerful even before he had to leave for work. "Now you text or call me if you need anything at all babe," Tom exclaims. They kiss goodbye as Tom accidentally on purpose grabs her boob. She laughs and smacks his ass on the way out. Making all his usual sales calls during the morning and into the afternoon, Tom calls Claudia every now and again checking in to make sure she's okay. Doing well, he continues about his day planning on seeing her again later tonight. "Shit," Tom exclaims after looking at his watch. Tom only has five minutes to get over to the precinct before he's late for the appointment he set with Angela. Not calling, he rushes over thinking maybe he can get there a few minutes late and play it off like he was talking with Butler. Turning down the hallway towards both of their offices, there they are standing in the middle talking with each other. "Fuck, there goes that plan," Tom mumbles under his breath. Looking at her phone for the time, Angela says, "You know I run a pretty tight ship here mister!" Tom comes up on both of them and says, "Ya it looks that way. You guys been sitting out here in the hallway wasting time not working? They all laugh a little as Butler leaves and Tom and Angela head for her office.

Sitting down in a chair that seems like it should be so much more comfortable for this type of setting, Tom gets cozy and looks up at Angela. Moving some paperwork around on one of the filing cabinets off to the side of her desk, she's looking amazing. Tom starts thinking she's doing this on purpose so he can check her out. Or maybe she's not doing anything at all and Tom's the one being a total asshole checking her out. Not as dressed up as before, she's wearing a pair of jeans that are stunning and show her tremendously fine ass. To my surprise or her purposeful action, she undoes her hair from the pony tail and lets it all hang down. "I hope you don't mind, but I've had my hair up since yesterday and just have to let it loose," she says halfway looking at Tom. Tom catches himself sitting there with his mouth hanging open and says, "Oh no, no problem at all." She sits down on the chair opposite his, puts a notepad in front of her and a pen in hand. "So, how do you want this to go?" she asks. Tom has no idea where this is going and no idea how to respond. All he can think about right now is how that top fits amazingly on her showing just enough cleavage to make him not pay attention. "Tom," she says. "Oh sorry," he says. "I'm not sure what you mean. Did you want me to start talking or something?" he asks. "Well, no. I'd like for us to do this together. The studies I do in regards to dream reading are unique in that they require the two of us talking as opposed to me simply listening to you and analyzing. Make sense?" she says. "Ya, I guess," Tom says. "The other psychology work I do here is quite different than this. In fact, after talking with the detective about you, I was more than excited to meet you Tom. And now that I have, I feel it's going to be an adventure together to figure this out. What do you think?" she asks smiling. Tom has absolutely no idea what to say now. He's so turned on by her he can't even think straight. But also feeling terribly guilty because of Claudia, he knows he has to refocus and get to work on this. "I think that would be great Angela. Where do we start?" he asks.

Catching up on what detective Butler explained to her along with filling in the little gaps of information, Tom and Angela get deep into the dreams and events that followed. Tom is surprised how Angela isn't just blowing this off like it's all bullshit like Butler did at first. In fact, she's been more than supportive than anyone about all this with ideas that make sense and advice that just might help him while he's in the next dream. They talk about the details like Butler did which is why Tom thinks the detective got that idea from her. Either way, it's all good stuff. Now all Tom has to do is not worry so much about his own death. For some reason, Angela has given him that confidence. Because of her insights, she's been able to show Tom a completely different outlook on that recent dream he had. She's assured him there is no significance with that dream and Tom seeing himself laying there dead. "You know, this has been very helpful Angela, thank you," Tom says. Leaning over in front of Tom, she sets her notepad and pen down on the table. Fooling around with her pen for a second or two, Tom can't help himself and takes a quick peek at her cleavage. Looking up just then, Angela says, "So, are we good for tomorrow? Same time?" Knowing he's totally busted for looking, Tom says, "ya, that should work fine. This time I'll be on-time." Angela stands up and moves to the side of him with her tight jeans and wonderfully fitting shirt and says, "you better be or else buddy!" Toms imagination runs wild at the torture he'd love to have her put him through for being late. Thinking he might be late tomorrow just to see what happens, he says, "or else what? You gonna tell on me or something?" he says laughing and leaves the room. On his way down the hallway, he wonders if he's flirting or just being himself. Either way, he thinks its fun. On his way back to Claudias place, he picks up his phone and gives her a call. "How ya feeling?" he asks. "I'm good babe, how was your meeting this afternoon? Or did you forget?" Claudia asks. With an excited tone, Tom says, "Oh it was great actually!" He thinks for a second he sounded a little too excited about this and comes back with, "Well, I was a little late. She didn't appreciate that," he says making her think Angela isn't as fun as what he really feels she might be. "So what would you like me to pick up for dinner?" he asks. "Nothing babe," she says. Toms heart drops for a second thinking maybe she saw right through his bullshit and she knows he's got something for Angela. Instead, Claudia says, "How about you just get your ass over here. I have something special for you!" Tom looks down at his phone, smiles and says, "On my way!"

Chapter 46

Just before entering Claudia's apartment, the smells of something good linger in the hallway. As she opens the door, the same smells come billowing out right in his face. "Oh my God does that smell good babe!" he exclaims. Claudia, finally wearing something other than sweat pants and a sweat shirt while she recovered, is in a sexy pair of Lululemon yoga pants and a belly shirt to match. Tom enters her apartment looking her up and down just as she planned. "You look great babe," Tom says. "Thanks hun," she says. "I felt it was about time you saw the me you used to love before I had to dress comfortable every second," laughing. "Well, you look fantastic as usual and babe, I enjoyed you even in sweats!" he says. Wandering into the kitchen, Tom looks over the pots and pans sitting out and says. "So you cooked?" he asks with the surprised look on his face. "What the fuck is that look for ya smart ass? Of course I cooked," she exclaims laughing. Rubbing his hands together like someone about to get something they're excited about, Tom says, "Other than you, what's for dinner?" he says with another sarcastic tone. "Oh I'm for desert babe!" she says with a devious smile. Putting her hand on his shoulder, she says, "Wait til you hear this. I made a Parmesan Risotto with Roasted Shrimp for dinner. It's on the list as one of the most romantic dinners for two," she says smiling next to him placing her head against his chest. Proud as hell of what she made for them, she tells Tom to sit down at the counter and get ready to be served. "Babe, why all the fuss for me?" he asks. "You've been taking care of me even before getting shot and especially after while I've been recovering. I can't say enough how thankful I am for you being in my life. I just feel so lucky is all and wanted to show you how thankful I really am," she explains.

Pouring Tom one of his favorite brews in a frosted glass from the freezer, she pours a glass of wine for herself and sits next to Tom. Holding up her glass to his and looking into his eyes, she says, "Cheers babe! Thank you for everything." The ding their glasses gently together, take a sip and engage in a long kiss where blindly, they put their glasses down on the counter without interruption. Pulling away from each other after a passionate kiss, Claudia gets up and starts to prepare plates for dinner. Drinking more of his beer, Tom watches as she moves elegantly through the kitchen area showing off her figure. "Whoever created those yoga pants is a genius you know," he says leaning over catching a nice shot of her ass. Smiling and being sarcastic, she says, "Oh really now? You say that to all the women wearing these?" Tom knows she's fucking with him and has to respond in a way that's going to fire her up in a good way. "Well, I couldn't say that to a complete stranger with an ass like yours now, can I? She throws a hot pad holder at him laughing, "jerk!" she says. Claudia fills each plate with the delicious food she's prepared and they begin to eat. During dinner, much of the conversation is around how well she's recovered and how she feels getting back to work is the best thing for her now. Making sure she's not rushing things, Tom relies on the information the doctor gave them about how much time she'll need to fully recover and when they feel she should return to work. Tom talks her into one more day at home which would be Friday and then having the weekend to relax too gives her three more days. She agrees and says, "I'll make some calls tomorrow just to let everyone know I'll be there Monday." Both finishing up with dinner, Tom convinces her that since she cooked, he'll clean. She has no problem with that, pours herself another glass of wine and heads into the living room to get comfortable. "You're really moving around well babe," Tom says. She looks at Tom with a sideways grin and says, "You haven't seen anything yet!"

Cuddling up on the couch and settling in, Claudia doesn't waste any time at all. Wanting to put her glass of wine down, she reaches over to Toms side of the couch while pushing her perky, full breasts into Toms face. She then throws one leg over the top of his, sets her glass down and sits on his lap. Sitting there with his arms wide open and a beer in one hand, he says, "Um, excuse me?" Not saying a word, she takes his beer and makes him sip it once more before setting down next to her wine. Placing her hands on the back of his neck and looking down into his eyes, she says, "It's been too long for this babe," and leans in for the kiss. Their kisses are always pretty passionate, but this one was new. With his tongue gently licking the inside of her lips, she suctions it between her lips and sucks ever so softly. His hands are all over her rubbing her legs, up her thighs and back onto her tight ass. The smoothness of the yoga pants allow his hands to slide with ease. Her hands on the side of his face, she twists and turns wincing just a little as she moves from one side to another. Hearing this, Tom pulls back and says, "Babe, you okay? Does this hurt?" Looking down at the wound, his fingers gently rub across the bandage that is covering up the stitches from where the bullet entered her body. She lifts his head up by his chin and says, "I'll be fine. Just keep doing what you're doing!" "Don't have to tell me twice," he says as he begins sliding his hand up onto her breasts over her belly shirt. With his other hand on her ass, he begins taking his thumb and lifting the middle of her shirt between her breasts. She leans back, crosses her arms while grabbing each side of her tiny little shirt and pulls it up over her head. "There they are," he exclaims with a look like a kid in a candy store! They both laugh as they are having so much fun with the situation. Toms hands wander all over while his lips and tongue focus entirely on those beautiful breasts. Placing one hand underneath her leg on her hamstring and the other on her ass, he says, "hold on baby!"

Being strong and somewhat muscular, he pushes off the couch and picks her up like she weighs nothing. Carrying her into the bedroom while they continue kissing, he bends over with her arms wrapped around his shoulders and gently lays her on the bed. Having only her yoga pants on, he stands up in front of her and takes his shirt off. Showing off his muscular shoulders, chest and arms, he gently pulls off her yoga pants revealing her tremendously sexy naked body. He then places a hand on both sides of her pressing his naked chest against hers. She rolls him over to the center of the bed wincing in pain again. "Babe," he laughs. She grabs his hands and pushes them down behind him and above his head. Another evening enjoying each other thoroughly and they fall in love even more. She falls to his side cuddling up to him while rubbing his chest and laying her one leg over the top of his. After a short conversation, he kisses her forehead and they fall asleep.

Chapter 47

Oh my God, this is great! I'm fading into one of my extremely lucid dreams where I can fly. I even say to myself, "sweet, I'm dreaming. Don't let this stop now." I start to look around me trying to figure out where I am. Below me is a large playfield like a professional stadium for baseball or football. It's too unclear to make out exactly what it is, but all the colorful people, cars everywhere surrounding it and the stadium lights give it away. Hovering over the top of it, I slowly start picking up speed racing away and into more of the city. I can feel the force on my body as my speed increases dramatically. My arms are out in front of me like I'm Superman or something. Maybe I think that's what I should do when I'm flying all by myself. I'm also wearing a blue shirt. Not sure that has any significance, but I see the dark blue color on my sleeves as I fly through the air. As I'm making my way further away from all the lights from the stadium, I find I'm racing further and further away from the ground as well making it almost impossible to see anything. Clouds now below me, I realize I've gone too far and tell myself to start heading back. Only having a limited amount of control, I begin speeding towards the ground only to use every bit of energy I have to stop from crashing. Once again, I can feel the force in my body from the speed of turning and trying not to hit the ground. Coming out of this dive, I begin cruising through the city again watching as I pass by all these huge buildings. I'm flying over the top of them noticing people everywhere as if the buildings have no roof or maybe all the people are out on their balconies. What's weird is the amount of people. They are everywhere as I fly by now at a much slower pace than before. What goes through my mind now is whether they can see me during my own dream. Because I know I'm dreaming, I wonder if they see me instead of this just being a weird dream of my own. The best part about this dream is that I can ask and answer my own questions. I'm also focusing on not waking up because that would fuck this up and I love flying in my dreams. Wondering if people below me can see me, I notice some lady dressed in a black shirt looking up at me while holding a camera and taking pictures of me as she follows me across the sky. I'm literally only about fifty feet away from everyone. It's like one huge party of people along the tops of all these buildings. Banking right to follow the structure of the building, I continue to watch as she follows me the entire way snapping shots with her large, silver and black camera. Now coming up on a straight building that extends for miles, my speed slows even more as I cruise even closer to the people below me. Again, I'm looking down at all these people and now find they're looking back at me. Trying to communicate with them, I find myself making some sort of yelling noise in my dream. I recall an old, bald man reaching up to me as I'm yelling back at him with my hand extended. What if I can touch this dudes hand? What would happen? I actually ask that to myself while I'm slowly hovering over the top of him. Not sure what I'm saying, but I'm trying so hard to communicate to this person knowing knowing I could wake up at any moment. I continue to yell something at this guy and suddenly fade out of the dream.

"Honey, Claudia says again. Tom shakes his head and says, "Did you hear that? Was I talking?" he says laughing. "Talking?" she says. "No, you were yelling. It was like you were humming really loud," Claudia says. Tom sits up in bed wiping his eyes and looks over at Claudia who's already kneeling up in bed towards him. "Oh man, that was so much fun. I was dreaming one of those fun flying dreams and this time, I tried to communicate with some old guy," Tom says cracking up. He continues to tell her about the dream entirely with all the flying and people and stadium and all the different colors and lights and everything. Tom was so excited about this dream because it was the first time he's ever noticed anyone noticing him. He tries his best to explain the dream and how it works when he knows he's actually dreaming. This isn't one of the dreams he needs to make detective Butler aware of because that thing didn't show up. Plus, he has little to no control when that happens. He has much more control in the fun ones where he gets to fly and determine what the outcome of the dream will be. "I guess what I'm trying to say is it's like going to another platform or level or something. I'm not sure how it works and like the other dreams I have, I don't know when it's going to occur. But I do know when I'm starting one of the flying dreams. Does that make any sense," he asks. Claudia shakes her head and giggles holding Tom around his shoulders and says, "maybe we can talk about this more tomorrow babe. It's still only three in the morning and you need your sleep. Who knows, maybe you'll have another dream before we get up." They lay back down getting all cuddled up as Tom watches her fall asleep in his arms. All wired up from the fun dream he just had, Tom can't fall asleep.

Exhausted from not sleeping since three in the morning, Tom slowly gets out of bed and ready for work. Knowing he's got a long day today with meetings this morning and another meeting with Angela this afternoon, he'll be dragging ass. Claudia is wide awake and refreshed with nowhere to go. Tom kisses her goodbye with eyes half open as she smacks him on the ass walking out the door. The morning goes by pretty quickly with one more appointment after his one o'clock meeting with Angela. After grabbing a quick sandwich for lunch, he heads over to the precinct to meet with Angela for their diagnosis of his dreams. Even as tired as he is, Tom's looking more forward to seeing what Angela looks like today than he is discussing his dreams with her. Stopping to say Hi to detective Butler, Tom catches up a bit with him and lets him know how Claudia is coming along. "No dreams lately?" Butler asks. "No bad ones," Tom says. Just then, a nudge from behind him makes him jump a little. "Hey, what are you two talking about?" Angela asks. In harmony, they both say, "Nothing!" She laughs and starts walking down to her office with Tom. Sitting in the same chairs as last time, Angela asks, "So how have you been?" Tom adjusts himself in the chair trying to get comfortable and realizes he could just fall asleep sitting here he's so tired. "I've been good," he exclaims. "Tired as hell though," he says. "Really, why is that?" she asks. Tom knows they are already bantering back and forth and doesn't really care if he says something inappropriate to her that might be funny. "Well, a lot of sex and little sleep is why," he says giggling. "Oh is that so?" she says with this little sexy tone. Without missing a beat she says, "And is the sex everything you DREAMED it would be?" Tom laughs and realizes she knows exactly what she's doing. Tom's screwed either way he answers that question. If he says yes, she might wonder if she'd do it better than Claudia. And if he says no which of course he wouldn't do, she'd see an opportunity to banter more with him making him think she wants to try. So instead, Tom jokes and says, "Oh it's fantastic! And one day, it would be great to try it with another person!" Angela cracks up, pulls out her notebook and pen and says, "Well Tom, maybe you'll get there one day."

They dive deeper into the dreams they've talked about previously along with some of the other information Butler was kind enough to share with her. She even goes as far back as his childhood trying to understand where all of this came from. Almost out of time with this meeting, Tom brings up the dream from last night and explains it to her in detail. "Wait, what did you say? she asks attentively. "Well, I finally was able to reach out to one of the guys I saw while I was hovering over him," he says again. "Do you realize what you might be doing Tom?" she asks while taking some notes. "I don't know. Just having fun with some dreams I guess," Tom says. Angela leans forward as if something new just came to her mind, something exciting. "You just might be Astral Projecting or Dream Traveling," she says. "Astro what?" he asks. Angela laughs and emphasizes the word, "Astral. You might be doing some dream traveling." Not sure what the hell she's talking about, Tom yawns and says, "Well, whatever it is, it's fun. I'm actually in more control with that dream than I am with any other. When I'm flying, I actually know I'm dreaming and can ask myself things, see things and do things that I normally can't or don't even think to do in other dreams." Angela is so intrigued by this, she gets up and goes to her bookshelf. Even half asleep, Tom still notices her great ass as she's perusing through all the books taking up most of the shelves. She grabs one and sits back down. "Tom, I'm going to study this a little more tonight and I want you to think more about the dream you just told me about. Maybe take some notes at home and we can talk more next week," she finishes. They both get up and walk towards the door. On the way out she says, "If you're doing what I think you're doing in those dreams, it might just open up a whole new area for us to discuss." "Just great," he says. "Why not make this more complicated?" he continues laughing and walks down the hall. On his way out, he waves to Butler and heads for the door. With one more appointment in a couple hours, Tom has a little time to grab an energy drink on the way.

Chapter 48

Sucking down his Monster Rehab ice tea and lemonade, Tom sits in his car in one of the local parks preparing for his next meeting. "Ya, the meeting went pretty well babe," Tom says to Claudia. "She said something about dream traveling or Astro dreams, I don't know," Tom continues. "So when is your next meeting babe?" she asks. "In about an hour or so. I'm drinking some energy and will head out there soon," he answers. "I'm so tired babe! I can't wait to get home and close my eyes," he exclaims. "Hang in there hun," she says. Tom hangs up and sucks down the remainder of his Monster. The park he's in is a quiet one. Facing the water's edge, a number of people come here to simply chill and take up the view.

I'm running as fast as I can through what looks like corn maze with vines growing all over the top and down the sides. Only these vines are black with leaves that look nothing like the normal leaves on a tree. The corn stalks are brown and brittle like a field that hasn't been picked for years. The walls on each side of me are tall, maybe ten feet with falling leaves from the vines all over the dirt covered ground. Not knowing what I'm running from, I stop and turn to see what's behind me. There it is! The eyes of this thing are recognizable and certainly unforgettable. "Shit," I scream. "I know now where I am and what's happening. Turning to run, I find myself dragging ass without the ability or control over my own body. The harder I try to run, the slower I get. I turn around again and see it's right on me! behind me stands this huge ten-foot tall being with arms shaped like skeletal bones stretching to both sides of the maze. Its huge fingers scratch their way through the corn stalks damaging them as each one practically cuts in half as its bones pass through them. Coming directly to me, I know this might be my chance to stay and communicate with this fucking thing. But I'm just too damn scared so I turn to run. Looking forward to where I'm running, I see Angela or what looks like her climbing into a large box that appears to be some sort of elevator. The growling behind me grows louder as the hair on the back of my neck stands up completely. Running and yelling to Angela, no sound comes from my voice. Somehow I knew that would happen. I yell again as the doors slowly start to close behind her. Once she's in the elevator, she turns, looks directly at me and smiles that sexy smile. The old, dark looking doors with vines and scratches all over them close and she disappears from sight. Falling against the doors, I reposition myself and try to pry them open with my fingertips. With all my might, I get one of the doors to budge, then the other.

With my hands almost entirely between them, I pull open the two slimy doors hoping to find Angela standing there. Instead, I gasp as I watch the elevator fall from view down into a black, endless hole. Almost losing my balance and falling in behind her, I turn around to gain my balance and come face to face with its awesome gray eyes and jagged teeth inches from my face.

With a knock at the car window, Tom lurches up banging his legs on the steering wheel as he comes out of this dream. He gathers himself for a minute wondering where he is and what's going on when another knock at the side window scares the shit out of him. Tom rolls his window down just enough to say, "Ya, can I help you?" The man standing next to the car says, "You okay bud? I saw you moving all over the place and figured you might be dreaming or having a seizure." Tom looks around himself making sure all is okay, still gaining clarity to where he is. "Oh yes, thanks. Just had a dream is all. Appreciate it," and rolls the window back up. Tom looks at his clock and notices he's late for the meeting. But now, that doesn't matter. He picks up the phone and calls Angela. Going right to voicemail, he realizes she might be in a meeting and rushes over to the precinct. On his way, he calls the detective just in case. "Hey Tom, what's up?" Butler says. "Do you know where Angela is right now?" he asks. "I think she's down in her office, hold on," the detective says while leaning out his door to see her office. Holding the phone to his side, Butler yells to

Angela, "Hey, Tom's on the phone for ya." "Tell him I'll call him back, gotta go see someone," she says. Angela is right in front of the elevator door holding it open with one hand while holding some folders with the other. "Did you hear that Tom?" the detective asks. "WAIT," Tom yells. "Don't let her get on that elevator," Tom screams through the phone. The detective immediately starts running for the elevator yelling for Angela, "Wait Angela!" Angela's hand gets between the doors just in time as she pulls the door back open. "What," she says. The detective motions for her to come out of the elevator and says, "Tom just yelled at me telling me not to let you get on there." The elevator doors close as she looks at the detective with a quirky smile and says, "what was that all about?" Butler puts Tom on speaker and holds the phone out between himself and Angela. "Hey Tom, you there?" he asks. "Yes, did you stop her?" Tom asks. "Ya," Angela says. "I'm standing right here." Just then, both Butler and Angela hear a loud crash as the building rumbles to the sound of an explosion. Feeling the vibrations from the crash, Tom yells out, "Are you guys okay?" Butler and Angela head for the stairs and run down four flights of stairs as other in the building are doing the same. "Ya Tom, we are," the detective yells to him as he's heading down the stairs. "I'll have to call you back Tom," and he hangs up the phone. Reaching the first floor, Butler and Angela enter a dusty filled hallway with people all around where the elevator door is. One after another, officers are trying to open the crushed doors to the elevator and finally crank them open.

"Nobody in here," one of them yells. A sigh of relief comes over everyone as Butler and Angela stop and stare right at each other.

Chapter 49

With fire trucks outside the building, Tom walks into the precinct noticing first responders and emergency personnel flooding the first floor. Immediately, Tom is confronted by Detective Butler and Angela once they see him coming in the door. Angela lunges towards Tom and says, "Come here you!" Dropping whatever she's holding to the floor, she grabs ahold of Tom and hugs him like he's never been hugged before. Her arms are wrapped tightly around his waist and lower back as her head rests softly against his chest. With her body so close to his, he can feel her firm breasts up against his midsection while he wraps his arms around her comforting her as she cries. Not letting go, Angela can't believe what just happened and is saying under her breath, "Thank God for you!" Toms hands are now on her upper back as he slowly rubs them up and down saying, "It's okay, it's going to be okay." Tom also senses the softness of her body and feels the guilty pleasure of this innocent hug turning into something dirty in his mind. Looking over at Butler, Tom sees the jealousy in his eyes. "What the hell was that," she barks at Tom. "How did you know?" she asks. Wondering what actually happens to an elevator when it falls from several floors up, Tom looks around at the damage and sees there is really no way someone would survive that if they were in there. The three of them go up to Butlers office while Tom explains the dream he had while he was in his car this afternoon. "I have no idea it would happen so fast and when I snapped out of it, the first thing I had to do was call you," Tom exclaims. "So you called me as soon as you woke up?" Butler says. "No, I called her," pointing to Angela. Looking at her he continues, "Your phone must've been off or something because it went right to voicemail. Then I called you." Tom says looking back at Butler. The detective sits back in his chair and sighs with relief knowing it was only a matter of seconds before Angela entered that elevator. Angela can't believe what she's hearing and from a psychologist's perspective, this is something that needs to be evaluated much further. "Tom," she says. "First of all, thank you! You saved my life. Secondly, I'll admit I was interested in your story after the detective told me about you, but I was a bit sceptic. I really wanted to have you come in and talk with me just to see how it all fit together," she says. "But now? Now I am fully in on this one and will make sure we work together to figure this out one way or another," she exclaims while putting her hand on his leg. After a long discussion on scheduling times with Angela and working more closely with the detective amongst other things, Tom leaves the precinct still tired as hell and heads for home.

On his way home, Tom starts thinking about all he's been through within the past several months. He also remembers when he was a kid and how this was affecting him. But now, it's like a huge weight has been lifted off of him since now he has other people not only interested in helping and working with him, but people that actually believe him. Totally forgetting about Claudia for some reason, he picks up his phone to give her a call. "Hey babe, how's your day going? Still tired?" she says. "Very tired, but had a full day that's for sure," he exclaims. They talk briefly about getting together tonight and hang up. Tom didn't want to talk on the phone about the fact that he had a dream that saved Angelas life, but didn't have a dream before an event that almost killed Claudia.

Getting to Claudia's house after stopping by home, changing and picking up something quick to eat, they are sitting at her kitchen counter eating pizza and having a couple beers. "So what was this full day you had today? Get a huge sale or something?" she asks. Claudia knows in her heart that it's not a big sale or anything having to do with work. She can see it in his eyes that he's got something to tell her and is waiting for just the right moment even though there probably isn't a right moment. "So I had another dream today babe," Tom says. "Today?" she exclaims. "Ya, I was so tired that I decided to take a quick nap in my car before my final meeting and that's when it happened," he says. "So you had a dream in your car? That's a new one," she says trying to be hopeful and positive. "What was the dream about? Is this something that's going to be happening soon?" she asks. Tom isn't quite sure how to tell her about it so he just blurts it out hoping she'll understand he has no control over this stuff. Explaining the short dream to her, who was involved and the events following his dream, Tom sits there in silence watching at Claudia soaks it all up. "So she's okay right?" she says. "Yes, she is fine," Tom says. Again, sitting in silence for what seems to be forever when it's only a few seconds, Claudia says, "I guess I'm a little confused Tom." Tom thinks, "Oh shit, here it comes." "You have a dream about someone you just met a few days ago and save HER life right?" she asks rhetorically, "But you don't have one about me before I got shot?" Tom doesn't want to look up because he knows she's staring at him waiting for his response. "Look, I feel terrible about that baby, you know I do. I have no control over these things and certainly feel guilty enough that I wasn't able to prevent what happened to you," he exclaims. Thinking that was a great answer and should resolve this conversation completely or have it turn back into a positive direction, Claudia gets up and walks into the living room area. "Shit," he mumbles. Following her, he grabs his beer then notices she's left hers on the counter. Taking a few steps back, he grabs her beer and heads into the living room. Usually, he'd have to squish himself beside her because they always sit very close together. This time however, there is plenty of room on the couch. She's sitting all the way over to one side with her elbow resting on the arm rest as she's staring at the wall in front of her. Placing her beer next to her on the table, he sits on the wide open couch and says, "babe, you okay?" If a pin dropped in another apartment way down the hall, you could've heard it. She turns to Tom sadly and says, "I'm okay. I don't understand your dreams, but I do feel a bit unimportant right now." "Oh baby," Tom leans in to her placing his hand on her leg. "You are SO important to me. Like I said, I have no idea when, where or why I have these dreams," he exclaims. Rubbing her leg a little and only a little, Tom feels he shouldn't even do that. It's like it just went down twenty degrees in the room. "I don't know what else to tell you babe," he exclaims. Again, silence. Then after a few minutes, the questions start coming at Tom like a 1918 Tommy Gun.

"So what is Angela like? Is she a younger psychologist? What background does she have? How long has she been working for the department? Is she pretty?" she asks without taking a break for breathing. Tom starts to laugh knowing he's going to get in trouble for the slightest hint of humor from this. "Is this funny," she says sternly. "No babe," he's still giggling a little knowing he's now in trouble. "I was just laughing because of all the questions at once, that's all." he says. Tom has nothing! In his mind, he's so busted for not even doing anything wrong. He tries to compose himself and take the humor out of this and says, "Okay, what did you ask again?" Thinking he's funny and trying to lighten the mood, all he gets back is a stare and an adjustment in her seat which only brings more cold air in between them. Taking a large drink of his beer and setting the glass back down on the table, Tom says, "I would say she's our age I guess. She looks a couple years older though," he says trying to make it look like she's old and undesirable. "Detective Butler recommended her to me and thought it would be a good idea for me and us to work with her," he exclaims. With every answer following this one, Tom does his best making sure Claudia feels included and tries to convince her that every conversation he has with Angela somehow involves her, even though they may not. The conversation continues as Tom describes the mayhem at the precinct and what a destroyed elevator looks like after crashing to the ground. They talk for the next thirty minutes or so about how all of them are going to work together moving forward. "So she almost died today! Babe, you saved her!" she exclaims. Tom says, "Yes!" Tom feels as if he's made a breakthrough and back out of the doghouse with Claudia. Just then she asks, "So is she pretty?" Tom mumbles under his breath, "Fuck!"

Chapter 50

The weekend goes by without a hitch and Claudia is anxious to get back to work on Monday. Feeling much better, she tells Tom she'd like to get out of the house and do something fun before this Sunday slides away. "How about a football game at the sports bar," he asks. "Perfect," she responds. They settle in at their favorite sports bar where they've watched many games either together or before. With a beer in hand, chips and a cheese dip on the table, they dig in enjoying what they would usually do on a Sunday afternoon. Many of the people in the bar know them and come up to see how she's feeling and love the fact that she's back out and on her feet. One guy in particular spends a little more time talking with her than others. He's tall with light brown hair, blue eyes and a muscular build. While Tom's talking with some of the others, this guy is spending a lot of time focused primarily on Claudia. His hand on her back and leaning in close as if he really cares about her well-being, they talk for quite a long time. Now that Tom's done chatting with some of the others, he sits quietly at the table and a little uncomfortable while Claudia and this guy finish up their conversation. The guy leaves and Claudia bashfully looks back at Tom, then sips her beer and grabs some chips like nothing's happening. Is this her way of getting back at me or something, Tom thinks kind of laughing in his own mind. Tom watches this guy to see where he goes to sit down. Across the other side of the bar, he sits with another guy and two chicks. A small amount of relief comes over Tom when he sees the guy is with his girlfriend or wife or something. Not being terribly bothered by this, Tom has always been a pretty confident guy and has never really had any trouble with the ladies. But for some reason, this made his senses perk up for just a minute.

As the football game continues and conversation with Claudia resumes as usual, they order up a couple of the main dishes off the menu. Claudia gets up from her bar stool and steps away from the table saying, "I have to use the bathroom babe. Could you order me another beer?" Tom loves the fact that she drinks beer with him and that she's into sports like he is. "Sure thing babe," Tom says as she walks towards the bathroom. The beers show up and Tom is wondering what's taking her so long to get back from the bathroom. He knows chicks take longer than dudes, but she's been gone for more time than she usually is. Not thinking much more of it, Tom sips his beer and glances over at that guy again sitting with his significant other and another couple. "What the fuck," he says sitting more upright. There is Claudia standing right beside this guy talking to him and the other three. For whatever reason, Toms heart skips a beat and his stomach loses it's appetite. He pretends not to notice and stares at the tv above the bar so that he can see them out of the corner of his eyes. What seems to take forever, only takes a few minutes as Claudia heads back towards Tom. "Hey babe, here's your beer," Tom says playing it off like nothing is up. "Thanks babe," she says looking back at the other table. Without knowing how to bring it up, Tom says, "Oh, I noticed you were over at that table. How do you know them?" Tom tries to include all of them so she won't think he's jealous or anything. What he really wants to know is who the fuck that guy is! "Oh that's an old friend, his sister and his sisters friends," she says. Tom trying to wrap his mind around what she just said still trying to figure out who that guy is says, "huh?" laughing. Claudia giggles and says, "ya, that did come out kind of confusing. An old friend of mine, his name is Josh. He has his sister in town and she met up with a couple of her old friends," she says clarifying things. "Oh, I get it now," tom says. Not liking this at all anymore, Toms confidence just dropped down a notch or two. "Oh, an old friend from your childhood?" he says while eating his burger as if to be nonchalant about it. "No, I met him when I came here," she says. Tom sits there wondering why each of her answers are short and totally not elaborating his questions. He knows that she knows he's interested in knowing more about this fuck. Frustrated, Tom simply responds, "Okay, well you don't have to tell me about him if you don't want to."

Tom just put himself back in the driver's seat of this extremely awkward conversation. He's showing her that he really doesn't give and that it doesn't bother him, even though it does. And now Toms making that sure she knows he doesn't really care who this guy is and how she knows him, even though he does. Toms head is spinning from all the stupid tricks they are both playing right now. She's being coy and he's being, well just curious for now. Finishing up their meals, they are getting ready to pay the bill and leave when suddenly without warning, he's standing right there. Without looking at Tom at all, this fucker looks right at Claudia and says, "It was really nice seeing you again. I hope I see you around soon," and leaves. Paying the bill and frustrated as all hell, Tom finally looks up at Claudia and says, "Okay, what gives?" Claudia says, "Fine, he was an old boyfriend kind of. I mean we were going to date, but didn't get a chance to because he had to move out of town for a while. We just decided not to at that time." Toms mind is going a hundred miles an hour right now. This guy wasn't around when he met Claudia and knowing now what he knows about this piece of shit, Tom for sure doesn't like it. "So why do you think he didn't even say Hi to me or introduce himself to me?" he says to Claudia. "I have no idea why he didn't say anything. He's really a nice guy," she says. Oh that pisses Tom off even more. No nice guy is going to blow off others at a table unless he's trying to prove a point. And for Claudia to say he's a nice guy, well that just means she must still have something for him. Tom calms himself down, finishes paying the bill and says, "Well, whatever. Some guys are more friendly than others I guess." Leaving the bar, they say goodbye to the few people still there that they know and head for Toms car. When Tom drops Claudia off at her apartment, he tries to play it all off like no big deal. "Are you excited to get back to work?" he asks. "Yes, I really am. And thank you for being so great while I was recovering babe," she says reconfirming her love for Tom. Tom leans over, gives her a nice warm kiss on the lips and watches as she goes into her apartment building. Driving away, he says to himself, "Okay you little asshole, it's on!"

Chapter 51

Tom walks into the office a little after eight thirty and everyone's there welcoming Claudia back to work. Putting his things down at his desk, he wanders over to see how things are going so far. With flowers and candy boxes all over her desk and chairs, the entire cubical looks like a giant party. Nosy Cheryl slides her chair over the second Tom comes into view. "So did you take good care of our little girl," she says annoyingly. "Oh she's a tough one and doesn't need too much help taking care of herself," Tom says with Claudia overhearing. Sitting at her desk like nothing ever happened, Claudia is back to work like everyone in the office needs her to be. The office hasn't been running smoothly without her and with the help of Cheryl, it was even worse. Trying to get caught up, Claudia's looking around at all the flowers thinking of all the thank you's she's gonna have to give. Leaning over the edge of the cubical, Tom says, "it's nice to see you back here babe." From the cubical next to her, you can hear giggling from you know who. "I can't tell you how nice it is to be here instead of laying on my couch,"

Claudia says. Tom stands up getting ready to leave and says, "let me know if you need help with all this stuff. I have a day in the office so I'll be here all day." "Thanks babe," she says. He's just about ready to head back to his desk when he sees one of the cards on a vase of flowers that is signed, "Josh!" He pretends not to notice and goes to his desk. In Toms mind, there has to be more than one Josh. Sitting as his desk, he goes through the company directory looking for another Josh. "Ah," he says to himself. "Two Josh's in this place. I knew it," he sighs.

A Monday morning as usual and everything is back to normal. Well, considering Claudia's been shot, Tom saved a hot chick from almost certain death, Claudia is worried about another woman around Tom and finally, Tom being concerned about this Josh guy. Other than that, it's a perfectly normal Monday. Early in the afternoon, Toms phone rings, "Hi Tom, it's Angela." Almost wanting to hide the fact that he got a call from her, Tom slouches down a bit and says, "Hi, what's up?" "I was wondering if we could move our meeting to later around six," she asks. "Well, I was planning on taking Claudia to dinner tonight and have six thirty reservations," he says. After this weekend being so weird with guilt, jealousy and insecurities, Tom was planning on taking Claudia to dinner not only to celebrate getting back to work, but to solidify their relationship after having such a fucked up weekend. "I could push it to five and then you guys could make your regular dinner reservations if that would be okay? Besides,

I'd like to meet her," she says making it almost impossible for Tom to say no. "I'm going to have to check with her if that's okay. She's in the office today and I can ask her shortly," he says. "Great!" she exclaims. "Text me if it's not going to work and if I don't hear from ya, I'll see you then. Thanks Tom," and she hangs up. The pit in Toms stomach grows into what feels like a watermelon he just swallowed. Having to go ask her if she'd like to meet the woman she's been questioning him about is the last thing Tom wants to do. After about twenty minutes contemplating how he's going to either get out of this or just get it over with, Tom gets up and heads for her desk.

"Hey babe, catching up on everything," Tom says laughing. Claudia rolls her eyes and says, "there is no way I'm gonna catch up today, I'm so far behind. I mean, I appreciate what everyone's done while I was gone, but it just made more work for me. I may have to stay late." Tom almost jumps for joy thinking he just got out of the cluster fuck of a meeting after work with Angela and Claudia in the same room. "Oh, I'm sorry to hear that babe. Well, Angela just called and asked if you and I could meet with her before we go to dinner. But I'll let her know you're too busy and we'll schedule it another day," Tom says with utter excitement. "What do you mean? Didn't you have that meeting this afternoon?" she asks. "Oh, she had to change the time to six and I told her we have reservations at six thirty. She then asked if we could make it at five and she also thought it would be nice to meet you," Tom pauses. "But we also have all these flowers to do something with so I'll just let her know you're too busy and," Tom's interrupted. "No, that would be fun," Claudia exclaims. "I'll finish getting caught up tomorrow or during the week. It's nothing too important and I'd love to meet her," she finishes with a big smile on her face. "Great!" he exclaims. "I'll let her know." Tom walks back to his desk mumbling "Oh ya, this is going to be a freakin blast!"

Chapter 52

Walking into Angela's office, Claudia looks her up and down in a way that isn't too obvious then looks at Tom. Oh Tom saw that and now knows he'll have some explaining to do later. Angela's looking fantastic! She's wearing another tight pair of jeans and a V-neck sweater showing off her fabulous figure and high heal shoes that say it all. Welcoming them both, Angela greets Claudia with a warm smile and a friendly handshake and directs both of them to sit down. Sitting side by side in the two chairs with Angela sitting across from them, she starts the meeting. "It's very nice to finally meet you. Tom talks about you all the time," she says to Claudia. Tom's feeling pretty good about this with that comment and feels this may not go as badly as he first thought. "Oh that's nice, thank you. H'es said some really nice things about you too," Claudia responds. Again, Tom's sitting there thinking this is going very well so far. "Awe, thank you Tom, that is very nice," Angela says looking at Tom with one of those smiles that you know damn well your girlfriend's gonna notice. Now, Tom's not so sure about this. "So let's get down to the details shall we?" she asks. Angela runs the meeting with lots of questions and evaluations based on answers from both Tom and Claudia. Their conversation includes Claudia and her terrible incident along with the many others Tom has had in the recent past. Angela does focus on the one recently where she was prevented from going into the elevator due to Toms quick phone call. "I don't know how, but he truly saved my life," Angela says. Grabbing Toms hand, Claudia responds, "I know, he told me all about it. I'm amazed at how quickly the dream and the event happened. It's still all very confusing to me, but I'm here for Tom in any way!" Tom thinks how awesome that was to hear especially in front of Angela. "Thanks babe," Tom says looking at his beautiful girlfriend. Realizing how fortunate he is having Claudia in his life, Tom squeezes her hand just a little more to show quietly his affection. The meeting ends with some key notes and future things to watch for during any of his upcoming dreams. As they are getting ready to leave, Claudia surprises Tom with a move he's not quite sure about. "Hey Angela, should we exchange phone numbers just in case we need to get in touch with one another?" she asks. "Oh absolutely," she says more than willingly. Tom stands by watching this clumsy exchange of cell phone numbers as his thoughts run wild with all the disastrous possibilities to come. Saying goodbye, they head for dinner.

A couple glasses of wine and some soft bread to dip in the plate of oil and spices, Tom and Claudia settle in to one of the nicer Italian restaurants in the area. It's dark, romantic and lit just right for the mood. "I thought the meeting went well, don't you?" Tom asks. Setting her glass of Caymus Cabernet Sauvignon down, she responds, "Actually, I did. I was quite impressed with her capabilities being so young." Tom's quite pleased at how Claudia is handling all this. She sees that Angela's gorgeous and frankly, pretty fucking hot. But that and the fact she's very friendly to Tom doesn't seem to bother her. "The dream reader stuff she talked about briefly," she says. "She mentioned that, but I'm not sure what it means," Claudia finishes. "The best I can describe it is that she understands dreams better than other psychologist I guess. That's about all I know about it. We can look it up if you'd like later and get a better idea of what I'm supposed to do," Tom says. "Sounds good, let's make sure you're doing everything you can to help Angela do her job," she says. Tom's beside himself. Either Claudia really likes Angela or she's trying to make sure she keeps her close enough to keep an eye on her. It kind of turns Tom on having Claudia so interested and wanting to protect what is hers. Tom starts to think about that Josh guy and feels the same way. Only Tom knows men play different games so he'll have to be on high alert after that bar bullshit. An eight ounce filet, potatoes and some veggies for Tom and Spring Pea Risotto for her. The evening turns out just perfect including great drinks, food and a romantic setting made for the two of them. Finishing up dinner, they head back to Claudia's apartment for a final cocktail.

Still a little early, they reconnect romantically starting at the kitchen counter ending up in the bedroom. As usual, the love making is unbelievable as they both feel very lucky to have each other. Tom heads back to his apartment feeling pretty damn good about his relationship with Claudia and the meeting from earlier.

I can't believe what my eyes are seeing! Why the hell is that Josh guy hanging all over her. Not only that, what the hell is he doing in her apartment. I'm at a party, I know that. Claudia didn't tell me she was having a party, but everyone's here. I'm not even sure who these people are quite honestly. Every time I look across the room to eyeball Claudia and get her attention, she's hanging on that asshole. She finally walks over to me laughing and smiling and says, "there you are!" I'm pissed at her and ask her what she's doing with him and why are they so fucking friendly together. All she can say is, "Oh don't be silly, there's nothing going on." "Bullshit," I say. She wanders off and right back to him. All of a sudden, I'm stuck behind a crowd of people and can see her clearly now sitting next to him on the couch. "That's where I sit fuck face!" I yell. She can't hear me, what the hell. I'm yelling at the top of my lungs, "Hey, what are you doing. Stop letting him touch you." He's all over her and all she's doing is laughing and having a great time. "I'm outa here," I say. Heading down the short hall to the front door of her apartment, I look back only to see her watching me leave. She doesn't even try to stop me!

The alarm goes off and Tom lays there fuming about the stupid dream he just had. He knows if he brings it up at work today, she's just going to make fun of him and that might just piss him off more. But instead, Tom reminds himself of the evening they just had and realizes, it's just a dream. A stupid dream that everyone has about shit they worry about. Taking his time to get in the office, he texts Claudia just to see if she'd like him to bring her a coffee since the coffee at the office sucks ass. Replying that she already has one, he skips the trip and heads to work. With all the flowers and candy still on her desk, she's standing over them with a cup of water from the kitchen trying to fill each vase to keep them all alive. "Are you gonna leave these all here," Tom asks. "I'm not sure. Maybe I'll take a few of them home and brighten up the place a bit," she says. Wanting so badly to bring up the dream just to put his mind at ease, Tom says, "Oh I had the weirdest dream last night." She stops abruptly and says, "Really? Was it a bad one?" Tom laughs and says, "No, no it was fine. Just a stupid dream is all. Uh, how about that, I forgot most of it. Oh well, maybe I'll remember and tell ya later," he says feeling like an idiot for even bringing it up. He helps her move a few of the vases around in her cubical giving her more room to work and get her little work space almost back to normal. As he's moving one of them, she gives him this really weird look as if she wondered if Tom saw who they were from. "What," he asks. "Nothing, it's nothing," she says. "Josh?" he says looking at the card on the flowers. The card with the name was right in front of him and he figured there's no way he wouldn't have noticed. "That's not who I think it is," Tom says. "Yes it is," she replies. She didn't seem happy or devious, just matter of fact when she said that. "Oh, does he know you work here or something?" Tom asks. "I'm not prying, I just didn't know and you haven't mentioned him until the other day at the bar. Sorry for being nosy," Tom says playing it off like it's no big deal. But now he's pissed. This is exactly the types of games dudes play when trying to get a woman. Well, that is if they know what they're doing. "Oh it's nothing Tom," she says. "I didn't even know he sent them until I went through each of them wondering who they were all from," she states. "When did you realize it was him and not one of the other guys here? I think there's another Josh that works here, not sure," Tom says. Tom is very sure and in fact, Tom knows there are two other Josh's here. "Oh I looked at all of them yesterday after I got here," she says. Tom is steaming and now she hid something from him about this tool, "Oh, that was nice of him," he says. Tom finishes up with Claudia and heads back to his desk, packs up his shit for the day and heads out.

The usual sales calls for the day and a pretty boring morning for sure. A quick call from detective Butler just to keep in touch turns into a long-winded discussion about how the precinct is going to be upgraded overall and how busy he's been. With one more call before lunch, he shoots Claudia a text just to see how it's going. "Hey babes, what's up? he texts. A few minutes go by then, "Not a lot, just working. You?" she responds. "One more call then lunch," he texts back. "Well, good luck hun," she sends. Tom didn't want this to drag, but wanted to see if she'd have lunch, "lunch?" he texts. Waiting for more than a few minutes and getting ready to walk into his next meeting, he gets a text back, "one of the girls are taking me, thx," she sends back. Tom is pleased to find that she's back to normal and going out to lunch was definitely one of the things she enjoyed with the girls from the office. He makes his last call ending around lunch time and decides to head to a small cafe for a quick sandwich and coke. It's a little place out of the way that nobody really goes to, but has really good tuna and egg salad sandwiches. As he walks in the place, he goes to his right and sits and one of the booth tables by the window. Not paying too much attention to who's around, he looks up and to the other side of the cafe. His heart drops to his stomach as the pain of what he sees takes over his appetite for anything. There she is! The woman who stole his heart, sitting right across the table from Josh.

Chapter 53

Before the waitress even comes to the table, Tom quietly gets up and makes his way to the door trying not to be noticed. Sliding by the curtains separating the cafe from the front entrance, he sneaks out and heads down the street the opposite way from where they're sitting. Finding a bench at a close by park, Tom realizes he's more hurt than he is pissed. But he's still very pissed off. Sitting there contemplating on what to do if he does or says anything, he's heart-broken at the lie she told him earlier when he asked her to lunch. "Am I being ridiculous to think we're monogamous? Is there more to this Josh asshole than I know about? I didn't fuck Angela!" all these things he's mumbling under his breath. Putting more thought into it, all Tom comes up with is two options. One is that there is much more to this Josh guy than she's telling him. The other option is pretty simple and makes the most sense. Even though he's done all he can do to convince her, Claudia still feels insignificant to Angela because of the dreams. He does know this, his heart is broken and he's just not sure how to handle this. Shaking his head in disbelief, Tom heads for his next sales call. Talking with some of the guys at his customer's office, Tom isn't his usually happy go lucky self. The meeting goes fine and he leaves with new orders for his company along with making some pretty decent commissions. Almost forgetting he has another meeting with the psychologist at the precinct, Tom decides to go there a little early.

"Hey detective, how's it going?" he asks. Butler happened to be out in the parking lot coming back from one of his meetings. "Boy, the cases I have coming in lately. Even a couple of the ones we worked on are still lingering around," Butler says. "Got your meeting with the psych?" he asks. "Ya," Tom says with no enthusiasm at all. Leaning down a little to catch Toms face, Butler says, "Ya? That's it? Usually officers or other guys within the district can't wait to see the psych. Some of them even make shit up to see her," he laughs. Noticing something's bothering Tom, detective Butler says, "Hey, is everything okay?" Tom looks at Butler almost ready to open up and get some shit off his chest when, "Hey," they hear from the parking lot. "What are you two guys talking about?" Angela says. Both Tom and Butler watch as she closes the door to her Ford pickup truck and head their way. Butler mumbles to Tom, "nothing sexier than a woman in a truck." "Two women in a truck," Tom says laughing. "So what's new? Tom, you're early!" she exclaims. Butler looks at Tom with one eyebrow higher than the other and heads into the building. With all the construction being done on the elevator and other upgrades, they all have to walk the stairs to their floor. With Angela ahead of them, they keep their eyes down and try not to burn a hole in her fabulous ass. Sitting across from her once again, Tom starts talking a little more about the dreams he's had while she interprets them from what she knows about reading dreams. During the meeting, Angela notices Tom is just not himself. "Tom, I'm noticing there's something off with you. Did you want to tell me anything?" she asks. "No, it's fine," he says with a voice that is less than convincing. She puts her hand on his knee and says, "I'm here to help. It doesn't always have to do with dreams!" A long pause silences the room as Tom finally says, "I saw Claudia with another guy today." "Oh Tom," she says sympathetically while moving from her chair to the chair next to him. "Are you sure it was something bad?" she asks. "I don't know. But I do know she lied to me today when I asked her to go to lunch. She said one of the girls were taking her and then I see her with him," he says. "Him? Is this someone you know?" she asks. Tom goes on explaining who this asshole is and what little he knows about him. He tells her they were doing great until this guy showed up and now he feels as if Claudia's rekindled something from the recent past. "Did you want me to talk with Claudia about it," she asks. "Holy shit, no! That would make it worse," he exclaims. "Worse? Why would it make it worse? I've done a lot of couples therapy in this position. I'm sure I'd be able to provide you guys with some help," she says. Tom starts fumbling around a little in his chair thinking of what to say next. So he just says the obvious, "I'll think about it, okay?" Before leaving, Angela let's Tom know he can reach out to her anytime if he wants to talk. She gives him a pat on the shoulder as he leaves.

Instead of heading back to the office to finish up some work, he decides to take his laptop back to his apartment and finish up there. Even if he's wrong, he saw what he saw. Not knowing if they are just friends or something more, Tom thinks all afternoon about Claudia and Josh sitting at the booth together. No texts or anything from Claudia and it's already almost five. Tom figures he'll just hang here until he hears from her and play it off like he's just had a lot to do while working from home. Another hour goes by and Toms mind is wandering off the charts as to what Claudia's doing and who she's with. Resisting the temptation to call or text her, his pride takes over and he doesn't even lift his phone. Knowing he has it on loud, he lets it sit on the kitchen counter waiting for her call or text. Seven thirty and nothing. Now Tom's worried instead of bothered. This isn't like her at all, he thinks. All kinds of things go through his mind until finally, his phone dings from a text. Practically jumping for the phone, Tom reads her text, "Ugh, finally home. How was your day?" Tom sighs a short breath then responds, "Wow, just getting home from work?" He figures this will open up something or maybe catch her in another lie. "Yes," she texts back. Tom is still waiting for a little more clarification than that and types, "Was everything okay at work?

Why so late?" Tom waits for a few minutes with all kinds of shit going through his mind like why is she taking so long to text back and what if he's with her and maybe she's trying to come up with another lie and just then, her long text comes in. "Well, I had to work a little late to catch up, but then had to take all those flowers and candy boxes back here with me remember? I know you were busy so I had to make several trips to my car with them and then from my car to here. I'm exhausted." Tom sits back on the couch and says to himself, "Oh crap! Forgot about that."

Chapter 54

The building had to be built over a hundred years ago. I think they call this the Ford Highland Park Plant and it's been vacant for many years. Still early in the evening, darkness hasn't quite set in. The dirty, gray brick walls extend hundreds of feet with holes where windows and doors used to be are scattered all through this place. Long corridors with endless space from side to side must have been used to manufacture something years ago. Above me is a concrete ceiling falling apart little by little. Sunlight still shines through some of the large openings on the side of the building. Standing above the ground one or two floors up looking out the opening, I can see overgrown vegetation taking control of the grounds surrounding this entire multi story building. Suddenly, I hear noises from the floor above. Banging like thunder rolling in from a storm rolling in miles away. Looking around me for any signs of movement or anyone else, I get the feeling I'm not alone. The sound from above gets louder and louder as if something heavy is running across the room. I look around me only to see darker rooms to the center of the building where the sunlight isn't touching. Running to the other side of this massive area, I stand tightly up against the wall right next to an opening the size of a large showroom window only there is nothing but empty space beyond it. On the floor, you can see divots and impressions where equipment must have been secured while they were making whatever they were making here. The echos of the thunder like sounds continue only down on the other side of the building. Peeking through the large opening to my right, darkness is all I see with the exception of some small spots of light coming from the other side of the building. Looking at the ground just inside the hole, I make sure it's as solid as where I'm standing now. I jump through, slide next to the hole and against the wall as to not be noticed by anyone or anything. I stop to take a look around. From the corner of my eye to my left, I see the light from where I just came from. In front of me is another large hole in the wall about thirty or forty feet away with still more darkness on the other side. To my right is another corridor leading down to an end only heading to the left from there. There seems to be a pattern in this building that I can't figure out and it's directing me to the other side. As carefully as possible watching every step that I can see along the way, I run to the other side and slam by back up against the wall facing the direction I just came from. Now I can see the light coming in from the outside and much more of the building to my right. The noise I heard from above has now moved below me, but now with voices I don't recognize. I look around for any staircases expecting something or someone to come flying up them and right at me. I run to the side where I can see some light and enter yet another opening in the wall landing on my ass as I fall on unstable ground. It's brittle like sand mixed with gravel and very uneven. I feel my body become sluggish trying to walk through this room to the other side. It's darker than the others with a musky smell like dead animals or even worse, dead people. My arms are swaying as hard as they can while I wrestle my way to the next wall opposite of where I came in. Turning around to gather my bearings, I don't see the openings I just came in from. All I see are dirty, gray walls from the little bit of light coming in to my right. The loud thunder like sounds I hear are now footsteps running through the rooms. It's much clearer now that I'm being chased. With my feet almost buried entirely under gravel, I wrestle with myself trying to move at all. The force that is not allowing me to move is too much as I rest against the wall knowing I'm stuck. Trying to pick up each foot one at a time, I can barely take steps to get anywhere. It's like I'm stuck in quick sand that isn't letting me go. Suddenly, the noises from all the footsteps becomes louder. Voices are yelling all kinds of things I don't understand. Not because it's a different language, but because there are so many of them. My heart is pounding and the rush of fear runs through me as I gather up the strength to jump through to the other room. Landing on the ground, I slide my body against the wall right beneath the opening I fell through. Laying stretched out under the opening, it shows itself. There it is again! Crap, another one of those fucking dreams. With nowhere to go, I lay as still as possible. The long black cape drapes over the top of me as it looks out into the room as if it's scanning to find me. Long skeletal fingers curve over the bottom edge of the window just inches away from my face while the others are almost touching my feet. Watching this thing look slowly from side to side, the sound of my breathing might give me away. I can almost hear my heartbeat come through my throat making noise I can't afford to make. Just then, the noise of footsteps and voices yelling terrible things is closing in. Everything is right on me! And at that moment, it looks right down at me. Reaching for me with one of its giant skeletal hands, it fades just after it barely touches my face. Just then, I'm surrounded by one of the most dangerous gangs in the city. Many of them looking down on me, one of them pulls the trigger.

Chapter 55

"**B**ang!" Waking from the gunshot, Tom jumps up out of bed and immediately grabs for his face. "Man!" he yells. Running his hands all over himself and especially his head, he makes sure he's all in one piece. Looking around the room he says, "shit, that wasn't a gunshot. What the hell was that?" He walks around his apartment in search of anything that fell off a shelf or something that got knocked over somehow and finds nothing. "Damnit, I better get in touch with Butler and Angela right away," he says going for his phone. Both calls go straight voicemail so he jumps in the shower, gets ready and heads out the door. "Bang," he jumps to a halt just before the elevator from the noise coming from another apartment. "Jesus," he says. "Fucking remodeling next door." He continues on knowing he's got to get to them quickly. Not a clue on how to interpret that dream, he's anxious as hell to get to Angela and get her view on this. Coming face to face with a gun is one thing, but seeing yourself dead like in the previous dream is another altogether. And combining the two scares the shit out of Tom. He also has to get in touch with Butler as quickly as possible. He's got to know this dream had that thing in it so there is a message there, just need to figure out what it is. "Details," he says to himself on his way to the precinct. "Shit, I'm gonna have to recall details just like the detective told me." Tom tries to remember all the little things about the dream. Writing down what he can while he drives, he comes up with a short list for Butler. On the ride over, he tries once again to get in touch with both of them. Neither answer.

Upon arriving at the precinct, Tom is glad to see both of their cars in the parking lot. But before he heads up there, he knows he's got to call Claudia. "Good morning babe, feeling better today?" he asks. "Yes, thank you Tom. You coming to the office?" she asks. Tom would love nothing more than to say yes and that everything is okay. But he has to let her in on this because the last time he tried keeping one of his dreams from her, it didn't work out so well. "I might, not sure. But babe, I need to tell you about a dream I had last night," he says. "Oh my goodness, are you okay? Was this one of those bad ones?" she asks. "Yes, it was," he says. Not having much time at all, Tom quickly explains the dream to her making her worry even more about him. But then he starts to think about what he saw yesterday at lunch and decided to cut it a little short. "Oh honey, is there anything I can do?" she asks. "I don't know babe, but I'm here at the precinct and as soon as I can figure this out, I'll let you know," he says. They say their goodbyes and hang up. Tom sits there for a minute contemplating on how he's going to handle that Josh thing. He caught her in a lie and not sure if that was something she had to do in order to tell this guy to go away or if it was something more. Not wanting to jump to conclusions again like he already has, he forgets about it for now and heads in.

All of the officers, administrative people, detectives and pretty much everyone else are hanging in the main hallway listening to someone talk. It's the Chief of Police speaking to everyone about some of the city issues they are having. Coincidentally, gangs in Detroit came up. Bounty Hunter Bloods, Seven Mile Bloods, Latin Counts and Vice Lords are just a few of the gang names Tom overheard. "That's it," Tom exclaims to himself. "That had to be a gang!" "What had to be a gang," he hears from behind him. Standing there is detective Butler sipping some coffee and listening in. "I saw you come in as I was coming down the stairs," Butler says. "What's this about a gang?" "Do you have to stay and listen to this," Tom asks. Butler responds, "I don't think he's going to miss me if that's what you mean." They head up to his office as Tom's explaining the dream to him and even hands him the piece of paper with some of the notes from the car ride over. It was almost like Tom was proud and thought he'd be getting extra credit for taking notes and remembering certain details about the dream. They sit in Butlers office diving deep into the dream studying the possibilities it could produce. Angela walks in, sees Tom sitting there and turns that beautiful smile on. "Hey, you missed it. Great speech today about violence in the city. Something we never hear about," she says sarcastically emphasizing the word never. "Hey get in here and listen to this," Butler says with conviction. "Oh shit," she says and sits down next to Tom. "What are we looking at Tom?" she asks. Tom and Butler bring her up to speed and show her the notes as well. "I'll be right back," she says. Running to her office, she comes back with a couple books about dream reading and starts looking up stuff. "After our meeting last time, I started reading more about this stuff," she says to Tom. "In one of the books, there's much about seeing yourself in the second person or seeing yourself somewhere else." Excited and eager to turn pages, she continues, "Another shows how dream alchemy can open things up and clear the way from blocks and limitations. It also promotes moving forward with more control of future outcomes in the dream. Tom," she exclaims, "This is where you are!" Not know at all what the hell she's talking about, Tom says, "Well, what the hell does that mean?" She goes on to explain how Tom's beginning to explore other dimensions of life through his dreams and how he has to be careful on the decisions he makes within those dreams. "I'm not making any decisions," he blares out. "Yes as a matter of fact, you are Tom," Angela exclaims. Butler just sits back and watches all of this unfold finally saying, "Angela. What is it we need to be watching for? He had this dream and with all the others he's had, we need to be looking for something." Angela sits there silent for a few moments, closes her books and stares at Tom. "I'm don't know," she says quietly. "Well, I guess I'm screwed!" Tom exclaims. The discussion takes on more depth, but with no real solutions as to what Tom needs to do or not to do. He decides to head to the office because of an overwhelming, unexplainable feeling he has that he just wants to be near Claudia. On the way there, he decides he's not going to bring up this Josh fuck incident. Instead, he's going to trust that if she wants to talk about it, she'll bring it up.

In the office, Tom goes right over to Claudia, walks into her cubical and stands right behind her. She sees him in the reflection of her computer monitor, smiles and turns to him. "Hey there handsome, how was the meeting with the detective?" she asks. Instead of answering her, he leans down and gives her a short, but sweet kiss on the lips. Surprised, she kisses him back for just a second blushing as she leans back in her chair. "Really?" she says in that sweet voice. Just then, a giggle and an "oh baby," comes from the cubical next to them. "I don't know babe, the meeting was kind of useless. Angela showed me some of that dream mumbo jumbo shit that might make sense to her, but certainly not to me. Butler, well he wants to help, but has no idea how. I guess they're putting their heads together and will get in touch with me if they figure something out. In the meantime, I just wanted to be here with you babe," he says. "Well, I'm glad you did. Lunch today?" she asks. "Definitely,"

Tom says and heads back to his desk. Feeling pretty good about not bringing up the loser Josh thing, he sits at his desk not getting any work done. His mind is too busy thinking about the dream and wondering what, if anything is going to happen. If history tells Tom anything, it's that something will for sure.

Lunch with Claudia brings things right back to normal. Sitting across from each other at a tiny little table where they've met for lunch before, they talk about all the crazy things they've been through since they met. Tom explains a little about the dream the night before and also about what Angela said about future outcomes and dimensions and stuff like that. With what seems to be a new connection to each other, they finish up lunch and head back for the office. Cutting through one of the alleys which is much shorter to the office than around the block, Tom and Claudia walk slowly hand in hand. "There is something I'd like to tell you Tom," she says with a concerned tone. Tom gives his best look of confusion pretending not to know what she's about to tell him. He's sure it's going to be about that Josh idiot. "What is it babe?" he asks. "I lied to you the other day," she says looking coy as if she's wanting forgiveness instantly. They stop in the middle of the alley facing each other when Tom says, "I think I know what you're going to tell me." A terrified face comes over Claudia as she yells as loud as she can, "No!" A loud CRACK rings out from the air deafening both of them. Tom's eyes clinch together when feeling a tremendous amount of pressure and pain to the back of his head. Running down the alley are two thugs ducking and hiding and before she can do anything, they're gone. Calling for help, she grabs her phone and dials the police. Holding Tom in her now bloody covered arms, she's crying and yelling for him to wake up. Moans and small movements come from his body as the emergency crews show up, address the situation and take off for the hospital. Meeting Butler at the emergency entrance to the medical center, Claudia says hysterically, "Everything happened so fast." As Tom gets wheeled down the hall, doctors surround Tom evaluating and dictating directions to all the nurses. Catching up with Tom, Claudia runs along-side the gurney looking directly at Tom watching as he doesn't respond to anything. Just before entering the surgery room, she yells, "Don't you die on me babe!" With no response at all, she uncontrollably sobs just outside the doors as detective Butler holds her from falling to the ground. Inside the surgery room, doctors are doing all they can to save him. With the noise of metal surgical tools, barking of directions from doctors, pumps and air pressure sounds and heart monitor beeps, the emergency team continue their efforts to keep Tom alive.

Looking up and to the entire group of medical personnel, Tom somehow watches as he's being operated on, but this is like a dream where everything's in slow motion. Tom knows now what he sees isn't real at all. Slowly, the room darkens as the operating table and even medical personnel disappear leaving an empty room with just his body lying there. Motionless, Tom is able to move his eyes from side to side trying to get a glance at what's moving around him. Moving towards him ever so slowly, large cape covered figures grow closer with every breath he takes as he's now completely surrounded by darkness. Tom believes he's in one of his dreams and tries to snap out of it for the moment, but unable to wake himself, he stares into each of these figures blackened, skeletal faces staring down on him. Having no body control, movement or sound to be screamed, Tom tightly closes his eyes knowing what's next to come. As the room grows completely silent, Tom opens his eyes only to be face to face with the Demon once again. Warm, moist air of breath flows from this monster into Tom's lungs as if he was taking his own deep breath of fresh air. Only this was the furthest from fresh at all. Inches away, the demon's eyes stare right through Tom's eyes like a burning migraine headache piercing through his brain. The skeletal, huge hands cover Tom's torso as the demon pushes down on Tom with great force. The ground begins to shake as my body jerks up, then down. The demon says something in a low, growling voice, but Tom can't understand. Sliding his boney cheek along the side of Tom's, the demon's mouth is now brushing against his ear. Being completely covered by this beast, the demon whispers into Tom's ear once again. Snapping out of this terror, Tom realizes his right hand is being tightly held by a warm and wonderful feeling. He opens his eyes, catches his breath knowing it's Claudia by his side. With tears in her eyes and a smile filled with joy, she leans down to Tom pressing her cheek against his whispering into his ear, "I love you Tom." With Tom somewhat still in shock, he whispers back the exact words he just heard moments ago, "I'm not done with you just yet." In disbelief, Claudia knows exactly why he said that as Tom grasps her hand even tighter.

The End